The Geology of Desire

Clint Wastling

Stairwell Books
//

Published by Stairwell Books
70 Barbara Drive
Norwalk
CT 06851 USA

161 Lowther Street
York, YO31 7LZ

The Geology of Desire©2014, 2015, Clint Wastling and Stairwell Books

All rights reserved. No part of this publication may be reproduced, stored in or introduced into a retrieval system, or transmitted, in any form, or by any means (electronic, mechanical, photocopying, recording, e-book or otherwise) without the prior written permission of the author. Any person who does any unauthorised act in relation to this publication may be liable to criminal prosecution and civil claims for damages. Purchase of this book in e-book format entitles you to store the original and one backup for your own personal use; it may not be resold, lent or given·away to other people and it may only be purchased from the publisher or an authorised agent.

This book is sold subject to the condition that it shall not, by way of trade or otherwise, be lent, resold, hired out, or otherwise circulated without the author's prior consent in any form of binding or cover other than that in which it is published and without a similar condition including this condition being imposed on the subsequent purchaser.

Second Printing

ISBN: 978-1-939269-33-1
Previously: 978-1-939269-22-5

Printed and bound in the UK by Russell Press
Layout design: Alan Gillott

To My Family and Geology!

Acknowledgements

In writing the Geology of Desire I used my old notes from Hull University and British Regional Geology: Eastern England. I was also helped by Roger Osborne's book, "The Floating Egg," particularly over the discovery of the plesiosaur. The Harker Geological Society Song, *Spodumeme,* was composed by Gareth Atkinson and Jon Elliott but as to who wrote each line, no one can remember! I'd like to thank my wife Brenda, who helped with the early edits and my friends June Cook and Linda Green for reading, editing and encouragement. Finally to Alan and Rose at Stairwell Books for having faith in my first novel.

North Yorkshire Coast between Whitby and Hayburn Wyke

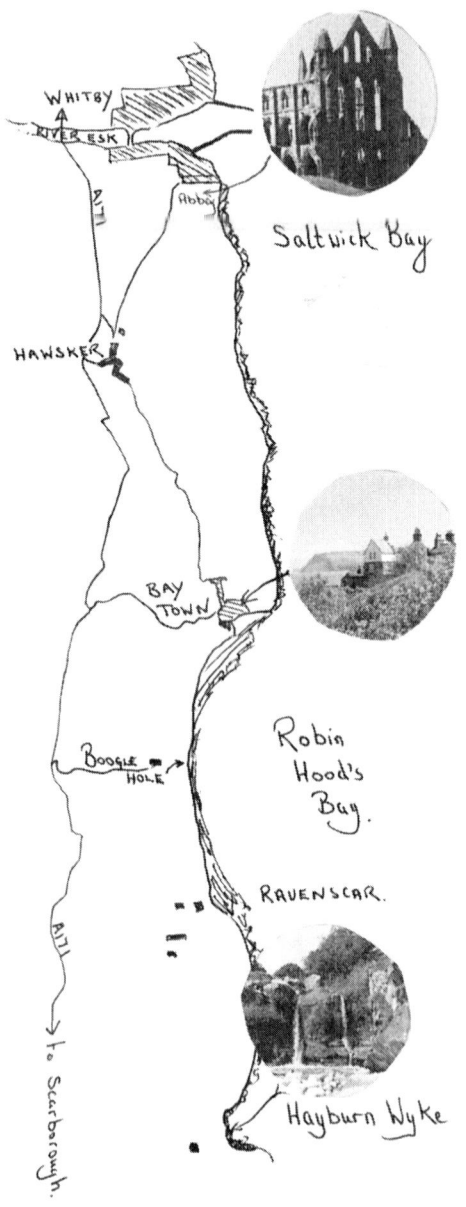

The Jurassic Rocks at Ravenscar

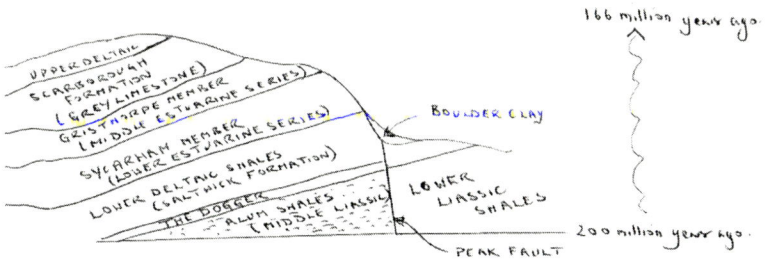

Dactylioceras commune

Prologue

Bartholomew Fair stood tall in the car park. I was taken aback by how distinguished he looked in his fleece jacket and black flat cap. I knew this man. He was Aunt Gertie's grandson and I knew she was proud of him serving with the North Yorkshire Constabulary. She'd say to me, "Davy Jones, you'd do half so well if you took a leaf from Barty's book!"

"David," mum would correct.

Of course she wasn't a real aunt but a friend of my grandparents. Every alternate Saturday she would arrive for tea complete with her own bread. Aunt Gertie was a coeliac. She made an issue of it in the same way some people do with their beliefs.

I'd known Barty so well, I had to stop myself from waving and calling his name. I was not supposed to be here. I was supposed to be lying in bed in Down's Hall. I pushed myself down in the driving seat of the hire car.

The rain beat on the windscreen. I risked a single stroke of the wipers to see outside. Drew pulled her collar tight. Her boyfriend put his arm around her and pulled her closer. A police car drove into the car park and they all got in. The driver discarded a bottle onto the tarmac and sped off. I followed. They weren't going far; this road was signed as a dead end. The abbey loomed above, its pinnacles hidden in the low cloud. I shivered. The arc lights revealed the sandstone blocks of the abbey perimeter through driving rain. I stopped the car and got out. Even in foul weather I felt compelled to take in the outline of this ancient ruin: its gothic windows filled with night. The gale which whistled through the empty panes sounded like the cries of lost souls. Saint Hild ordered all the poisonous snakes to leave this sacred place. As they fell from the cliff they coiled up and turned to stone. The ammonites on the foreshore are their remains. It is a beautiful piece of folklore but the truth of these coiled fossils reveals far more.

The police car had already stopped by the great nave of the abbey, its walls rising spectral through the blasts of rain and floodlighting. The officers walked round the corner. Drew and her friend followed. I had to run to catch up a little but stopped when I feared the sound of my shoes would be heard.

Bartholomew held out his hand and prevented Drew and her boyfriend going any further. The young man looked around as if he was expecting to see someone. The more portly officer took the opportunity to handcuff him. Together they walked headlong into the squall which shrieked across the headland.

I followed, keeping to the contours of St. Mary's Church where the shadows were deeper. Wiping rain from my eyes I slipped behind an eroded grave stone and waited to see what was going on before moving closer. The rain continued to beat into my face and I felt chilled. Using the sandstone memorials as cover I managed to get closer and catch brief extracts of an argument. The meaning of the sentences was snatched away by the wind.

Drew's boyfriend hit Barty with his cuffed hands and some shoving started. Drew screamed at the officers and flailed with her fists. Barty grabbed hold of her and pushed her to the edge. He smiled at his compatriot, who nodded. I clearly saw Bartholomew push Drew over the cliff. I gagged a scream. I thought I would be sick. Doubled up I stumbled towards the church. I saw less clearly from here with my eyes watering but I'm convinced the cuffs were removed from Drew's boyfriend. He looked down. He moved towards the officers and lashed out. He caught the older officer on the face, so they pinioned him and dragged him towards the precipice. The sounds of his fall were muffled by the gale blowing from the east. Driving rain mingled with my tears. I panicked and ran. I heard shouts but I got back to my car before the officers reached theirs. I drove without lights for several hundred yards and took a minor road into Whitby.

At first light I drove back to Hull with my stomach still writhing and my eyes searching the rear view mirror for pursuit. I arrived back at my flat just before Barbara leant her bicycle against the wall and opened the front door with her pass key. The kettle went on. I lay on the bed, then got up and opened a book on my desk, intending to skim through the contents. I looked at the packet of cigarettes, my hand hovered, I looked at my watch, it was too early. I studied the geological map of Britain and the fantasy posters I used to disguise the unrelenting magnolia of the institutional walls. The posters depicted rugged heroes and dragons. Finally I gave in and opened the patio door to light up a cigarette on the balcony. The cold damp smell of heavy rain augmented my mood. A gentle tap on the door was followed by Barbara's voice. "Morning, David."

"Morning." Barbara already had her university cleaners apron on. A cigarette drooped from her lips as she carried in two mugs of tea.

"A good night?" She asked.
For a moment I didn't speak. "Awful," I said.
"Looks like you'll be in need of a cup of tea and a ciggie."
I smiled. "You know the way to a man's heart."
"I've been married twenty five years. I've used every combination."
"I get confused by it all," I confessed.
"I can see that, just looking at these posters tells me not everything is clear cut." She inhaled and leant against the balcony rail. "Still, there are worse things, David. You could be a murderer."
I laughed, almost to the point of hysteria. I could have been. I really might have killed Drew. No, I might have but I was beaten to it. "Have you ever felt like murdering someone you love?" I asked.
Barbara smiled. "Only my husband."
Barbara was a smoker, her face creased with lines round the eyes and her makeup applied with the uneven tones of someone not quite ready to start the day. "Better get on."
I agreed. I sat at my desk and perused *The Stratigraphy of the North Yorkshire Coast*. A section of the headland at Whitby stared from the page with every layer of rock named. I pencilled the line of Drew's descent. Why had Drew been pushed? Had England really become like a South American Republic where the police routinely mete out justice?
Bartholomew Fair.
Drew knew him too. We had been childhood friends. I'd been brought up in a posh 1930's house on James Reckitt Avenue. Aunt Gertie's house was the other side of East Park and my grandparents lived out at Thearne until the day they died. "Godwyn." that was the name of the bungalow, a delightful place with an almost circular doorway ending at two plinths of Yorkshire stone. Somewhere at home there was a picture of nan and grandpa sitting at the threshold and smoking whilst starring out at the unknown photographer.
The questions about what I'd witnessed flooded back, my stomach knotted and thought I might be sick again.

Chapter 1: Absence of Evidence

I woke with my heart racing and a feeling of panic. I'd seen Drew pushed to her death, only in this nightmare I was behind her and I reached out. I clearly saw my hands touch the skin of my one time lover. She slipped silently from the cliff into the boiling ocean. Disorientated, I realised I was not in bed and the crick in my neck informed of my discomfort. I had slept on the eminent papers of several Victorian geologists.

My research wasn't going well. *The absence of evidence is not evidence of absence*, as Professor Piasecki frequently informed us. The first floor of the Brynmor Jones library was dull. The leather book bindings were complimented by a plain carpet and leatherette covered desks. The place hadn't always been so lifeless. For the first term Drew had shared my desk. Drew had placed books at all angles to study the nature of fossils, sediments and magma. Time had slowed. Time had burrowed into the pages of the ancient tomes allowing the past to intrude upon the present.

Outside the late June sun was setting. In a bored moment I had tried to work out how many times the sun had set on this planet since it formed from elemental dust. The calculator showed an indecisive E. Scribbling out the figures provided a clearer idea but the result contained too many zeros for the mind to encompass. It was a number rendered useless by its immensity.

Geology is alternately pompous and practical. Here I was in a library, trying to work out which rocks I would discover if I walked along the cliffs of North Yorkshire. The irony of the research wasn't lost on me. Pictures of the layers of sediments and drawings of fossils provided a clue to what I might find if I actually stepped foot on *terra firma*. Actually doing something seemed to sum up my problems. The modern and easily read versions of Earth history were layered beneath reprints of Philips and Smith. A dangerous stratigraphy in which the oldest book lies above youngest. I checked my watch just as the bell rang. There were ten minutes to pack up and go and another twenty before I met the gang for a pint at The Queen's. I took the stairs two at a time and almost knocked over the corpulent librarian. I muttered an apology, expecting him to swear or break into lines of poetry. He stared angrily and as I passed I smelt brandy on his breath.

I quickly piled books and notes into the bike basket and replaced the lights. At the end of my first year at Hull University, the shortest route from the library to The Queen's was well practised. My fellow members of the course would have arrived hours earlier. They somehow learnt their work by a process of osmosis as alcohol replaced water in their bodies. It struck me that I must be doing something wrong, either missing connections or bowed under the weight of grief.

Nigel my flatmate would get a First just because he was a nice person and incidentally the organiser of the Harker Geological Society and creator of Captain Geology. Tucker would get there by good luck rather than good judgement. I had drawn the short straw and just had to work hard. It was a warm evening and smells from the takeaways mingled with diesel from the blue and white buses.

Tucker and Nigel were standing in the car park smoking, their silhouettes instantly recognisable, one tall and thin, the other squat. 'I'm ready for a pint,' I said applying the lock to my bike.

"Don't wait on us," Tucker said in his Geordie lilt, "the girls are in and you know how they don't like..." he drew on the fag then flicked it over the fence.

"Is Carrie in?"

Tucker laughed. "They just about got her arse through the door!"

I gave him the finger, lit up a fag and went in.

Smoke curled out of the door and a cacophony of conversation and laughter mingled with muzak. I pushed my way to the bar and ordered the cheapest bitter. A hand reached out and grabbed my shoulder. Carrie stood smiling. Her other hand rubbed against my crotch then squeezed. "Ever thought of being a porn star?" She asked leading me to a table at which two other girls sat. One began wafting the air with a beer mat as I sat down.

"I'm not big enough," I replied.

"It's not size that counts but physique, you have to give punters somebody they can identify with."

"Oh! Yes!" I smiled with embarrassment and downed the rest of my pint. I should have asked her how she knew but the moment passed.

Tucker and Nigel joined us. "Are you all sorted out?" Nigel pushed next to Carrie.

"Yes. The ten forty train to Scarborough. Then onto somewhere near Whitby by bus."

"Isn't that a bit…" Nigel's voice trailed off. Everyone looked at me.

"Somehow it feels right," I said realising the implication. "I want to stand at the very point where Drew jumped. I think it will help," I lit another cigarette and smiled weakly.

Carrie put her hand on my knee. "If you want to talk, or anything." I muttered thanks.

I was shocked when I found out that Drew had taken her life. I knew it wasn't true but that's what the paper said. There was a picture in the Hull Daily Mail identical to the one I used to keep on the bookshelf but I couldn't stand the photo of someone dead looking at me. It was as if a portal to beyond might seek me out. "My choice of mapping area wasn't academic. I knew I had to look over the edge and see with my own eyes the path of her descent."

"So long as you don't jump." Carrie added.

"We took a more phlegmatic approach and swapped parents for a month. Cheapest way of doing it and old Prof Durham won't know any different. He'll just get the geology of Weardale versus the Mendips," Nigel sounded pleased with himself for thinking up the plan.

"Aye man, with you it'll all be flat and boring. I suppose you could do the philosophy. It would go well with those crappy poems you write." I felt myself flush at Tucker's remark.

"Speaking of crappy poetry, I've written a song," Tucker cleared his throat and looked around. "I thought it might be the Harker Society's anthem.

Spodumeme! Spodumeme!
We all love spodumene!
$Li\ Al\ Si_2\ O_6$,
Monoclinic symmetry
and a hardness more than six!
Spodumeme! Spodumeme!
We all love spodumeme!"

"You're madder than a Geordie on Newkie Brown!" Nigel announced swigging the dregs of his pint.

"I am a Geordie on Newkie brown!" Tucker replied indignantly, "I thought we'd call it the Geology Song. And... well... I haven't worked the rest out yet." Tucker confessed.

"Like I say, mad," Nigel concluded.

"Well," I said draining my pint. "I'd better be off. A long day etcetera." As I stood to leave Carrie announced she'd better escort me home. Tucker wolf whistled. Nigel searched for something under the table. I put my arm around Carrie's shoulder. As we left the room, I could clearly hear Tucker's voice singing "*Spodumene…*"

When we got to her flat, Carrie made me camomile tea in a white china mug. It sported a picture of John Lennon in a black frame.

"Ever appropriate," I commented, tapping the item with a spoon.

"Sometimes it's good to know others have suffered like you." Carrie snuggled next to me.

"I meant what I said. If you're hard up and let's face it you'd have to be, my aunt makes porn movies."

"Your aunt?"

Carrie nodded, "women enjoy sex as well as men you know."

I kissed her on the forehead. "I must be going, busy day tomorrow. Packing. I've got a train to catch. I must get my mapping over with by late July or I'll never earn enough money for next term." I pushed her auburn hair from her face. This was only half true. Carrie shifted her position on the bed and slightly opened her legs. At this signal my cock stiffened against the inside of my trousers. She noticed immediately and smiled. I had lost.

Whenever I touched Carrie's breasts I thought of Drew. The soft contours of Carrie's body were never the turn on Drew provided. Her body had been muscular, her small breasts shapely with nipples which sprang erect. It was only afterwards that I realised I'd spent the whole fuck thinking of Drew. I'd superimposed her dead body onto Carrie's dead soul. The fit was perfect.

I got back to my flat with the sounds of a bass line coming through the ceiling. The desk lamp was still on and a cigarette lay burnt out in the ashtray. The geological map of North Yorkshire was propped up by several books. Pink, red and orange, the colours given each layer of rock, gave way to white and brown. Thin black lines marked faults. I noticed how they clustered around the coast. It was as if the crust was weak at the very point where Drew had been pushed. Here a life might easily fall into the brimstone pit. I undressed and stood in front of the mirror. I'd have to put up with what I saw, my blue eyes caught the light and emphasised my squint. I never wore glasses outside the library or lecture hall. I looked at my body full length. In every respect I felt I was average: height, build, looks and physique. I had to play to my best qualities, whatever they might be. The dark rings beneath my eyes emphasised my need for sleep. *"Time for bed, said Zebedee"* I said before crashing out.

My heart raced in panic. I woke disorientated then realised that light was coming though the curtains. Drew had been sitting at the cliff edge. She turned and smiled and at the decisive moment my hands had emerged and pushed. Drew vanished into the ocean. A frantic knocking at the door jolted me from dwelling on the scene.

"David are you alright?" It was Barbara. "I've made you a cuppa."

"Thanks," I said pulling my head under the pillow and wishing the light would go away. It was no use. I couldn't deny the facts. I had only a few hours to pack my meagre possessions. I had a ninety-minute journey by train followed by twenty miles by bus. I hated the idea of travelling, of being forced out of my cosy little world and into meeting new people.

"Morning Barbara," I said as I emerged.

She smiled and put a cigarette next to my cup of tea.

"You're a bad influence," I said. "Don't suppose you fancy sharing a caravan by the sea?"

"I'm a married woman," She laughed. "And more to the point, I don't like the sea. Nasty dirty stuff with bits of shit in it. No, it wouldn't do for me," she stubbed out her fag and pulled the hoover roughly from its cupboard. "I've often thought of pushing him indoors over a cliff. The higher the better." She stared at me for signs of a hangover then flicked on the switch.

Women were an enduring problem in my life. I realised the cause was my own inability to be honest. I'm unsuited to telling the truth or of recognising it in others. I am unable to scrape away the soil and reveal the rock beneath. I peeled away the layers of clothes scattered around my room; stowed posters in the lockable portion of the wardrobe, removed items that showed the accumulation of dust and sticky circles where drinks had stood. Looking at the empty room, I realised that I'd smoked, drunk, wanked and fucked in this bedsit without ever having to consider the consequences. I pulled open the patio window and stepped onto the balcony.

"We're only supposed to hoover you know," Barbara lent against the door. "But considering you're back here next year, I suppose I'll have to look after you." She swept her finger across the desk and tutted. In consolation she added, "I've seen worse."

"Is that supposed to make me feel better?"

"No. It's supposed to make you appreciate me more."

We both laughed and after I'd carried my case to the hall, I made us a cup of tea.

"Where are you going to do your fieldwork?" Barbara asked. It was the first time I'd heard her enquire about anyone's studies.

"Hawsker. It's a little village outside Whitby. I've heard the cliffs are a reasonable walk and I'll guess there'll be a bus to get me to town."

"The only thing I know about Whitby is that Dracula's buried there."

I was going to tell her but refrained. "So long as it's not my last resting place," I joked, "I always promised my dad I'd take the plot next to him."

"Oh! I don't fancy being buried myself, too messy," she didn't elaborate.

"Well," I took a gulp of tea; "I'll see you in October."

Barbara stopped me and patted her cheek. I kissed her soft downy skin like a dutiful nephew.

I reflected that my problems with women were similar to my problem with geology. I knew I had been born, the evidence stared at me from the mirror but I had no recollection of events from nought to three, four possibly… all the earth-shattering events of teething, speech and first steps were lost. There were the family complications, the things usually left unsaid which happened just after I was born in 1962. Yet at nineteen there was obvious evidence of what had happened. These events were lost in a half-formed mind unable to articulate their complexity. Not so much an absence of evidence as evidence of absence.

The train from Cottingham to Scarborough arrived late. It was a modern push-me, pull-me with no room for substantial luggage, so I travelled with the case wedged between my knees. I peered through dirty windows at the scenery. The rich clay of Holderness had given way to chalk. The embankments were steep and the cuttings narrow. At Hunmanby a great many people got on, all hikers. They brought the smell of sweat, damp wool, and tobacco into the carriage. As the guard secured the doors all these odours mixed with my hunger pangs and I began to feel sick.

It was an interminable journey to Scarborough. Once there I piled my belongings into a locker so I could explore the town unencumbered. Across the road was the art deco facade of the Odeon but I took the route downhill, enjoying the fresh sea breeze. The street got narrower and noisier. Eventually I found the fish and chip cafe mum had always finished our excursions with. I sat in the corner seat and feeling like an oversized child ordered haddock and chips. A lager was the only nod at adulthood. I finished lunch fuelled with optimism and energy. I had two hours before the bus to Whitby, so I walked round the foreshore passing lads in tight t-shirts and girls in polka dot bikinis. I bought an ice cream and dawdled a little, taking in the sights and sounds but it was the smells which over whelmed me. Chips, vinegar, hot dogs and waffles and the smell of the sea. There was even the delicate aroma of vanilla as my nose passed close to the frozen confectionery.

All the time I was nearing the place I had to visit. The sandstone building hugged the landscaped cliff. I walked in and paid. I climbed the stairs. The Rotunda was the first purpose built museum in the world and the central section was created for a panoramic map. The coast of Yorkshire was painted layer-by-layer and annotated by rock type. John Philips had drawn the details from his uncle's notes and the result was a scientific spectacle.

All this had been constructed for William Smith and geology. It didn't matter that the curved cabinets were now full of ephemera, saucy postcards, model ships and the like, so long as the map remained. I sought out the area I'd be working on, it consisted of Liassic shales and deltaic sediments from the Jurassic. This was geology everyone knew about. The era of dinosaurs. It was possible I might even find some part of one. Such luck would definitely help pad out the thesis I had to create from all this work. Over four billion years had passed since the creation of the Earth. All this time must underlie the rocks I was here to study but there was scant evidence of them. Oceans opened and closed, mountains rose and were eroded, to create what we see today. I stayed a little too long in my homage to The Father of Geology and had to run up the hill to the station to collect my belongings. After crossing the road to the bus station, I spent a worrying ten minutes in a long queue. Finally I reached the driver.

"Two pounds forty."

I searched my pockets and produced a five-pound note.

The driver tapped the sign.

I read it slowly. *Exact change please.*

I searched my pockets again. I found two pounds, then thirty pence but no more.

The driver huffed and rang in the amount. "I should make you get off a mile early but I'm a reasonable man."

I swallowed and said thanks, feeling obliged and flustered at the same time. I tucked myself away at a window seat. I took out the geological guide to North Yorkshire and read its authoritative passages. The bus bumped and jolted along for an hour or more. I'd given up reading after a large woman sat next to me and made it impossible to move my arms without pushing against her right breast. Instead I studied the bleak moors and isolated farmsteads we passed. In the distance a stout church tower emerged from the green fields. Its slate roof descended to dour sandstone walls and nearby was a large building I took to be the schoolhouse. I had finally arrived.

I got off in the centre of Hawsker village. As the bus pulled away the smell of its diesel lingered. I looked up and down the road. There was one pub. There was a small shop with a post office but it was the church tower which dominated, sucking out light and the life from the village. Traffic echoed down the narrow main street. I realised that standing by the roadside wouldn't do, no one was going to collect me. I would have to walk. I set out for Soulgrave Farm, case in hand, coat over arm, bag over shoulder. I found the farm just at the village edge. I pulled open the massive iron gate and began to walk down the drive. Two inquisitive dogs came barking around my legs. A woman emerged from the farmhouse rubbing her hands on her apron. She shaded her eyes.

"Yes, what can I do for you?" She asked with caution.

"Mrs. Moralis? I'm David, the geologist from Hull. I wrote to..."

"Why didn't you say so? Come on in," The woman ushered me into the parlour. "I'll take it you've got the balance of the rent?" She held out her hand.

I counted out the agreed amount. She snatched it from me and stuffed it into an apron pocket.

"You'll be wanting a cup of tea?"

"That would be nice," I said.

"Well take this old kettle with you and you'll be able to brew yourself a cup."

I was handed a stained aluminium kettle and was asked to follow my landlady across the yard. The shower and toilet were at the back of the barn and looked serviceable. The caravan was bigger than I expected and tucked into the edge of an orchard.

"We put it here so visitors can have their privacy," She unlocked the door and handed me the key. "I think you'll find it clean and comfortable."

I stepped inside. It looked and smelt clean. I noticed Mrs. Moralis stayed outside.

"Well, I'll leave you. You must have lots to sort out. Knock at the door at any time up to nine if you've a question," the lady walked back round the corner of the barn, leaving me the sole occupant of the caravan.

The Formica surfaces were clean, even the corners of the wardrobe lacked dust. I unpacked my bag. Finally I put the kettle on. The smell of camping gas diffused round the room. I relaxed on the sofa seat and warmed my hands round the mug. I looked around. It was a startling revelation that there was no television. I felt a wave of panic: no News at Ten, Blake's Seven or Dr. Who. I opened my case and removed any means of entertainment. A *Walkman* and several tapes, a torch with batteries running low, a geological guide to North Yorkshire, slightly battered, the collected short stories of Somerset Maugham, secondhand, a notebook and pad of A4 paper.

I sighed.

A little later I began to feel hungry. I knew I had to organise myself. In my wallet I had one hundred pounds and a cashpoint card. There was no alternative, I plugged in the fridge, locked the door behind me and walked back to the village. An aunt had impressed on me the nutritional value of baked beans. My shopping took this fully into account. Tea consisted of beans on toast and an apple. Afterwards I read a story, then another.

Looking out I noticed the different shades of green amongst the apple trees with their unripened fruit and the buzz of flies. I looked at my watch. I examined the map. I planned the first day of mapping: a long walk along the coast to get an overview of the area. I read a third story. I was beginning to appreciate why the Victorian's loved long novels. Finally I picked up the torch and decided to walk to the pub. I'd noticed the Cook Arms on my arrival. The lounge was unexpectedly busy. A quiz evening. I sat on a barstool, drinking and listening.

"Hey, d'you know who was king in 1415?" The woman lent towards me.

"Henry the Fifth."

"Thanks," she said as she resumed her position.

In the interval the bar became a great crush. I lit a cigarette. The woman I'd spoken to earlier came up to me again. "You must be new here?"

"I'm staying at Soulgrave Farm. I'm doing my thesis here, so you'll see a lot of me."

"The Moralis place? Here Ricky, you didn't tell me you had a visitor."

"I didn't know," The lad stood in front of me. He wasn't as tall as me and possessed a slender frame like Drew. He also had slightly unkempt jet-black hair and piercing blue eyes.

"I'm staying in the caravan," I said. "Nice place."

Ricky sucked on his cigarette and looked me up and down. "I remember now, you're the student." He turned around and went back to his friends.

"He's like that sometimes. By the way, I'm Gabby, the landlady of this place. So you'll get to know me. What subject do you study?"

"Geology."

I was ready to add the usual explanation but she replied, "figures, the only geologist I know is this I guy on the telly." She didn't elaborate.

How could you know someone on television? I suppose you have the evidence of what you see and hear unlike geology were you have the rocks and what is preserved in them. Geology is a peculiar science. I literally fell into it by accident. Walking along Lebberston cliffs, I was so engrossed by the coloured layers that I tripped. I only avoided a two hundred foot drop by the tenacity of my grip. As I shouted for help, I saw at close quarters the peculiar markings in the sandstone. From that moment on I was hooked.

The deciding factor in my study of rocks was my failure to grasp maths. A grade D at O' level put paid to that subject and I'd never got on with physics, so I jumped at the opportunity to join Mr. Caine's Earth Science group. It promised two weeks of fieldwork in exotic places like Seahouses and Duror. Just the sort of thing I needed to get out from under mum's feet. We were an ill-matched assortment of individuals: a reformed junkie, a mother's boy, and Drew. I might have avoided Drew because we'd been childhood friends who had drifted apart when adolescence kicked in. However Mr Caine's seating plan placed Drew next to David. Five hours a week we sat next to each other, hardly speaking but then we both got drunk at the Sixth Form Christmas party. As we walked back through East Park, we started groping and kissing. I leant Drew against the bridge parapet. I placed my hand inside her bra and felt the solid erect nipple. Finally I got down on my knees and did something I'd seen on a video. From that night on we were confidants, hopeless gossips and lovers.

I looked over at the group of lads in the pub. Briefly Ricky's eyes met mine. I wondered why he'd snubbed me.

"Who had a hit with *Someone like you*? Number seventeen, who was Gordon of Khartoum's adversary? Eighteen: which football team won…"

The trouble with Drew was that she was both a good friend and a good lover. The mix was exhilarating. It wound me into an emotional whirl. I stopped working at college and it was only when I got threatened with the axe that I realised months had passed by unaccounted for. Seventeen became eighteen. Somehow I got the grades required by Hull University and despite living only a few miles down the road - I got a place in Down's Hall. Finally I realised if you were voted onto a committee you'd get a place in the second year. I nominated myself. There was no opposition. Drew didn't want the more regimented life so she moved to a private house on Lambert Street. One of those nice places rich parents buy for their kids, then sub-let.

Within days our relationship was over. Drew found there were just too many distractions. It was as though she was determined to extract every minute from her life. At a fresher's disco I found her in the arms of another man. That was the night I met Carrie. I'd felt her eyes seek me out but she waited before making her move. Drew and I went our separate ways. We stopped speaking. Occasionally we sat near each other in the library but I couldn't look her in the eye. I'd been foolish. She'd been foolish but neither of us knew how to bridge the gap. I couldn't walk over and say "I'm sorry," it wasn't in my nature. So we saw each other but everything went unsaid. When Carrie gave me the ultimatum, I accepted. It wasn't love with Carrie; it was lust.

How we deceive. How I deceived myself. Carrie was just the catalyst I needed to get over Drew but there was something else, Jonathan had come up to me after a poetry society meeting and told me he fancied me. I looked him over. He was of short stature and had long dark hair which partly hid his olive eyes. I put my arm round his waist and felt his ribs. He smiled. All the evidence was adding up to a conclusion I'd long chosen to ignore. Around me I was learning about rocks building by the layer into Earth History. In North Yorkshire I would see the layers of rock and the very fossils that had destroyed our faith in God, oldest sediments at the bottom and perching on the brink from which Drew had been cast into the void, the youngest.

Chapter 2: Extinction

The development of geology could only happen in a country with the freedom to express new ideas. First the observations were made, then connections and finally a theory grew. It wasn't meant to challenge God but by a quirk of fate several men of the cloth were involved in His demise.

Drew was pushed from right here. It was daylight and a wide blue sky kept my fears at bay. I bought a local paper, the coroner's report had brought in a verdict of suicide. Even after all these months there was still no mention of the boyfriend. I knew differently. I staved off a panic attack by doing deep breathing exercises. I was aware of everything below me and the compelling patterns of waves drawing me down. I double-checked my position before sitting. I felt calmer. I looked around to ensure no one was close enough to push me over before taking out a letter from Carrie. Her use of English would be unacceptable to either science or God as it contained too many *fucks*, used as either adjectives or verbs. I folded the pretty pink paper into a neat dart and launched it.

Rocks are the natural effect of the Great Flood, the one Noah sailed away on and that idea might still be in vogue today except for the quick wits of Chapman and Wooler. These two men found some solidified remains embedded in the cliffs at Saltwick. They removed the bones and by observation decided they had found the fossilised remains of an alligator.

Each wrote a considered description of the find for the learned journals of the time. The information presented might well have been dismissed except for the problem a fossilised animal conceived. God created the world. He created the animals. So how could an animal be preserved in rock? Rock was created before life. The Bible said so.

Of course one fossil could be dismissed. It is a matter of irony that the second stone alligator was found by the Reverend George Young. It was embedded in the alum rock at Whitby. Like many parsons with time on his hands, the Rev. Young was a scientist. He studied the fossil and was bemused. Although the creature looked like an alligator, it shared few characteristics. It was obviously oceanic and had bones like a fish. It was a matter of inconvenience that no living relative could be found. God created all animals, so he certainly wasn't going to let any become extinct. Extinction was a word that raised the reverend's hackles. He found a get out clause, he agreed that despite finding this unknown species in fossil form, its living relative must be awaiting discovery. This was his conclusion as George found it absurd to think of animals dying out before people were here to appreciate them.

Two fossilized sea creatures might well be God's little joke to test the faith of scientists. Unfortunately a third specimen was discovered petrified. This skeleton was more complete and the creature could be seen for what it was, a great sea crocodile. It was purchased by the Whitby Museum for £7 in 1825.

By the time a fifth fossil was found at Saltwick in the 1840's the marine animal sported the smart name of plesiosaurus. Science had gained the upper hand. Lamark had broken free of The Bible with thoughts of evolution. This was the final irony. Animals had lived for a billion years before we had evolved to our present condition. This placed the plesiosaur as just one reptile amongst many, hunting through Jurassic Oceans.

I sat on the cliff edge watching another pink dart descend. Under me ranged 80 metres of Jurassic sediments, the layers perfectly preserved and brilliantly cut by centuries of erosion and all inaccessible. I'd walked the coast path from Mawe Wyke Hole to Robin Hood's Bay. There wasn't a single point at which any sane person could descend. My feet ached. In fact my feet throbbed! I'd made a serious mistake. My tutor at university told me to ensure I chose an accessible area. Clearly I had not. I pushed my head and neck over the edge. It was a long way down and one thing I refused to do was jump. The image somersaulted in my mind and I thought of Drew's last vision. Perhaps I should have said more when she rang. The night before she was murdered Drew remembered me. I found that difficult to understand. If it was a plea for help it fell on deaf ears. I listened politely. She told me that the coast would be perfect for my mapping area. That was helpful. Finally Drew told me about the local boy she'd met. Mike Astor.

"Aren't you jealous?" She asked.

I thought about my feelings, "I would have been last October but now," and for once I was honest, "I've found my Jonathan."

"So you don't love Carrie?"

"No." It was quite simple, I felt relieved I'd told someone. "I don't love Carrie." I had loved Drew in the way only first love engenders, a hopeless confusion of what should have been or what might have been. The line went quiet and then the pips started. I think Drew said *goodbye*, or maybe I convinced myself she had so I'd feel better.

It must be true that more creatures have become extinct than are now living. But that's the impersonal nature of fossils. Each remain we delight in was a tragedy. I pushed myself to the edge and looked down again. My own tragedy beckoned. I could hear the sea crash against the cliffs. I could smell damp earth, straw and salt. The wind sighed through the field of barley behind me. I stood and brushed myself down. I picked up my bag and made for the houses clustered against the cliff.

The footpath ended at a street of Victorian semis each sporting an initial and a date. I made my way downhill. A seagull's cry echoed round the narrow lanes. I passed a second hand bookshop and resisted the temptation to buy one of the local geology guides on display. *Day one and not yet desperate.* I mused and bought a newspaper before entering a pub called The Dolphin. I ordered some food and sat at a window seat drinking a lager shandy. I read.

"It's you," the voice said.

I looked up, "Hello, Ricky."

"Your sort make me sick," Ricky added, "always on holiday, always drunk."

I tried to think of a witty put-down, but my mind went blank. "I thought I deserved a break after three hours."

"Did you find what you were after?"

"It's not a question of finding- the rocks are always here- but mapping the rock type, the thickness of bed, angle of dip, distinguishing features, fossils. It's a detective game. A great 3D puzzle, only I don't know what the pieces are yet."

"You've lost me," Ricky picked up his canvas bag. The tools sounded metallic.

"Join me on Saturday and I'll show you?" I offered.

"Saturday's are for footy and fucking," he swung the bag over his shoulder. "But I'll take you up on Sunday."

"Fine," I said.

Ricky walked out of the pub. He didn't turn round once as he walked down the hill.

The girl brought my food over and I ate whilst reading. I looked up the tide times in the paper and as it was going out, I decided to start some mapping. The north cliff had the atmospheric name of Dungeon Holes and began where the sea defences ended. Granite boulders scattered over the wave cut platform were backed up by huge pillars of reinforced concrete to protect the town. From this angle the buildings dug precariously into the cliff looked in dire need of further protection.

I returned to the caravan with a great many notes and felt more optimistic about my prospects. After tea I drew a rough sketch of my work. I must have fallen asleep at the table because I woke with a crick in my neck. I eased it with gentle movement. Finally, without bothering to turn on a light, I fumbled my way to the bed I hadn't bothered making that morning.

I spent the next day at Robin Hood's Bay. I treated myself to the same lunch. I didn't see Ricky. I'd collected a number of fossils and carrying their weight made my shoulders ache. I'd found several Devil's toenails, the much more romantic name for a filter feeding mollusc called, Gryphaea. I'd even recovered the impression of a fish body but by far the most beautiful where the ammonites. Each whorl preserved in pyrites and iridescent in the sunlight. When I got back to the caravan I spread out my finds on the table and started cutting up plasters and writing information on them. There was a knock at the door.

"I made too much of this," Mrs. Moralis passed me a plate with a second inverted over it.

"Thanks," I said, savouring the aroma. I lifted the lid to reveal a large slab of steak and kidney pie with all the trimmings. I pushed the specimens to one side then cut the pie with my fork edge. Mum would not have approved.

I only noticed the police car as I returned the plates. Mrs. Moralis took them from me without a word. I hovered. "Is everything alright?"

"Fine," she said closing the door. I could see Ricky and two officers in conversation, one was Bartholomew Fair. I moved quickly when he glanced out of the window and returned to the caravan to complete labelling the days finds.

As the tide permitted I spent the next three days mapping the North Cheek at Bay Town. I felt part of the place knowing the local name for this tourist trap. The wave cut platform was hard grey shale into which fossils were flattened. The casts of ammonites were preserved, the originals had long since been hacked out as they were worth so much. I'd heard rumours of fossil hunters – professionals under the protection of rich collectors.

I had lots of measurements to do. The remains of long, thin shells all possessed the same orientation. I began recording the data hoping to prove the direction of a current which flowed two hundred million years before the Great Flood. Finally I'd use my limited knowledge of FORTRAN to process the data through the main frame computer.

The great roar of the sea reminded me that the tide was on the turn. I looked up at the cliff tops. The sheer face provided no escape so I realised I'd have to move quickly towards the town. I noticed a women and a man at the edge. From this distance the girl's pink skirt was the most obvious item of clothing. I looked at layer upon layer of rock rising as a barrier before I collected my possessions.

I broke into a jog in an effort to beat the incoming tide but slipped on the wet shale, cursed and picked myself up. I heard the scream and looked round. A man was falling, his arms and legs desperately flailing and as he got closer I could see his mouth was open wide and his eyes black with fear. The man's jacket swung back like an angel's wings. He hit the rocks in silence. The thud seemed to come later.

Stunned, I approached the victim. The contents of his body had splattered across the Calcareous limestone but his head looked intact. The smell travelled quickly. I retched. Just when I'd straightened up enough to look, I retched again. I moved back a few paces and I stared at the sky, trying to keep the sick down. That's when I saw the woman standing at the cliff edge. She clearly saw me because she waved.

I reached into my rucksack for my camera and forced myself to take a couple of photos. As I looked through the view finder I realized I knew the face. I thought I might be sick again. It was Bartholomew Fair. I looked up at the cliff. Had I imagined a girl standing there? Had I imagined it all? I looked back at the body. It was definitely Bartholomew. I thought of having to break the news to Aunt Gertie. She'd been so proud. What a dreadful accident.

The last time I had seen him, he had been interrogating Ricky. I also remembered how he'd flung Drew over the edge and how he'd cuffed Mike. This was an unlikely coincidence, even the police might mange to connect one event with another. I stumbled towards Baytown. I willed myself to breath and walked ahead to beat the tide. The slope from the beach nearly defeated me. A police officer took my arm and guided me through the crowd. My head spun and I must have fainted.

When at last the doctor had seen me and I was able to drink sweet tea, I talked more lucidly. The officer put the tape in the machine and introduced himself, "I am DCI Birbeck and this is DS Laing. The detective had a leathery skin creased around the eyes and forehead. I imagined straightening it out to reveal a secret message. His boss was overweight.

DS Laing went through the procedures and offered a legal representative. I agreed and one was found. The woman who entered looked harassed, her greying hair windswept and her eyes hidden behind dark glasses. She introduced herself, tidied forms, clicked her pen and nodded. The interview commenced at three fifteen pm. "Please state your name and address."

"David Jones of 556, James Reckitt Avenue, Hull, currently residing in a caravan at Soulgrave Farm."

I told the two officers everything I'd seen. They nodded but their faces remained implacable. I realised Birbeck was the man I should concentrate on. His face was flabby and his clothes untidy and occasionally I caught a snatch of stale breath which reminded me of an alcoholic lecturer. I kept steeling glances at the man, the more I looked the more I was certain he was with Bartholomew the night Drew was pushed. He spoke less often than Laing and I had the uncomfortable feeling he was scrutinising everything about me.

"A tragic accident," I said despite thinking the girl on the cliff had pushed him. "There was a woman on the cliff. She had a pink skirt. She might be a good witness to the accident."

"Accident?" The officer appeared to have some agenda.

"Accident," I confirmed despite remembering the argument. The cross examination started again. Questions about the girl, questions about why I was in Bay Town, questions about Ricky. By the time they'd finished I could no longer be certain what I'd seen.

"We're inclined to treat the fall as a tragic accident. The cliffs are treacherous when wet." DS Laing concluded. "But it's a sad day for the North Yorkshire Constabulary."

I agreed. "I know how dangerous cliffs can be. I nearly fell to my death some years ago. That's how I became a geologist."

Laing thought I was being frivolous. He rounded on me. "You do realise you witnessed the death of one of our officers, a very popular young man?" Laing continued.

"I do. I knew him as well. He was Aunt Gertie's grandson. Bartholomew."

DCI Birbeck starred at me as if connecting several facts. He said nothing and eventually he looked at DS Laing, "I think Mr Jones should go home to rest. I take it we can contact you at Soulgrave Farm for…"

"The next month," I added helpfully.

"Interview suspended at 7.45pm…."

"Well young man, the doctor's given you some sleeping tablets. The instructions are written on the packet," The DCI looked at me, trying to weigh me up. I smiled weakly.

I hadn't realised the passage of time. It was nearly dark outside. A uniformed cop, probably traffic had offered to drive me back to Hawsker. He was pleasant, asking no questions but insisting politely to see me inside the caravan. He said "Good night," but in a way that lacked conviction and I saw in his eyes the dreadful burden of his work. A friend of mine had joined the force at eighteen but left within a year. He told me it was the unexpected which broke him. Not death. Not the dying he'd witnessed but simply the fear of the unknown with every shift.

I wasn't going to take the tablets at first but when I lay down on the bed the image of death returned. I punched out a tablet from the foil and washed it down.

Morning came too quickly. I snapped awake, my mouth feeling dry and my head boxed full of fuzz. I stumbled to the kitchen, fumbled in the fridge, dropped the top and drank from the bottle. The lemonade washed into me. I felt renewed. I felt sick with hunger so I opened a packet of cereal and spooned handfuls into my mouth. I returned to bed and folded myself into the warm sheets.

The tapping at the window took me by surprise. I felt a wave of panic, and then I saw it was Ricky. I pushed open the door.

Ricky stood there, "Can I come in?"

"It's a bit early."

"I think we've got some talking to do," He put down the packet of cigarettes on the table. He pulled a jar of coffee from his coat pocket and a packet of digestive biscuits. "Are we in business?"

"You've got the goods, I've got the party," I smiled.

Ricky smiled but it soon faded. He looked out. It had started raining. "News travels fast round here, especially when you don't want it to. We heard about the accident in the pub last night."

I thought about the word accident. I started to speak but changed my mind, "Tragic."

"It seems our village is cursed. We've had more than our fair share with Mick going off the edge with that girl and before... before that there was my brother."

"Your brother?" I thought about the loss of someone so close. Of course I'd lost my dad, but I was only eight. I didn't fully understand. It's just that one day he was there, all smiles -- his moustache stained yellow from cigarettes-- and the next he was lying cold on the kitchen floor. Mum found him when she got up to make breakfast. I watched her calmly ring for the ambulance.

"He was everything to me," Ricky lit a cigarette, his hand trembling. "I loved Jevan."

"Why are you telling me this?" I looked directly into Ricky's dark eyes.

"Because it's not right! Something connects them all. I'm sure of it."

"And you think I might know something?"

I realised how lean and muscular he was and the line his pecs made under the t-shirt.

"I do care," I reassured. "I'm just emotionally drained after yesterday. It's all a bit raw."

Ricky stubbed his cigarette into the ashtray, "Eight o'clock and Jevan was going out to his girlfriend's. He got in the car and drove off. The next we knew the police were knocking at the door. Jevan's car had been driven into an abandoned quarry and torched. There was no body. The police closed the file. Suicide. Their best guess is he jumped from the cliff after his girl had finished with him. He couldn't take rejection, that was Birbeck's theory. But it's not true. I know it's not true. She hadn't finished with him and he would never have left without telling me, he just wouldn't do it, the fucking bastard. It wasn't what we'd planned." Ricky lit another cigarette. He put on the kettle. "We had money saved. We were going to buy a sheep farm in New Zealand. Our futures were mapped out. God damn it! Brothers don't do that to brothers."

"I don't have any experience of brothers. I'm an only child. I know my dad fell out with his brother when the big house was sold from under his nose. They never spoke again." I pulled a fag out of the packet. I looked at Ricky. He looked at me. The kettle whistled. I waited. He waited. I got up to make the coffee. I slid the cups across the white Formica. "And what about Drew?" I asked.

Ricky nearly choked on cigarette smoke. He took a mouthful of water from the tap. When he'd collected himself he just stared at me. "I didn't think it was an accident, you being here."

"Drew suggested the place. She said it would be perfect for my mapping area. In fact she rang me the night before she was murdered. She sounded happy. She sounded like the future was all rolled out before her and waiting to be walked on."

"Murdered?" Ricky asked.

"Yes, pushed by Bartholomew Fair and Birbeck."

"How do you know?"

"I saw it," I confessed. "And do you know it was Fair who died yesterday. He was pushed by some girl in a pink skirt."

Ricky smiled and made himself more comfortable. "Wow! You and me might be on opposite sides but I reckon we could bridge the gap."

"I'd have thought we might be on the same side."

Ricky eyed me suspiciously. He drank his coffee. "Drew knew a bit about fossils, so she came in handy when these German guys arrived wanting to know where to find good specimens. They gave her a cut. When I visited the Canon, he had some new specimens on show. It didn't connect at first but then Carrie told me about the private collection in the tower."

"Carrie?"

"Tall, university type, big arse."

"Yes, that's Carrie. She's the Canon's niece."

"She's my girlfriend when I'm that way inclined."

"You're not a part time puff are you?"

I didn't say anything. I just smiled. Ricky collected the jar of coffee and what remained of the biscuits and left the caravan. I watched him cross the yard and enter the farmhouse.

I opened all the windows and cleared out the rubbish. I wanted to delay going to the coast and so cleaned the caravan. When everything was completed I looked at my watch. The bus for Whitby left in about fifteen minutes. I decided to change direction. I packed my bag with the requisite materials, rolled up an unflattering blue Cagoule and headed off. The was no queue at the bus stop but various people joined me from assorted shelters, as the engine pukked and revved round the corner. I was glad of the company. I listened to the conversations. None of them concerned the cliff fall or geology; they were all blissfully unaware of extinction, being preoccupied with shopping lists and hernias.

"Aunt Muriel's a coeliac you know," the woman behind me confided.

"They never seem to have much luck in the horoscopes," her friend retorted.

I concentrated on the view of Whitby with its abbey on the headland and the town clinging to the sides of the Esk Valley. When I was five or six, nan and grandpa brought me to Whitby on the way back from a wedding. We counted the steps of Caedmon's Trod and walked round the abbey in the sunshine. Finally we went for a fish and chip supper at *The Magpie*. That was the bit I enjoyed most. I remember that as we walked back to the car the heavens opened.

The clouds looked equally ominous today. The driver turned on the windscreen wipers. The windows began to steam up. I wiped the surface of the glass. I hadn't intended to go to Whitby Museum but as it was raining I decided I might make use of the occasion. My grandparents had brought me here and I remembered why it was so important to them. In 1938 they too had sheltered from the rain and grandpa had brought out a ring and proposed right here on the wooden bench under the *fossile bones of an allegator*.

After braving the rain and pulling off my cagoule, I left rings of water on the floor. I could see the plesiosaurs as they were now called on display and I hoped I could glean a few ideas about the geology of the area, particularly those coves only accessible by boat. Perhaps, and this was unlikely, I could find someone who could ferry me to such bays as William Smith had been. The notion was fanciful. I could never afford the hire of a boat and I doubted I had the stomach for seafaring. A windy afternoon on East Park boating lake was enough for me.

I held out my damp student card and was nodded through the turnstile by the attendant. It wasn't what I expected. The large room was crammed full of objects, some in cases, others hung at dubious angles from the walls. The famous fossils were mounted as plaques. The contorted skeleton of the first pleisiosaur suggested death by asphyxiation. Next was George Young's own find Teleosaurus chapmani. This black lacquered specimen looked dusty and neglected. It was named after Chapman, one half of the duo who discovered the first fossil and set us on the road to our knowledge of evolution and extinction. The skull showed two definite eye sockets. Only one fin could be seen clearly and within the skeleton were the remains of its last meal: ammonites. The condemned ate a hearty meal but never had chance for digestion. For a long time I stared in wonder at the reptile. It was smaller than expected but clearly a sea creature, streamlined, adapted for hunting. It must have been formidable. I took out my notebook. It was only later as I stared at a tattooed and shrunken Maori head that I realised I'd left my notes behind. I retraced my steps. The book was where I'd left it on top of a glass case of assorted fossils. As I lifted it a piece of paper fluttered to the floor. I picked it up and unfolded it. The pink scented paper stirred memories. The message was simple:

Don't try to find me. Love Drew.

As I turned around my eyes wouldn't focus and I felt panic make me light-headed. I sat by the exhibit and calmed myself. I could see no one in the hall except a family with two bored children. I read the note again. I held it to the light. It was exactly the paper Drew had used. Had it really been there eight months? I dismissed the idea. Someone was playing a joke in bad taste. It was a forgery. I suspected everyone but who knew I'd be here in Whitby? Who might have followed me and why? I folded up the note again and placed it back in the book.

I found myself drawn to the shrivelled Maori head. I stared at it for a long time. My dad always said to me that unless you had children your genes became extinct. He fretted about the family name continuing, pointing out the names on the family tree and saying each one with pride. Even when I was eight he pestered me about getting married before I was twenty-five. He insisted I should have kids whilst I was young enough to enjoy them maintaining that that was a mistake he'd made, leaving having a kid until late. Perhaps he knew he was dying and that sowing the idea of procreation in one so young would eventually bear fruit.

I don't think he thought a lot of me. I was a wimpy child, not a footballer and certainly not a rugger player – a game he was passionate about. I'd once asked Dad if I could take piano lessons. The beating I received ensured I never asked again. I remember mum would let me spend hours painting in our sunny kitchen. She still keeps samples of the work that impressed her. I suppose that's the double sting. I was a bit of a disappointment to mum because I didn't take up art. About all I use it for now is drawing pictures of fossils. I suppose I'm good because people ask if they can photocopy my work. Usually I agree for a token payment. Drew hated that about me, my mercenary streak. I looked at the intricate faded tattoos and tried to imagine what a long dead head might be thinking of. Did it dwell on the disappointment of its own sons or was it just slowly decaying into oblivion? Someone tapped me on the shoulder. I jumped.

"You're not one of those activists are you?" The curator seemed quite genuine in her concern.

"No. At least not in the returning heads to their homeland sort of way." I smiled but the woman didn't see the joke. I shrugged and walked on. It was later inside that museum that I committed the cardinal sin. I began copying notes about the detailed geology of the coast. I also realised there was a caravan park above Saltwick Bay and that if the conditions were good, I'd be able to gain access to the beach there.

Even though it was still raining when I emerged, I felt better about myself. I'd briefly forgotten yesterday's dreadful event. I wandered round a couple of antique shops. I saw a porcelain figure of a faun riding a tortoise. I yearned to hold it. I asked the price and then the best cash figure. Both were way out of my league. I moved on. I studied windows full of Whitby jet and coiled ammonites. I opened my backpack and went into a rock shop.

"What sort of price would a specimen like this fetch?" I pulled open the two halves of a nodule and handed it to the owner.

"Quite nice. Dactylioceras commune. I could give you a fiver."

I smiled. I'd already seen a battered version in the window for fifteen quid. "I'll bear your offer in mind," I lied and left the shop. It was useful though. If I ran out of money, I wouldn't have to ring up mum for a sub, I could make my own way. Independence was important to me. I'd seen how other parent's had emotionally blackmailed my friends. I just allowed myself to be emotionally blackmailed by Drew and now Carrie.

As I turned the corner I saw the girl in the pink dress. Her dark hair was plastered to her forehead where the hood ended. Instead of darting out of the way, I shouted. She turned, saw me and ran. The crowd of tourists was too thick to make speedy progress. I last saw the flash of pink mingling with the crowd, the umbrellas, coats and rain concealed her. There was something familiar about the girl. I couldn't work out the connection. I stood in the rain before taking a right into a dimly lit pub. I sat down on the red velour seat and regained my composure. Eventually I took off my coat and walked to the bar. I pushed my way through the crowd of mostly older men and ordered. A musician began playing the hurdy-gurdy. The humming continuo reminded me of a concert in Beverley Minster. I quietly whistled the song. A middle aged man sat opposite me. He smiled.

"Do you like this sort of music?" His accent had a Geordie lilt.

"Yes. Tradition." I drained the last of my bitter.

"You don't look the hippy sort."

I looked more closely at the man. His thinning grey hair suggested someone who might be enjoying his seventies. He put a carton of old Virginian on the table and began making a roll up.

"Help yourself," he said.

With this comment I knew he was on the make for something. My chip butty arrived, so I couldn't just walk away.

"Sorry," he said, turning to light the fag away from me. I had a few minutes of peace whilst the musician played and the old man smoked. I'd barely finished my sandwich before he popped the question, "green or brown?"

Now green makes me hyper and I don't sleep well. Brown can be good but sometimes they add pig tranquillisers. There again green has a taste... "green."

He looked at me very carefully, "roll yourself a fag and slip a tenner under the table if you like what you see."

I did as he suggested. There was no doubting the quality. Good dried back garden stuff.

"This is your first time, isn't it?" I asked, proffering the correct denomination.

"Is it that obvious?" The old man looked a little nervous.

"Yes."

"I need to supplement my pension. I thought..."

"Well it's as good a way as any. If you'll take some advice. Only sell to people you know. It reduces the risk."

"Risk?" The old man said. "There's only one cop on duty for the whole of Whitby on a Friday and he's on a liquid lunch."

I leant closer to him. "That's not the risk," I surveyed the room, no one seemed to be looking. "This is someone else's territory. It's all divided up. There's as much research in selling dope as there is positioning baked beans in Sainsbury's."

"I'll take your word for that," the man finished his drink. He looked around the pub and left. Sure enough a woman with tattooed arms followed him out. Coincidence maybe.

I didn't read of anything in the press that night, nor was the Cook Arms filled with seething indignation at another local crime. After the bus dropped me off, I had wandered in, damp and cold. I sat by the fire and warmed myself. My drink soon finished, I reluctantly went out into the rain again. The walk to the farm seemed to take forever. Extinction has many forms, the ending of life, the emptying of a soul. Tonight the extinction was my own.

Chapter 3: 1941

The Defiant dived low over the fields before waving its wings and banking steeply into the evening sun. Ernie smiled and listened to the cheers of other passengers. It was in the paper that three German bombers had been shot down by Defiants and people were feeling a bit more positive about events.

It had been a long night with the all clear sounding just after 2 a.m. and tiredness made it an even longer day with people being crotchety or just plain bad tempered in his boss's case. It was a relief to get out into the May sunlight and queue for the bus home.

The bell rang and a heavily pregnant woman was escorted off the bus by a dapper young man. "That's not her husband!" The woman in front remarked to her neighbour. Her neighbour tutted in reply.

Ernie stubbed out his cigarette then stood, unsteadily for a moment, before regaining his balance. His built up shoe echoed on the footplate.

"Same time tomorrow, God willing," the conductor touched his hat brim.

"Same time whether He's willing or not," Ernie smiled and put his good foot on terra firma before swinging down. As the bus pulled away he noticed the men walking out from the glasshouses. He waved, both waved back. As he crossed the road a crow took flight trailing entrails from the remains of a rabbit. Ernie took a deep breath. It reminded him of the child's body lying broken amongst the rubble during his last fire watch.

Ernie never got tired of admiring the sweep of the arch around the front door. He stood for a moment at the gate before entering.

Marjorie beat him to the door. "A small glass of sherry?" His wife asked.

"You've been buying on the black market again," Ernie commented then untied the Windsor knot and threw the tie over the banister.

"Eldedt says we shouldn't want for anything."

Ernie sat at the table and unfolded his paper. Marjorie smoothed his collar over his tweed jacket then pushed a stray wisp of hair into place. "You're going thin on top."

"I'm thirty one; it's only to be expected. What time are they due?"

"Seven. Blackout starts at twenty one fifty three," Marjorie stood with the evening sunlight falling on her face. It lit up her green eyes and highlighted the leaves in the pattern on her blouse.

"Can't you say seven minutes to ten?"

"I've washed and ironed your ARP uniform."

Ernie smiled. "Thanks," he squeezed her hand. "It can't be easy. All the unknowns."

"If only I smoked like you or drank like your dad but I haven't got it in me. Some character defect I suspect," Marjorie smiled. Her face shone with expectation.

Ernie pushed the table away and patted his knees. "Come here."

Marjorie sat obligingly. "We don't get enough time together with bulge getting bigger and our friends round night after night."

"And Eldedt staying in the front room. He has funny habits."

"Yes, I saw as I alighted from the bus. Still the life expectancy of a fighter pilot," Ernie mused. He slapped his wife's thighs and after she stood he hoisted himself back onto his feet. He moved over to the pan, lifted the lid and sniffed.

"Minced cobbler," Marjorie took the lid off him.

"Cobbler?"

"It's cobblers it's got mince in!" She smiled.

A plane flew low over the acres of glass houses. "One of ours!" Marjorie waved at it then looked back.

"Do you wish I was up there?"

"You do your bit," Marjorie stirred the stew. "Is that what's eating you?"

"Yes. No. I don't know. If it was just an ordinary night, you, me, Berny Loban and a few dances. I built this place for us."

"Soon there will be three."

"Three but tonight it will be six maybe seven."

"Five," Marjorie corrected and reeled off the names.

"We really are doing our bit," Ernie suggested with irony.

The meal was a sombre affair, bland but adequate. After listening to the Home Service Ernie changed into cords and donned his Wellingtons. He looked out at the clear blue sky and the faint moon rising. For a moment there was silence, he leant on his hoe and lit a cigarette before pegging up the beans. He noticed a dead rat which he removed on a shovel. Its one remaining eye stared accusingly before rippling with the maggots within. He threw the body on the incinerator. As Ernie replaced the tools in the shed he studied the paraphernalia of his pre-war hobby: photography. He had taken only a few pictures since the war started, who would want to see suffering and destruction on such a scale?

"A penny for them?" Cyril placed a hand on Ernie's shoulder making him jump.

"You gave me quite a shock. Hello there," Ernie replaced the gardening tools. "I was thinking that when bulge is my age, it'll be 1972!"

"And in 1972 you'll be a sad old git leaning on the gate and waiting for God!"

"Talking of old gits. I was always sweet on Gertie. Make certain you look after her, particularly now she's in the club!"

"I don't know what you mean," Cyril shifted uncomfortably.

"I think you do." Ernie left it at that for now. He changed the subject. "It's a nice evening. We might walk down to the Ship Inn and have a pint."

Cyril opened his mouth to say something.

"Don't worry, the worst that can happen is I over do it and get laid up tomorrow," Ernie tapped his knee.

They both looked into the evening sky. The distant exhaust trails of planes dispersed like italic script spreading a transitory message.

Ernie stooped over Gertie and kissed her on the cheek. He patted her bump. "How long now?"

"Four weeks, if I've got my dates right," Gertie winked.

"Another a few weeks more and the baby will have company."

"Yes," Marjorie looked over her glasses, "we can be broody mums together, pushing prams in search of decent food with our coupons."

Gertie clicked away with her knitting needles. "Why don't you two go for a pint? We can manage and there's always the telephone if one of us pops!"

"You have a way of making it sound so unpleasant!" Cyril snapped as he put on his jacket. Ernie stared at the two ladies who both engrossed themselves in their tasks. He knew as soon as the door closed they'd be talking. Conspiracy was in the air. "If we're delayed, blackout's at ten fifty three."

"Enjoy yourselves."

Outside the evening had turned chilly. The moon was now silvery bright and the blue hue presaged approaching summer. "Nights like this worry me. They're a gift for bombers," Ernie again searched the skies.

"When will it bally well be over?" Cyril lit a cigarette. He looked uneasily back towards the bungalow. He was going to ask about Eldedt but thought better of it.

Ernie waited saying nothing. They moved as quickly as Ernie's gait would allow and reached the pub just as a group of farm labourers were going in. There were one or two knowing nudges. "Evening Ernie," one lanky young man acknowledged his neighbour.

"Good evening. How's your grandpa after…"

"He'll get over it," the young man replied. "It took him half a bottle of whiskey before he could tell us anything about jumping in a ditch to avoid being strafed."

"Well pass on my regards."

"Will do," the lads clustered around the bar then migrated to the dart board.

"You've got yourself a reputation," Ernie whispered to Cyril before ordering two pints of mild but Cyril pushed past Ernie and left the bar. Ernie looked around and finding no table free he hoisted himself onto a bar stool and lit a cigarette.

"Got a real shirt lifter there." the farm labourer remarked, "caught amongst the cucumbers with that Dutch chap."

Ernie drew on the cigarette. "Sometimes a war can do strange things to people. They live for today and not tomorrow."

The labourer appreciated the sentiment. "But some things go beyond. He aught to watch his step. Don't see why you should put up with him, you've done your bit."

Ernie defended Cyril. "He married my fiancée. Turned her head with his money and social climbing."

"Them's the sort that loses everything fastest," he philosophised and turned his attention to the darts match.

Ernie felt light headed after drinking two pints and smoking. He'd spoken to villagers he hadn't seen in many weeks. In the farming community life went on. Their reserved occupation meant families stayed close. The idea of a family seemed oddly positive now, something to look forward to and not hide from. His father had drilled it into him these past few years. *A man must be a father by forty.* Well he hoped to make it with nine years to spare.

The walk home seemed so much easier as if the alcohol had lubricated the stiffened joints in his gammy leg. He pushed open the door and heard Eldedt's voice charming the ladies. "Hello!" He shouted and entered the warm room. There was silence. Ernie looked around. He took out his pocket watch. "Time for blackout."

"Where's Cyril?" Gertie bit her lip.

"I thought he'd be here. We quarrelled. He left an hour ago."

"Quarrelled?"

Ernie shot her a glance and she starred into the embers of the fire. "I'd better put that out." he poured sand over the glowing coals until they hissed and smoked. Ernie lit a cigarette and sat down. He caressed his leg and knee and shook his head. The air raid siren sounded. Gertie sucked in her breath between her teeth.

"I'll go and look for him," Eldedt volunteered, "I'll be careful." He turned up his collar and disappeared into the darkness. They all listened to the drone of planes overhead.

"Someone's in for it!" Ernie turned on the radio as Teddy Foster played the tunes from Covent Garden. Only then did he realise his unintentional double entendre. He hid his face in the shadows until only the red hot ember of his cigarette could be seen.

The telephone rang. For a moment everyone ignored it. The ring was persistent. Ernie got up. The conversation was brief. Ernie put on his coat and left the house without saying a word. He returned just as the bombs began landing on Hull. Eldedt's motorcycle fired up and the sound of its engine faded, to be replaced by distant sounds of destruction.

"He's been recalled. The balloon's gone up."

There was no reply except for the breathing of three people in the darkened room.

"And Cyril?" Gertie asked.

"I expect he's alright," Ernie reassured but it was hollow. He bade the women good night and carefully climbed the stairs. He pulled back the curtains and watched the orange glow take hold in the sky. Sometimes he fancied he could see the planes circle the city like mechanical vultures. He undressed and pulled the curtains closed as Marjorie arrived. "Don't look," he said, "it's too distressing." She pushed a stray wisp of hair behind his ear and kissed him.

The door downstairs slammed closed. There were steps in the hallway then the most almighty row. Gertie and Cyril's voices could be heard clearly through the floor boards and rugs. Eventually the voices subsided into sobs.

"Does she know?" Ernie asked.

Marjorie nodded. "The strange thing is the child is Eldedt's and Cyril doesn't seem to care."

Ernie laughed. He tried to stifle it but the sound still came.

In the morning Ernie shaved and put on his shirt, collar, tie and waist coat. Sleeve garters held the cuffs just below the jacket, so his engine turned gold cufflinks could display his aspirations. He unfurled a white napkin over his clothes. "Scrambled eggs." Marjorie spooned the contents of the pan over the plate. Cyril sat down opposite similarly attired. The same was ladled onto his plate.

"Sleep well?" Cyril asked.

"Like a log."

"Likewise," Cyril rucked up his shirt sleeves. "Lovely."

"Great. Better get a move on. The eight fifteen's due in ten minutes. There's bound to be delays."

"You're right."

Ernie kissed his wife's cheek.

"Gertie is feeling a little delicate this morning, perhaps you could..."

"Don't worry, Cyril, I'll help her as much as I can."

"Thanks. She's not a bad person you know."

"I know." Marjorie patted his arm. She stood in the shadows of the hall and waved. Eldedt returned on his old Norton, exhaust fumes billowing and dispersing behind. Cyril cast a second backward glance.

"Aren't you bothered?" Ernie asked.

"No," Cyril replied in earnest. "When he goes there'll always be evidence of his love no matter what happens. The child will be a common bond, something to keep us together."

Ernie stood at the roadside and for a moment didn't move. Only the site of the bus on the main road goaded him into action.

"Will you leave Hull tonight?" Ernie asked.

"I think we should. A good moon in May gives those bastards excellent targets." Cyril stepped onto the footplate then turned and offered Ernie a hand.

"Thanks," He said, pulling himself up. "You know we always offer a safe haven."

"A more ordinary night couldn't be had in times of war," Cyril joked as they found seats and sorted change.

I read the story. It was a fictionalised account of the family history with names changed to protect the innocent. Mum enjoyed putting our story into words; it helped her remember and gave her the excuse to send copies to the next generation. Of course the main protagonists weren't around any more, despite this mum studiously avoided Aunt Gertie, still going strong at seventy five and then there was her daughter and grandson. I sat back and arched my fingers in thought. I felt sad for them and wondered how they would take the news of Barty's death. I reached for a cup of tea. It had gone cold. Maybe it wasn't a very good story but from what Grandpa told me I knew it was true. Mum ought to send them away but it needed a title. Half way through showering it came to me. *Ordinary Night*. Yes, that would do nicely. It conveyed everything and what more could be asked? I made a mental note to tell mum.

Chapter 4: Fossil

A fossil is the remains of past life preserved in rock. The definition was indelibly etched in my memory. Some people learn Keats or Coleridge by rote. I learnt the zonal fossils of the Liassic, poetry I do in my spare time. I'd developed this fondness for the deeply unfashionable Walter de la Mare. Poems like *Silver*, stories with a hint of the supernatural like *Seaton's Aunt*. I had copied out the poems I liked in the back of my field notes. Sometimes I'd take a moment to read them aloud to the sea. There was something therapeutic about declaiming to the roar of an ocean.

"Slowly, silently, now the moon
Walks the night in her silver shoon,"

A voice replied:

"this way, and that, she peers, and sees
Silver fruit upon silver trees,"

For a moment neither of us said anything. The owner of the voice was about my age but taller, gaunt.

"I'm David Jones."

"Wojek Maric."

We shook hands.

His palm was calloused, his fingers large. I perhaps held on a little longer than I should as he became embarrassed and stammered, "I'm a mining geologist from the Cranbourne School."

"You must be really good to get in there?"

"Dedicated."

"I'm not certain I could describe myself as dedicated. I've set myself the target of getting an upper second from Hull. I'd like to think I could get a first but I've ruffled too many feathers," I looked up at the cliffs. The fault line that had brought me to this location was visible even to the untrained eye.

"How long are you here for?" The chap asked, trying not to look me in the eye.

"Another three weeks. I've got to produce a geological map from Whitby to Ravenscar. It's all coast plus the disused railway cuttings and quarries."

"I have to study the structure of the Dome. Folding, micro faulting, bedding fractures; that sort of thing. I've set myself a week so I'm working twelve hours a day in the field."

"Dedicated."

"Not really, I have work here as well. The usual, I need money to fund my dissolute lifestyle at uni and a little spare to visit relatives. Well it's been nice talking to another geologist, but I must get on. See you around," Wojek walked away.

I was about to open my mouth to ask him if he wanted to share some green. But perhaps it was for the best, I've never been a good judge of character. I looked up at the cliff then south along the bay. I could no longer see him. For some reason, this introduction galvanised me to action. I'd exaggerated my grade prospects. At least one of my lecturers told me I was a wet Nellie, Prof Piasecki said that to my face in a tutorial. In my defence I have to say I was trying not to be. It was difficult. I'd spent ten years growing up with just mum. Dad was a picture on the wall, a Sunday visit with a bunch of seasonal flowers. I believe it was Oscar Wilde who said, "*All women become like their mothers-- that is their tragedy*," well, from my limited perspective: all men become like their fathers and that indeed is their tragedy. My problem was that I didn't know. Time had erased his character. We are all in our way fossils. Casts of stone made in our parent's image with good and bad perpetuated in our genes.

I took out the tape measure and measured the thickness of the beds. At Ravenscar the sediments slope gently towards the south, so I found a bedding plane and used a clinometer to find the angle of dip and a compass for the direction. Afterwards I spent an hour searching the weathered face of the Dogger. This is a hard iron rich limestone full of fossils. I measured it out making careful notes and oblivious to the incoming tide. I turned my attention to the softer beds underneath next.

"We're both fools."

I recognised Wojek's voice.

"What do you mean?"

He pointed with his hammer.

I looked out to sea and finally down. Waves crashed against the cliffs cutting off our retreat to the path. "What's it like that way?" I asked.

"The good news is we aren't going to drown. The bad news is there's no way up," Wojek slid down the rock face next to me, "I've got some fish paste sandwiches."

"I've got a pork pie and a bottle of mineral water and," I searched in the bottom of my bag, "an apple and more unhealthily some fags."

"Good then we can keep each other company for an hour."

We shared our food, then lay back on the rocks and smoked.

"This is my girlfriend," Wojek pulled a photo from his wallet and passed it too me.

"She's good looking," I said.

"Beautiful," he added as though she might be listening.

"I don't have a girlfriend anymore."

Wojek looked at me.

"She threw herself off a cliff not far from here. With her new boyfriend."

Wojek sat up and crossed himself. "Mick and Drew? I met them both when I was doing a preliminary visit at Easter. They were very nice to me. Showed me the best places to get down the cliffs and gave me the address of a cheap place to stay. It turned out to be a very large vicarage where a Canon Franklin lived with part set aside as a retreat for contemplation and prayer."

"I didn't know Drew was into religion."

"I don't think she was but she put me on to a good job. Well paid. Are you interested in earning a bit more?"

"Always."

"Well I'll ask my employer and see if she has any opportunities."

"Thanks."

"I'm sure once we've escaped from here, we'll meet again."

"Very likely. There's so much work to do in this bay alone."

"You knew Drew from university?"

"We did A levels together then fell out at uni."

"She was sad about that. She told me it was one of those things...two people unable to bridge a gap."

I watched the wind flick through Wojek's hair before confessing, "We hadn't spoken for some time and then I got this telephone call out of the blue." I flicked the cigarette into the foaming ocean.

"I remember Mick asking Drew to do that. He looked like bad news but he had a heart of gold. He's not been seen since Drew's suicide. Can't believe that."

I looked away. I thought about what I'd seen that stormy night but knew I could not confide in anyone.

Wojek looked out to sea, oblivious to my dilemma. "Drew wanted to be loved so very much but somewhere down the line she confused love with sex."

I nearly choked. When I'd recovered some composure I confessed, "That's it. That's why we fell out. She said it was my fault and that I'd become too possessive. In her mind sex with another man wasn't love. In my book it was. It was selfish really. We'd had some great times. Perhaps neither of us was mature enough?" I wondered why I was confessing all this. Somehow it was liberating. Drew was a difficult person to get over. I continued, "When she rang she sounded so full of life. That's why suicide..." I couldn't go on.

"I know, we were all shocked."

I nodded.

"There had been a big argument that night and she had stormed out of the retreat. I never saw her again. That whole thing made me very sad."

"What was Mick like?"

"A reformed druggie. Says it all! He'd done time for theft and GBH. I know this is going to sound like I'm some woolly liberal but he was a nice person. Can you understand that?" Wojek stood and looked at the tide. Already the waves licked up the incline towards our feet. He looked up at the sheer face of the cliff with a little nervous smile.

"There's an under-cliff," I said calmly, "besides there's not a lot of debris up here. I don't think the tide gets this far. Not in summer."

It struck me as odd that a chance meeting provided so much information about the dead. Perhaps that's how life works. After all with so many rocks around it's pretty obvious that two geologists might bump into each other. Meeting Wojek with his intimate knowledge of past events left many questions, but I got the impression I was on the edge of it all. Where mum and I lived was equally on the edge. It was a long street of semis backing onto East Park -- a haven of suburbia. The next wave wet the limestone beneath us. I picked up my rucksack and walked sideways along the slope. Above me a narrow ledge appeared with tufts of grass. I pulled myself up onto it. There was nowhere else to go. Wojek had followed me.

"And how do you propose we get down from here?"

"You could slide into the sea," I smiled.

He ignored me.

"It strikes me that this rock marks the end of the Liassic," I looked up at the daunting cliffs, then below at the weaker shales. I followed the line of dip to the south. It was true, the rock that saved us was the Dogger, the very one I'd studied earlier, only I'd been looking at just one layer, not broadening my outlook to see its place in the scheme of things. It struck me that I'd done this with Drew. I hadn't established her position in the wider events which lead to her murder.

In the long silence that followed I stared out to sea and wished the tide would turn. I was beginning to feel uneasy about Wojek. Several things he said didn't add up. I couldn't imagine Drew staying at a religious retreat; she just wasn't into God. I couldn't believe she'd turn Christian for a boyfriend. It wasn't in her nature to compromise. Boy, did I know that! The trouble with Drew was that I lusted helplessly after her body and forgot to fall in love with the person. Maybe I did fall in love but along the way I started looking elsewhere. All I knew was that Carrie didn't fit the bill as a replacement. In fact I knew it was me who didn't fit the bill. I don't know why I set myself up as the boyfriend. I couldn't explain that at all.

Wojek was still looking out to sea himself. He was so busy thinking, I don't believe he realised my own long contemplation. I tapped him with another cigarette. He smiled. At that moment my doubts were dispelled. He couldn't possibly be acting all this for my benefit. No one could appear so genuine. And yet there was something. He cupped his hands round the match and inhaled.

"Are you still at the Retreat?" I asked.

"A good Catholic at a C of E retreat! It is cheap. Do you think God will forgive me?"

"I don't believe in God. The more I study geology the more I realise there is no place for a creator, only the natural processes of geology. My mum tells me that's naive because as I get older I'll need the crutch of religion."

"We all need a crutch of some sort," Wojek slid a little closer, "it's a funny thing, all the intolerance, the division. Perhaps we'd be better off without it?"

The layers of damp rock showed the tide was now going out.

"I stay at the prayer centre because I met this beautiful lady called Jocaster De Vile. She inspired me with confidence and when I found out what really happens," he confided, "it's all about fucking. Lots of fucking! They use a building dedicated to prayer as a base for making porn films!""

"That really surprises me?"

"It did me! But it makes sense being under the protection of the church. Mind the local police know about it. One of the officers is a regular visitor." Wojek slid down to the shale below. His feet sank in the wet debris. He looked up, waved. "See you soon," he said and ran to the safety of the steps before the next wave broke or I could ask him anymore questions.

I thought about what had happened to me, the murder of Bartholomew, the note in the museum, Ricky's confession and now Wojek. It seemed that everything was centred on me. A storm winding itself closer to my skin. The hairs on the back of my neck stood on end. Out here the geology was in control, it looked passive, virtually unchanged in terms of our brief lifespan, but if I sat back for long enough I'd notice the small changes: rocks falling or boulder clay slipping down the cliffs. I looked out to sea and watched the mast of a yacht climb up onto the horizon. I knew the storm wasn't centred on me, it dwelt on Drew. That idea was more alarming because it meant I could be sucked into the vortex and vomited onto the shore: just another broken body on the strand. I shuddered and felt a knot twist tighter in my stomach.

I picked up my belongings. Once more the bag was heavy with fossils. I skidded down the slope onto the shore and heard my steps crackle in the wet gravel. The sounds of my own feet were joined by others moving more quickly. I looked behind. Two men were jogging towards me. I had a premonition something was wrong even before I saw the chisel and drill they were carrying.

"There's one of the bastards who's nicking our fossils!" One said. His accent was thick.

"He needs teaching a lesson. This area is ours. All paid for and you aint getting a cut."

"He is. Grab the bastard and I'll drill him." His partner held up a drill like a gun.

I looked around. I started to run and gained the first steps. I took them two at a time, even though they were uneven. I tripped and fell heavily on my side. I looked up into the faces of the two men. One smiled as he turned on the drill. I could smell the motor heating up. I swung my bag at his balls. Man and drill toppled backwards. I regained my footing and jumped another few steps before I was felled. I felt a burning in my ribs and for a few moments I struggled to breathe. I felt the blows rain on my head. It was instinct. I swung my hammer round, hoping to catch anyone in the way. I heard a crack. For a moment my assailant stood transfixed. He fell to his knees. "My God!" I exclaimed. I thought I'd killed him but then he screamed. He screamed again then whimpered. I grabbed my bag and ran. I ran and I didn't look back.

Later I reported what had happened to the police. It was nearly 8pm when a white car pulled up outside the caravan. I recognised the DCI. It was Birbeck.

"Well," he said, "you seem to attract trouble David Jones. So, you lashed out with this?"

"Yes," I replied.

"A geological hammer?"

"I am a geologist!" I reminded him.

The DCI scrutinised me. "An offensive weapon used to inflict grievous bodily harm," he said matter of factly.

"Hey! I was the victim here. I was attacked; you seem to be forgetting that!"

The DC looked at his watch, "we've only your word for what happened. It doesn't add up. Why would anyone want fossils?"

"Some people collect them. Rare specimens can be valuable and ammonites sell well in craft shops around here. Selling a few of these might get a druggie another fix but these two weren't druggies, they were organised, professional."

"Professional, don't make me laugh." Birbeck analysed a specimen of Dactylioceras commune preserved in iron pyrites. "Ugly thing," he said putting it down. Birbeck lent over me until I could smell the brandy on his breath.

I felt uncomfortable. "Aren't you supposed to get a doctor to examine my bruises, photograph them or something?"

"There's only one doctor available and he's on another case. He might be back by seven tomorrow."

"Staff shortages?" I enquired. Another man got out of the car. "This is DS Laing. You remember him?"

I did indeed, he looked older than Birbeck but his tanned and wiry physique made it difficult to gauge.

"So half the police force of North Yorkshire is here trying to screw a confession out of the victim of crime?"

"I don't like your attitude," DS Laing interjected, "I've just heard on the radio Pete. A man checked into Scarborough Hospital two hours ago with a broken rib and concussion. He's a German national. Says he fell whilst climbing the cliffs at Ravenscar."

"There you are! Are you going to question him?" I asked indignantly.

The DCI stared at me. "Falling down a cliff isn't a crime. Meanwhile, you're free, at least for now. We'll keep the hammer."

"What am I going to use for my work?"

"It might take a week to process it with all these staff shortages but come along and collect it next Monday." Birbeck arched an eyebrow and smiled, "have you had anymore thoughts about Bartholomew?"

"Nothing I haven't already told you," I was feeling tired now

"It struck me that you might have known Drew?"

"Who?" I lied not wanting to get involved in another witness statement.

"Well Liang. It seems Mr. Jones is a one man crime wave breaking on our shores!" He laughed at his joke.

Laing smiled, "I could get a confession if we did it the old fashioned way." He left me in no doubt what this might involve.

"It's a good job we're more civilised now," I noted. The detectives got back in their car. As they drove off, I wondered why I'd bothered ringing the police.

It was already nine. I closed the curtains, took a couple of sleeping pills and got into bed.

Knock, knock. Unnatural sleep was slow to yield. *Knock! Knock!* I don't know whether I heard my name or felt the pain of daylight. It was a girl's voice. It had a familiarity to it, but not here, "David. David," she said, "it's me, Carrie."

Her scented body enveloped me and I realised this wasn't a dream. I kissed her. The embrace became a wrenching off of clothes. The soft contours of Carrie's body aroused me. The scent of her, stiffened my cock. My tongue glided over her skin. Gently she caressed mine with baby oil then her finger penetrated. "Relax," she said and I giggled. Finally she rose above me and let me enter. Her arse sank over my thighs like a warm wet blanket. I came in one great pulse which threatened never to subside. When it did I was disappointed. Carrie sensed my change in mood. She kissed me then slapped me. She put on my dressing gown and asked for directions to the shower.

I told her and turned over to sleep. When she returned she got back into the bed next to me. "It's your turn now," She said.

"Beans on toast for breakfast. Don't worry. I brought some decent coffee. I know your tastes," I lit the stove and warmed my hands before placing the pan on the hob.

We sat and ate. We laughed about mutual friends and finally she coaxed me out into the open. We walked to the cliff edge. We dangled our feet over the precipice and I told her all that had happened. She was an attentive listener.

"You know David," she said, "if we were married I'd say you'd been having an affair."

"Well I haven't -- unless you can call flirting with my cleaning lady an affair," I reassured, brushing her hair from her face.

"No, it's worse than that. You're having an affair with the dead." Carrie looked at me. "With Drew, how else could you explain this hysteria? I'm certain the note you found was from Drew but placed there on your first field trip. It's just lay there unnoticed, perhaps stuck in place by a blob from one of those revolting jam sandwiches you insist on packing up." Carrie's theory was plausible. I felt heartened by what she said. It was easy to be a sceptic in her presence. Then it dawned on me that I'd never mentioned the note.

"What note?" I asked.

"The one in your note book," she said all innocence. "The one you told me about."

Now I knew she was lying. Now I needed to know what to do about it. If she knew about the note, she must have put it there. I looked again at Carrie's dark hair. Was she the girl in the pink skirt who'd pushed Bartholomew Fair? I didn't think it wise to ask and I could see Carrie was trying to remain one step ahead of me.

Sunday arrived. On a whim I decided to do us both breakfast. Croissants and hot coffee. I lay the tray next to Carrie. Slowly her senses were roused.

"So it's not all self?" She woke and smiled. Stretched. We ate, then fucked. Finally we drank black coffee and lay on crumpled sheets looking up at the ceiling. There was a knock on the door. I wrapped a sheet round my body, and peered through the curtains. It was Ricky. I unlocked the door and smiled. He smiled back.

"Haven't seen you around."

"Distractions…"

"I heard what happened," Ricky stepped in, then stopped abruptly.

"Don't mind me," Carrie said, "I'm going for a shower." With that she unashamedly rose from the bed, collected her sponge bag and dressing gown and went off across the yard. We looked at each other again.

Ricky flopped down on the bed, "I thought you were going to show me the ropes," he stroked the sheet smelt his fingers and smiled, "on how to become a geologist."

"Yes, I'd love to but you'll have to give me a few minutes to get ready." I thought he'd get up and leave but he just sat there and talked about his week at work while I dressed. He was a trained plumber but in the last five days he'd done everything from helping to make coffins to plastering his uncle's house. I was impressed. I'd never been any good at the sort of jobs men were expected to do.

"It's about having the right tools," Ricky smiled knowingly, "that's ninety percent of it. The rest is having a good eye."

"I'll have to remember that, though I'm sure my mum will still prefer to pay a tradesman."

Ricky cocked his head to one side, "I haven't heard that expression for a while, *tradesman,* it smacks of the 'them and us' of my parent's generation."

"I didn't mean it like that. I meant... well it's like me…training to be a geologist. You devote years of your life to something hoping it'll all work out. I envy you, because you've got there. You're earning."

"You mean you want me to buy the beers?"

"Well, money is short!"

"So, what's it to be, Liassic shale or Jurassic sandstone?" Ricky smiled smugly.

I gave Ricky a playful tap on the shoulder. "You've been reading up."

He looked a little awkward for a moment then recovered his composure, "I can't let you have too big an advantage."

I saw right to the heart of his insecurity.

Ricky hovered for a moment, "I'll go and get my boots on and bring round the car. Where do you want to go?"

"Saltwick Bay," I said without hesitation.

"Okay. Let me give you some advice…"

Carrie barged past Ricky and made for her clothes at the bottom of the bed.

"…Beware of beautiful women." He looked at Carrie.

I looked at Carrie.

She turned and presented her middle finger, "just cos you fancy my man!" She said with venom. "You can wait outside!" Carrie pushed Ricky out, closed the door and emphatically locked it. "I wish I didn't have to go back tomorrow. I reckon you need protecting from the likes of him but I've got to earn enough to keep me at uni. We're not so different after all. It's just that I'm doing a useful degree."

I pulled the towel from around her. Carrie stood defiant. Her shape hardly the turn on it proved under the sheets. Nevertheless I smiled and kissed her. She seemed mollified.

Saltwick Bay was busy. The morning light made the tops of the sandstone cliffs appear golden. To the north Saltwick Nab jutted out into the sea like an island, further over Black Nab stood like a sentinel of death looking out over the ocean and the contorted wreck hard by told of lives lost. The tide was low and people were out walking, racing dogs, skimming pebbles. Children laughed and bawled, seagulls circled filling the cliffs with the echo of their cries.

"Why have you brought us here?" Carrie looked miserably at the bay.

"This is the birthplace of geology. Of all the possible places in the world, it happened here with the discovery of one fossil crocodile."

"Don't tell me. You want to find one," Carrie brushed sand from a rock and sat down.

"Yes I do! One pleisiosaur, one vertebrae, one tooth, dinosaur footprints, anything! You can't possibly know what it would mean to my thesis. The fossil would allow me to bring in the theory of evolution and to leave something behind. A specimen in a glass case -- with my name on it!"

"Well we'd better get looking," Ricky threw himself into the task. He'd been labouring as we descended as though loaded with some extra burden.

Carrie sat and looked out to sea.

Slowly the tide turned. The breaking waves pushed a fine spray into the bay leaving the taste of salt. I placed my hand lens on a boulder from the cliff and photographed some convincing tridactyl footprints. After writing this up I found my interest waning. It would be like winning the lottery finding a good fossil here. I straightened my back and looked at the layers of rock in the cliff. A further half hour's searching gained me a specimen of an ammonite. I realised I'd have to come back and map the strata properly.

I looked up until the rocks ended and vegetation cascaded over the edge. Carrie had walked to the Nab but Ricky was prising away at layers of fallen debris. I walked over and joined him.

"I thought this looked a good place," he said.

"A bloody stupid one!" I pointed up at the overhanging rock. "I once got caught in a rock fall. Frightening. A great roar. The sound seemed to bear down on me. I thought I was dead but the slide missed me. A great pile of detritus collected a few meters away and I went on with my business."

"Lucky. You could have become a fossil yourself."

I looked at Ricky. He knew more than he was letting on. "Keep still," I said. I gently pushed him to one side. The rock he'd been standing on turned and slid. Ricky picked up another dark grey rock. He smiled and held it out. "Is this what you were looking for?"

I picked it up and staggered backwards with the weight. Ricky helped set the rock on the ground.

"It doesn't look much," he said.

I took out my hammer and chisel. He stayed my hand. "I would wait. You might damage it and now I've got my eye in, I can see its part of a skull."

"Wow!" I clicked my tongue. A fossil about the size of my palm presented itself. It was distorted by the compaction of millions of years but recognisably a skull with several peg like teeth. I looked up to the top of the cliff.

"Oh, no!" Ricky shouted in realisation.

"At least you've brought the car," I added.

Carrie ignored us both as we climbed slowly to the car park at the summit. Once there we treated ourselves to an ice cream and sat on the car bonnet like little children. Carrie ate demurely whilst sitting on a green bench overlooking the sea. I stared at the dark figure of Black Nab, from this angle it rose like a chess piece waiting on a gaming board. I realised there was a lot of work to do on this one bay alone.

"What do you think then?" Ricky asked.

I shrugged, not knowing what to say.

"About us," Ricky gestured, "working as a team?"

"I'll mention you in the acknowledgements," I said unkindly and went to sit by Carrie.

She didn't speak until after the last crunch of biscuit. "He fancies you," she said, deliberately in his earshot.

"Who?" I said rather densely.

Carrie patted me on the cheek. "Just don't come back to Hull telling me you only take it up the arse. I'd be disappointed!"

"I think I should experience everything."

"Then you two will get along fine," Carrie replied knowingly but refusing to be drawn further.

None of us talked on the journey home. Ricky left me to carry the trophy into the caravan. He followed the smell of roast beef and vanished into the farmhouse. Later we met briefly at the pub. Ricky followed me into the toilet and lent against the wall whilst I pissed,

"I enjoyed today. Makes me realise there's a lot I don't know and a lot I don't understand."

"I'd be glad to teach you," I said innocently.

Ricky laughed, "just one piece of advice. Ditch the bitch."

I opened my mouth to speak but Ricky had already left. I wanted to be angry but I knew that's really what I wanted to do. Not the ending of my friendship with Carrie but the ending of the affair. Perhaps she was an impediment.

"Did he proposition you?" she asked, "I saw him go in after you."

I felt myself go bright red, "no, he asked me to ditch you."

"Don't be ashamed. You're business not pleasure and I'll be gone in the morning and then you'll see what he can do to people like you."

"What do you mean?" I asked finishing my drink and lighting another cigarette.

"You ought to stop smoking, it's bad for your health, one of these days there'll be a ban and then what?" Carrie picked up her jacket. "Well, you can take me back to the caravan."

I obliged but looked back once too often.

I set Carrie on the 7.55a.m. bus to Whitby. I waved. We didn't kiss, I could tell Carrie was disappointed in me. After this diversion I caught a bus in the opposite direction. Notebook in hand I spent the day in the old alum works above Ravenscar. It was an easy walk along the disused railway track and I covered a lot of ground. Even after eighty years of neglect there were still substantial scars of rock left in the quarries.

The beauty of Ravenscar derives from industry. The cliffs blasted from the landscape altered the whole shape of the coastline. The clinker track which once took tourists to Whitby and Scarborough by steam train, now took hikers to Bay Town and geologists into the kingdom of shale. Here and there a large rusting block reminded me that great furnaces once operated twenty four/seven to extract the alum.

In the distance the Baytown cottages clung grimly to the cliff and beyond these low tide revealed the eroded dome of sediments which Wojek was studying. From this vantage I looked at the coast. There was so much to do to complete a thesis on the geology of the area. I resolved to redouble my efforts now Carrie was gone. I was determined no one else was going to trap me in to a relationship as there were other more important considerations, like getting an upper second.

Above me towered 30 meters of soft grey shale. Its scarred surfaces rose bleakly from green fields. Bricks lined part of the path and were indelibly impressed with the Ravenscar stamp. I needed to do more research about alum. I knew it was used as a mordant for wool. It enabled the fabric to maintain a brighter colour but the step by step process which could take over a year eluded me. Here in a place of great beauty a poisonous industry once stood, its chimneys belching sulphurous fumes, its drains running with piss from Newcastle. All has passed away. What remained couldn't even be described as fossilised, it was evidence of sorts but perhaps it told more poignantly that nothing people do endures. As the Great King found when he asked his daughters for the universal truth and they came up with. '*And this too shall pass away.*'

Chapter 5: 1942

Eldedt had found a bottle of champagne to celebrate shooting down a Junkers JU88. Gertie sat tutting from her arm chair and looking exhausted because baby Margaret had developed croup and neither had slept. The heavy bombing of Hull the previous night had also frayed her nerves. Cyril remained at their home in The Broadway and Ernie was on fire watch after work. Somewhere at the top of the Guildhall Ernie observed the destruction through army issue binoculars with a wind up telephone hard by to bark out orders. The three glasses chinked without enthusiasm.

If the birth of Margaret had brought the *ménage à trois* closer, the birth of Elizabeth had placed a distance between Marjorie and Ernie. It wasn't a falling out or a lack of love, just an obstacle, a mewling, crawling baby girl, a beautiful baby who slept in the family cot at the foot of the bed.
"If I'd had a boy, I'd have called him Bartholomew after my dad but Margaret will be an only one. I know that," Gertie confessed. "I haven't told Cyril or Eldedt. The infection afterwards, well the doctor thinks the damage has been too great."
Marjorie squeezed her friend's shoulder as she passed. She didn't want to tell her that Ernie was determined on more children. He said he'd never met anything other than a spoilt only child.
Both ladies pushed silver cross prams down Thearne Lane. It was a warm May morning and Gertie wore a standard utility suit in tweed whereas Marjorie wore a woollen suit over a Fair Isle waistcoat and a pancake hat. Marjorie never went anywhere without a hat even if they were getting a little battered with age. Out here in the countryside the war might not be happening. Old Wazza stopped his push bike and spat out the cigarette butt. He doffed his cap. "Morning ladies. How's them young uns doing?" He peered into the prams and smiled, "must be a source of great joy," he stared right at Gertie as though trying to read her mind. She squirmed a little uncomfortably. He desisted.
"Are you going as far as the ferry?" He asked, "only I've a letter for Rose Turnbridge."
Marjorie smiled, "what's a man of your age doing writing letters to an old widow?"

"I'm only seventy eight and a man has his needs like anyone else," Again he looked at Gertie.

"I'd be delighted. It'll give us an excuse to get some honey for tea," Marjorie unclipped the brake, "good afternoon."

They hadn't gone very far when Gertie hissed, "Did you see the way he looked at me? Is there anyone in the village who doesn't know?"

Marjorie tried hard to think of an answer which would appease her friend and finding none said, "He's a new man since the Germans tried to strafe him."

"Funny how war changes people," Gertie said with venom.

Marjorie opened her mouth to speak but knew whatever she said would give offence.

The may was in flower and the lane was sweet with the perfume and the buzz of flies. It was a good mile to the banks of the river and when they got there, they were hot and thirsty. Marjorie climbed the embankment and waved at the ferryman. "If we were men," Gertie remarked, "we could take the ferry and sit and drink in the lounge of the Crab Apple."

"I'm shocked Gertie," Marjorie patted her chest, "ladies of our station don't do that type of thing."

This time it was Gertie who didn't reply for fear of offending. "Well then, let's visit Rose Turnbridge and see what she has on offer." They pushed the prams into the shade of the farmyard.

"Hello. Mrs. Crawford. How can I help you?" She leaned over the pram and pulled up the net. "Ah! How they grow."

"This is Mrs. Barlby," Marjorie gestured her friend but the introduction was ignored.

"I'd like some honey, if you have any and I don't suppose you've got any greens?"

Mrs. Turnbridge touched her nose and smiled. "The honey's last years, so it's set over winter. Mind it tasted good on toast this morning."

Marjorie passed over a few coppers and placed the jar and greens under the pram cover.

"Well that was a turn up for the books," Gertie remarked. "Cut dead by a farmer's widow."

"I think it's something you'll have to get used to. Out here everyone knows everything about you and anything they don't know they'll invent."

Gertie thought about this, "That's why Cyril prefers to stay at home. If it wasn't for this war…" Gertie didn't finish her sentence.

"You'd never have met Eldedt," Marjorie smiled.

Gertie brightened up a bit. "Yes, I must talk with him when we get back."

The cloud was building on their return and a cool breeze funnelled down the lane reminding them it was still spring.

"It's a beautiful bungalow. I always wondered why Ernie had it built so close to the lane."

Marjorie smiled, "that was my doing. I hate front gardens. All those impressions made and broken just by the wrong flowers in the wrong place. Instead we have a long back garden. It's private, we can sit out on an evening and no one would know we were there."

"It's not quite as intended with the lawn going for potatoes and beans."

Gertie looked at the curves of the front, with the two bay windows framing the almost circular porch which concealed the front door. To her it shouted of new money, of townies escaping to the rural idyll. The problem was she enjoyed it as well but no amount of cajoling could persuade Cyril to move to a village. Their charming semi-detached house on The Broadway would have to do if it survived the bombing.

Eldedt was cleaning the spark plugs of his trusted Norton. Gertie stood and watched, gently rocking the pram. Marjorie slipped away.

"How is the beautiful Margaret?" He asked.

"Without her father," Gertie was eaten up with this limbo she'd help create. "I could divorce Cyril and marry you."

Eldedt stopped what he was doing and kissed Gertie gently on the forehead. "It is not possible."

"When the war's ended. When you're not a pilot anymore. We could do it then."

Eldedt shifted uncomfortably. His sandy hair fell across his face momentarily. He pushed it back with oily hands, "I love both of you. To hurt one would hurt the other."

Gertie stomped her foot and woke the baby, "you'll have to choose. It isn't right that a man should love another man. In fact it's illegal!" Gertie bit her lip and bent to pick up the baby.

"We are old enough to make our own rules but we also have to be old enough to live with the consequences." Eldedt returned to mechanics.

"I insist that you marry me," Gertie was in high dudgeon.

"If only I could." Eldedt picked up a rag and cleaned his hands.

Gertie was in no mood to take *no* for an answer. "Wouldn't you like us to bring Margaret up together?"

Eldedt picked up the baby and placed an arm round Gertie. "It isn't a question of love or like. It's just impossible. Back home in Texel I already have a wife."

Gertie stood rigid and as the enormity of Eldedt's words sank in she pushed the man away. "You've done all this to me knowing…"

"Done! Nothing has been done to you. You were as willing as I." He passed back the baby, picked his jacket off the bike seat and walked away. Gertie replaced Margaret in her pram and fought back the tears.

Chapter 6: Orogeny

An orogeny is the formation of mountain ranges. When plates of continental crust collide, they cast up layers of sediment from the seabed to form the tops of mountains. Climb the highest Himalayan peak and you'll find sedimentary rocks from a long lost sea. No one believed the scientist who first propounded the theory of plate techtonics. It seemed preposterous. No one could discern this movement. Plates move a centimetre or so a year, so a lifetime might witness a metre's progress. Accurate measurement by satellites has proved the effect. The last Orogeny to buckle Britain contorted the rocks of North Yorkshire into domes and basins. A German friend of mine said it was the gentle landscape that caused the character of the English. He pointed to the Jura Mountains when describing his own disposition.

I remember grandpa cutting out the continents and placing them back together as one great land mass. He laughed and pushed them back to their correct positions. He had been intrigued by the ideas of Wegener in the 1920's and the article in the *New Scientist* outlined further evidence that he'd been right.

"It was a hair-brained idea when I was at school. Now it's an accepted part of the science curriculum."

"We've studied it twice already, once in geography and then in chemistry. It didn't get any better," I confessed and pushed the scraps of paper back together.

"You should watch out for that. Ideas you think are secure and suddenly, pow! A scientist comes along and sweeps it all away." Grandpa sat back down on his chair and picked up the magazine again, "take oil, people used to think it came from fossilised sea-creatures, now they're not so certain that's the whole story."

I watched the old man for a moment. I wondered what it was like to be sixty four. His face was lined and his nose possessed deep pores. His gammy leg made getting up from a chair difficult and he always turned sideways to push himself up. Finally there was the sadness which went with bereavement. I'd only known grandpa with lines around his eyes and very little hair but the photos around the house showed a fashionable young man in the 1930's and a successful manager during the war. I looked out at the rain. There was no chance of getting into the park, grey puddles lying on the grass told how wet it was.

"Tell me about the war, grandpa?"

Grandpa put the magazine down again and smiled. "The war," he said and I saw that twinkle in his eyes. "I guess you're old enough to hear about 1943."

1943

"It was inevitable. Eldedt had been shot down. There had been no word. Gertie did not wear weeds because she wasn't going to advertise her relationship but she wore a black hat with a half veil as a token of mourning. Marjorie was teaching your mum to walk. That's the picture on the chest of drawers."

I looked at the photograph with fresh eyes, noticing Gran's hands guiding mum along.

Gertie took less interest in Margaret rolling across the rug laid out on the lawn. The girls played with coloured blocks, stacking them into towers which momentarily defied gravity.

"Looks like a storm," Marjorie announced.

Gertie didn't look up at the clouds when she replied, "Maybe." In front of her was her salvation and her demise, baby Margaret. No one on The Broadway would speak to her. She had defied convention and been ostracised. Out here Marjorie never judged, no that wasn't true, she judged and remained silent which Gertie thought was kinder.

"Ernie told me that the continents are moving slowly across the planet. We're getting further from America with every day," Gertie announced with a smile.

"What a lot of rot! I've threatened to throw out his science texts but I know if I did I'd be ending our marriage."

"Really?" Gertie was intrigued, "before the war Ernie wanted to be a professional photographer. He was very good. He made quite a lot of money taking wedding pictures," Gertie closely observed Marjorie for her reply.

"Maggie, look after the girls."

The girl in a gingham apron nodded.

Marjorie ushered Gertie inside. She looked uncomfortable, "I didn't approve of him spending hours taking photographs of others celebrating their love. Weekends are for families. Of course we miss the money and he still spends hours in the shed – his dark room he calls it!"

Gertie enjoyed the admission. "He's still taking pictures?"

"Despite the war. He thinks when it's all over people will be interested in what happened to Hull. He showed me this dreadful image of a child's hand emerging from the rubble of a house on Summergangs. I told him to destroy it but he said it shows the horror of war."

"He's right, though there'll be no appetite for that sort of picture until everything's over. I always liked Ernie's humanity," Gertie tried to score a point from her friend.

"I always liked his honesty," Marjorie scored a touché, "that's why I invited you here for lunch. Ernie's had this opportunity."

The sound of two girls spatting then crying came from outside. There was silence and the ladies heard the nanny mollycoddling any hurt feelings.

"What opportunity?" Gertie asked.

"My father has offered to buy Ernie a photographer's studio in Harrogate."

"It sounds brilliant but I can hear from your voice that there's a catch."

Marjorie got up and ensured the door was closed, "There are two problems. One is inconvenient timing, the other insurmountable bureaucracy."

"Timing," Gertie smiled then remembered her own inabilities, "that can only mean one thing."

Marjorie nodded. The women held hands.

"The other?"

"Ernie's boss at The Guildhall won't release him. He's insistent Ernie is indispensable to the war effort."

"And Ernie?"

Marjorie looked uncomfortable, "he told me not to ask but I want him to have a free hand in the decision. He's not keen on leaving Thearne and I can understand that, after all he built this place from scratch and having a young family. It's a lot of upheaval. But, I want him to be free to go if he wants it, so I was hoping you'd ask Cyril to try and use his Masonic influence." The silence became a wall between the women.

Gertie took a sharp intake of breath and pursed her lips, "I'll ask. That's all I can say."

"That's all I can ask," Marjorie stood in the bay window and looked out at the sky. Gertie stood by her side and looked upwards into the empty blue ether. Neither said anything about Eldedt. "Shall we take the girls out for a walk down the lane?"

"Good idea!"

"Maggie!" Marjorie shouted, "Get the girls ready for some fresh air would you?"

"Right away ma'am."

Gertie smiled at the affection before going into the hall and bringing back two coats and her pillar box hat with the half veil, "Well, I've got you to look after now."

"Silly, I don't need looking after."

Gertie helped her on with her coat and fastened the top button. Marjorie held her hand. "Are you really ok?"

"Yes, I'm resigned to remaining married to Cyril. We've come to an understanding."

"Good. That's alright then." Marjorie didn't enquire further.

* * * * *

"Marjorie only told me about that as her heart gave out. She didn't want anyone to know she'd tried to help. The life of a photographer wasn't to be mine. That old bastard Birbeck wouldn't let me go. Revenge is a dish best served cold and eventually I found out what Birbeck was up to and amassed the evidence." Grandpa sat down in the chair again and stared at the wedding picture in the alcove. For a few moments I believed he was back on that beautiful day which I would only ever know through silver salts preserved on paper in black and white.

Layers of history build like the sediments in geology from the oldest to the youngest. From my grandparent's wedding in September, 1937 to my own memories and still the present bleeds from the past, with each heart beat the present becomes history and eventually geology.

I remember grandpa cutting out the continents and placing them back together as one great land mass. Funny how odd moments stick in the memory.

Pangaea eventually broke apart, the continents free to wander on their conveyor belt of mantle convection currents. It was the much later collision of Africa with Europe which made the Yorkshire coast a more interesting place geologically. There was however a single unexpected event. About 80 miles off the coast a perfectly preserved meteor impact crater had been found. The oil exploration company who discovered it thought 65 million years a good age but as yet there was no evidence. I folded the newspaper article into my notebook. The impact was many millions of years after the rocks of my mapping area formed. I was unlikely to find any evidence from my fieldwork but Wojek might with his structural survey. I made a note to ask him when we met again. I certainly needed something dramatic to show my professors at Hull and some impressive evidence if I was to get an upper second.

I had a tedious day searching overgrown cuttings along the old railway line noting and recording the angle of dip and strike, rock type, thickness…. All the time I knew others had already mapped the area, starting with William Smith in the early nineteenth century, then his nephew and now myself. The question was, what would I find which was different? There was no point copying if I wanted a good degree. It was soul destroying but if I was to reinterpret the structure it was unavoidable. I nursed the scratches from a brier and several nettle stings. At one point the road curved over the disused railway line. A woman was watching out, she shielded her eyes from the sun. She waved.

I ignored her.

"Hello." She said waving again. "Can you help?"

"Depends," I replied.

"My sports car has a flat tyre."

"Ok, I'll take a look." I scrambled along the narrow path and saw the yellow sports car pulled into the roadside. "That's well and truly shredded."

"Gave me quite a turn, I can tell you. I thought I was going to skid off the road."

"Certainly you might have slipped down the embankment." I gauged the drop. "Don't look; it'll just make you feel worse." I got down cross legged by the back wheel. The lady passed me a jack and wheel wrench. "It'd be good to do something positive today, it's been a bit repetitive so far. I'm producing a geological map of the area and all I've done is get hot, bothered and scratched!"

The lady seemed to understand, "My friend Wojek is a geologist of some sort. Have you met him?" She asked.

I nodded. "We were both cut off by the tide and had a late lunch on the Dogger."

"Now I know that's a layer of rock but nothing more."

"Yes, that's right!" The lane was quiet and there was no one else around. I banged on the wrench until the nuts loosened. I carefully placed the jack at the required point and slowly the vehicle lifted. A minute later and the damaged wheel was off. I went to the boot.

The lady gave me a quizzical look.

"I presume the spare's in here?" I pressed the chrome button and found spare tyre set into a hollow below the carpet. The car looked and smelt new.

"I've been walking along the coast, looking for a secluded sunny cove." The lady said fanning herself with a straw hat. "The light's better in the morning. I love the way the shadows of clouds skid over the fields."

I tried to study the lady between pinches of conversation. She was slender, quite refined in the way she dressed and I assumed she was rich: the new yellow sports car and the stones which glinted on her fingers gave that away. I placed the spare into position and span the nuts back. Finally I took out my hammer to ensure the nuts were secure and let down the jack. Once back on four wheels, I checked the wheel was properly fixed.

"You'll need to get this replaced. " I said placing the wheel with its punctured tyre in the boot. "There's a lot of grit on this road you don't want to get caught out without a spare."

"You've been really helpful. Thank you." The lady smiled. Now she looked more like a French Film star, elegant, demure and dressed with Parisian chic. "Can I offer you a lift? I'm going to Whitby."

"Can you drop me at Hawsker?" I felt a wave of tiredness wash over me.

She nodded, "I'm Jocaster," her voice purred. She got in the MG and turned the ignition.

"David Jones, pleased to meet you. No jokes about sea-lockers."

Jocaster even had the tan of someone who visits The Med often. I brushed the dirt off my trousers and slid onto the leather seat.

"It's not every day I meet a knight in shining armour. You must allow me to buy you a drink. I'm having supper in The Cook Arms tonight, you might like to join me after nine?"

"I'm made up having a lift in a brand new MG B GT. The drink would be a nice extra!" The journey was all too short, particularly at the speeds Jocaster took the minor roads onto the A171. The result was I got back to the caravan early. I didn't get much peace. Ricky knocked at the door and came in. "Has she gone?"

"Carrie?" I put down the book, "yes."

"You haven't forgotten our…"

"No…" I asked Ricky to sit down and made him a cup of tea before telling him about the day I'd had.

"Mine was boring too," Ricky confided, "except for Mr. Rideout touching my arse."

"What did you do?" I enquired, wondering where this conversation might lead.

"He said he'd seen me in a porn movie and thought I'd be up for it. That's what happens when you get involved with Jocaster De Vile."

"Jocaster?"

"He's an ugly git so I told him I'd ram twelve inches of copper pipe up his backside if he touched me again!" Ricky said ignoring me.

I nodded whilst trying to conceal my disappointment that Ricky hadn't found a more original approach to protect his honour. I tried again. "The highlight of my day was helping this woman change her car tyre. Nice car too, a brand new MG B GT. Funny thing, just seeing a yellow sports car waiting at the side of the road."

"Yellow?" Ricky took more interest, "describe the woman."

"Her name's Jocaster, she's about fifty, sophisticated in a Catherine Deneuve kind of way. I'd have taken her for younger but her neck had developed a criss-cross of lines. She wore heavy perfume. Overpowering."

"Jet black hair, rubies on her right hand, emeralds on the other?"

"Yes, do you know her?"

"Unfortunately. Remember I told you to beware of beautiful women?"

"I thought that was just cos you fancied me?"

Ricky ignored my remark, which was curious, "Jocaster and Josephine De Vile were the ones I had in mind." He lit a cigarette, "What I was going to show you tonight will tell you all about them and help you understand what's going on." Ricky stood to leave. "Oh! And as my parents are out, you can come for tea. I'll microwave us something. Can't say fairer than that can you?"

It appeared people were attempting to bribe me with food. I thought about the offer and wondered if Ricky would have any cold lager in the fridge. I looked at the contents of my wallet. Money was getting tight. "Eight?"

"Seven. Watch out for dad's Volvo leaving, come round any time after that."

I read another of Somerset Maugham's stories after Ricky left. It seemed familiar, then I remembered Dirk Bogarde playing the character in an old film. Finally I gazed out of the window and watched the shifting light on the leaves and the subtle way the greens changed hue as the breeze rippled through them. I started listening to a concert on Radio Three: Ravel's String Quartet. It had been my favourite piece of music since a concert last summer at Beverley Minster.

Aunt Gertie mentioned the piece had been Eldedt's favourite and insisted on taking me. I couldn't understand why her eyes filled with tears until she said. "He was the man I loved."

I thought about Uncle Cyril who was queuing for coffees. I looked down the aisle of the minster, he saw me and waved.

"You mean?"

Aunt Gertie nodded.

That's when I realised that all those stories grandpa told me about the war had been *U* certificate. The stories Mum had written down were more honest and I'd also done some research: what they actually spent the six years doing was living and letting life continue as normal despite rationing and bombing. There were many tragedies but mostly village life continued much as ever. When grandpa talked about the war, it sounded like a social, with all the friends who left Hull and stayed in Thearne overnight and at weekends to escape the bombing. On tranquil summer evenings they used to sit on the porch and smoke whilst lives in the city were blown apart. There was little they could do in practical terms. Grandpa completed his shifts on firewatch and Cyril wandered the streets of East Hull as an ARP warden. I suppose they watched the distant flames with a sense of foreboding. When mum talked about the war it was all about hardship, make do and mend but pretty early on I realised she was only four when the war ended. Her stories were apocryphal or concerned the even harsher post war days. If only I'd been old enough to find out the truth, I might discover a novel in all that family history.

The only person left from that era now was Aunt Gertie and she would be in mourning for her dearly beloved Bartholomew Fair. There was a part of me still shocked at his death but I'd balanced this with my knowledge of his part in Drew's murder. Then I had to ask myself, who would want revenge on him?

Slowly time moved toward seven o'clock. I got myself ready. Ricky's parent's left. I wandered towards the back door. Ricky took me by the shoulder and led me in. We stood in the kitchen whilst first chilli and then chips revolved in the microwave. We took our food through to the lounge. I sat in a damask armchair and sank into the cushions.

Ricky opened a can. "Did you make any money?" Ricky's hand hovered over the glass before he poured.

"What a student, making money! I'm unlikely to find Monday's as profitable as you."

"You have this way of sounding educated and old-fashioned at the same time. It makes me smile!"

"I think you know a lot more than you're letting on Ricky."

"There's nothing like being direct. Don't I get to eat first? After all I'm doing you a favour."

The meal was warm and spicy and my tongue tingled with the mix despite the lager. I washed up the plates to remove the evidence of my visit. Afterwards we had a fag on the patio. I smiled and Ricky mirrored the gesture his dark eyes alive with desire. Before I could comment Ricky nudged me and I followed him inside.

Ricky put a video on. He sat back in the chair and covered his crotch with a cushion. It was a porn movie and I was bored by the lesbian scene that opened it. The chap who disturbed them was familiar.

I opened my mouth to speak.

Ricky nodded. "That's Jevan." He looked at me then fast-forwarded through the scene.

"Your twin?"

"My twin brother," he nodded. "This will be of greater interest."

The dark haired lad took down his trousers and started wanking. The girl from room service knocked then opened the door. When she saw what the lad was doing, she took hold of his hand, it was only at that moment the camera dwelt on her face. It was Drew. My mouth fell open and I felt my head pounding. "Stop it!" I ordered and flung myself toward the back door. I took a deep breath of air.

"See what I mean…" Ricky said with a leer.

I nodded. I don't know who cried first but I felt the warm tears fill my eyes and for a while the world was blurred. I felt Ricky's hand on my shoulder. I took another deep breath.

"And Mike," Ricky replied, "I met him once. Well not met exactly. I… well you might as well know, I propositioned him in the toilet of The Cook Arms. The whole film crew were down for a meal. I think that's the night I met Drew as well. Anyway he wasn't impressed but he had the sense to tell Jocaster. Later that evening she approached me with a better proposition and one which paid well: a part in one of her porn flicks. They'll be filming up at the centre soon."

I let this all sink in. I'd been saturated by facts. The telephone broke my reverie. Ricky listened for a long time. "Girl trouble," he announced. "My brother's ex. I go round sometimes. She finds seeing his double comforting. Though I suspect there's more to it than that." He picked up the car keys. I was slow to respond. Ricky rattled the keys in front of me. I moved to the front door..

"You'd better put the video away," I cautioned.

"You take it." He said before he got in the car.

Stupidly I did.

The air outside smelt of cattle. I took another deep breath. Ricky fired up the car and drove off, leaving a cloud of dust lingering on the farm track. I walked through it. I was half way to the pub before I realised what I was doing.

I looked at my watch. Jocaster said she'd be in the Cook Arms from nine, she'd offered to buy me a drink and I was in the mood to accept. It was curious that I'd been unable to find anything which had pierced the tread. Jocaster had put it down to the large amounts of grit or a faulty valve. Armed with three fags, two quid and only enough green for one joint, things were beginning to look desperate. I knew I wouldn't have sufficient money to last the remaining weeks if I withdrew more before Friday.

It seemed Jocaster wasn't a woman of her word. There were five men in the bar, occasionally they passed a comment or two but mostly they were on their own, smoking and staring into their pints in the way I remember my dad doing. I pulled myself up onto a bar stool. Gabby didn't bother to ask what I wanted. She placed a pint of lager in front of me. "Shame about Ricky," she said matter-of-factly. "He's gone out to Andrea's place. I mean that was never going to work, replacing the dead brother with the live one. Andrea is just a lost soul really, a bit like Ricky."

I shrugged and played the red hot end of my fag round the ashtray.

" I hope you don't mind me being frank?" Gabby polished another glass, "besides there have been rumours…"

"Meaning?"

Gabby smiled, "just rumours, nothing more." She let this hang mid-air as she rang in the amount on the till and held her hand out for money.

"I just thought, well I wondered why he left so quickly." I moved uncomfortably on the seat and lit a cigarette.

A bell rang. "Must go," Gabby said, "Jo's in the lounge and she'll be wanting another Martini."

"Jocaster?" I asked.

"Yes and if I were you I'd leave well alone. I'd walk out of here and go back to your caravan."

I stared after Gabby. I drank quickly. It was an old ruse. Give out a little information and expect a lot in return. I was just about at the pub door when Gabby shouted.

"She wants to see you." That was all Gabby said. It was a summons.

I walked round to the lounge. "Hello again."

Jocaster stood up and shook my hand. "My knight in shining armour," she took hold of my arm and led me to the seat next to her. Her perfume was heavy with citrus fragrances. "There. We can be a little more private now," She smiled. "Gabby, another pint for David and a Martini for me." Ricky had been right about the jewels: rubies on the right hand, emeralds on the left.

Jocaster asked me about my research.

"I've got four weeks this year and four next year to survey the area from Robin Hood's Bay to Whitby and produce a geological map."

"Sounds interesting but lonely."

"You'd be surprised at the people you meet, like Wojek."

"Wojek, how lovely, he's one of my rising stars." She took out a black Sobrane and offered me one.

I accepted. "I've never tried one," I replied savouring the tobacco.

"In my experience you should try everything at least twice.

"Twice?"

"The first time might not be with the right person."

There was some merit in the idea.

She continued, "there's no sense in going to your grave regretting." Jocaster smiled, "my sister and I have lived here for many years, I returned last summer having spent some time in Saintes. Have you ever been to France?" Jocaster blew smoke across the table.

"I'm not well travelled outside the UK."

"Let me see your palm." I held out my left hand, she tilted it into the light and stroked my skin. "I think you will have many adventures abroad, young David, you might even have one here. How would you feel about taking part one of my films? A gay scene with Ricky, perhaps? Do say yes."

"With Ricky?" I was thrilled and appalled by the idea. "But isn't it illegal?"

"In the UK unfortunately, yes, but I have my protectors." She touched her nose.

"Would I have a big part?"

Jocaster laughed, "I hope so. You'd be the virgin seduced by a young man and rescued by our leading lady." she stared at me searching for my response.

"You should try everything once," I lifted my glass in salute, "More importantly does it pay cash?"

"If that's what you want. Well that's settled, come to dinner and meet the cast tomorrow night." Her hand brushed over my cheek then held my chin. I looked at her. Jocaster moved her head slightly. "By the way, Ricky will drive you into Scarborough in the morning, I'll organise an appointment with Dr. McGregor at 10a.m., we'll need a blood test and examination. Merely precautions."

It was only after I said, "goodnight," that I realised Jocaster had known I'd accept. Everything was mapped out, the layers of rock and the movements of the people upon them.

I went over and propped up the bar.

Gabby came over. "She knew you were holding something back. She won't be satisfied until everything connects. You've got to be thorough in her game."

"Just what is Jocaster's game?" I smiled knowing the answer.

Gabby looked at me, "You've got to be joking? Jocaster makes porn movies."

I laughed, "It's no wonder she thought it funny when I asked if I'd have a big part."

Gabby's steely glance melted. "That's worth one on the house," and she poured me another drink.

"I thought porn was made in Amsterdam?" I remembered my eighteenth birthday. Drew got into trouble with a Dutch guy who wanted me to video as he fucked. We both refused and ran out into the night.

"Home grown," Gabby said. "New decade, new opportunities. That's how I come to be here and coincidently how I paid for this place." Gabby smiled.

"You mean you made your money in porn?"

"Enough to buy a pub. But I don't recommend it as a career. It's degrading. I was so doped up I don't remember half of what I did. Probably just as well or I might kill someone!" Gabby laughed nervously at the confession. She leaned closer to me, "but I did get to meet someone special." She sighed, "guess I'm destined to live alone now."

Later than expected and a little light-headed from drink I found myself leaning against the pub wall taking deep breaths before walking back. I looked around. The last car in the car park was a German registered Opel. There were two men inside. They pointed me out and for a moment I was caught in the headlights. The door behind me was locked so I vaulted a dry stone wall and ran for cover.

The men got out and shone powerful torches, their beams played over the fields and walls but I was concealed.

"Come on Hans we must report back."

The car doors slammed and they drove off. I took the back route to the caravan. I saw their car decelerate and turn into Soulgrave Farm. I thought they were on to me but it waited a few seconds before reversing out. Slowly the car was driven back in the direction of the pub. I cut across the field.

In the farmyard, I saw a light on in Ricky's room. I threw a pebble against the window. I waited then threw up another. The curtains parted and the window opened. "Who is it?" Ricky peered blindly into the darkness.

"It's me, Dave. I should've listened to your advice. Just thought I'd let you know."

"Oh!" Ricky sounded relieved.

"Everything alright?" I asked.

"Fine. Aren't you going to shout, make a scene or something? Tell me I let you down?"

"Why tell you what you already know?" I said and took a step or two forward into the light cast from the window, "I've been given a part in a film."

Ricky sat down on the window ledge. "You're a bigger fool than I thought," then he smiled. "Who are you doing the scene with?"

"You."

Another voice sounded from within.

"You should try everything twice."

Ricky pulled the window closed. I stepped back into the shadows. That night I slept fitfully. Just once I thought I heard footsteps cross the yard. In the morning I pulled the sheets around me and began writing: Once all the continents were tiled into a great landmass called Pangaea. Throughout the Jurassic the island of the Northern Pennines allowed sediment to accumulate in a shallow basin. The Liassic shales I was studying formed in a shallow sea at the western end of an ocean. All around in the rocks there is evidence of change, of plates shifting and rifting, of the North Atlantic opening up and separating Europe and America. This split caused changes in the rocks while all around the age of the dinosaurs had begun.

When I was a boy Uncle Rob stood me on top of Long Nab and told me to look north, I did so with the eye of a photographer, taking everything in.

"What do you see?" He asked with sudden ferocity.

"Cliffs, blue sky. Sea?" I replied, insulted he should ask.

"Then you haven't seen anything," he replied and walked off.

I stood and stared until my uncle was in the distance but I could see nothing more. The change came on me slowly. Every year I must have stood at that same spot and studied the coast. I suppose first of all I noticed the different layers of rock: sandstone, limestone, and shale. Finally as a teenager I looked north and was amazed that I hadn't seen this before, a great meandering river was preserved, its sinuous banks picked out by coloured sediment. I climbed down the cliffs and spent hours studying layer upon layer of rock. The only thing I could say with certainty was that I stood on the fossilised banks of a river which flowed when the dinosaurs roamed. I based this not on theory but the industry of two youths who were carrying a slab of stone from the beach. Clearly impressed in the rock were dinosaur footprints.

It was the summer of my sixteenth when my uncle told me more about the war. "I'd like you to do some maths," he said, stroking his grey moustache, "which year was your mother born?"

"1941, June ," I added for the sake of completeness.

"Now do the maths for Margaret, when do you think she was conceived?" He looked at me through the pint of shandy he'd bought us both. "Subtract nine months from May 41."

I remember my heart sank, this was to be another of my uncle's detective stories. I'd completed one in my interpretation of the rocks and here was another. I looked out through the window of the pub and glanced at the high tide pounding the sea defences. "August, 1940," I said and wondered where this conversation about his wife was leading.

My uncle looked at me, his moustache dipped in the froth of his shandy. He wiped himself clean on the back of his sleeve. "Does that prove Aunty Margaret's Eldedt's daughter?"

I thought about this, "It's evidence but perhaps you need some sort of genetic test. I mean Aunty Margaret doesn't look like Uncle Cyril but then I guess you wouldn't want a woman to!"

"The birth certificate says it's Uncle Cyril who's the father. Everyone seems preoccupied with the idea, as if the single sperm determines everything about a person." Bob drained his glass.

"Well it must fix half the genes." I concluded.

My uncle grunted and stared passed me at some argument developing in the bar. I changed the subject.

"You must be very proud of Bartholomew." I said.

"Barty's doing fine. He's been working with The North Yorkshire CID for a year now." Bob went to the bar and had himself another pint of real ale pulled. "Did your grandpa tell you anything about the war?"

I realised immediately that my uncle was fishing for information. "He told me lots of stories about the war and photography but nothing about Margaret," I knew I had to do more research on this topic, another conversation with Grandpa only this time I'd record it all on tape.

"Well something's afoot; Gertie had this letter from Holland." My uncle shook his head but said nothing more.

Even though I am standing still. Even though I am standing at the edge of Long Nab, I know the Earth is changing. A centimetre a year adds to the distance between Europe and America. Another year casts me further adrift from mum at home. Standing here in the July sunshine I feel that something binds me to this place.

Just as Jocaster promised, Ricky drove me to Scarborough. The doctor was a well built man with asthmatic breathing.

"Good morning Ricky and this is?"

"David."

"David Jones," I added.

"Well David, you're going to be in one of Jocaster's films. I'll look forward to seeing that." His smiled stretched lecherously across his face and I wondered again at the wisdom of my decision.

"I'll need a sample of blood for analysis, so sit down." He swabbed my arm with iodine and took up a syringe. I looked away as the needle penetrated.

"Good." He labelled it all up and placed it in an envelope. "Now the bit I enjoy the most. Take off your clothes and get up on all fours on the couch." The doctor pulled on a rubber glove and with a small amount of lubricant penetrating my anal sphincter. I was embarrassed by the squeal I let out as his finger entered.

"Just checking there are no obstructions and that your prostate gland isn't enlarged. There's no reason why it should be in one of your age but we have to be thorough." He smiled and told me everything was okay and provided information on some interesting stretching exercises.

I put on my clothes again.

"Doesn't that worry you?" Ricky asked.

"What?"

"Knowing there'll be men out there wanking to our scene on a video whilst their wife's are out shopping."

I hadn't thought about the implications. "No," I confessed, "when Jocaster said I'd be with you I was…"

Ricky smiled. "You were?"

"Over the moon."

Ricky put his hand round my waist and gently ran his fingers along my ribs. "I've got some work to do, can you manage on your own till I get back?"

"Sure." I said.

I stayed in Scarborough's North Bay, wandering round the outcrops looking for dinosaur footprints. I found some on a fallen boulder, the three toed impressions of Theropods, filled with water. I dried them out, measured them and drew them in my note book. The bedding plane on which they were preserved was rippled like the beach beyond. There was no chance of cutting these from the rock without specialist equipment. This reminded me of Hans and his companion. I'd become nervous about these fossil collectors. There was also Jocaster. Pretty soon I would be a part of her world. I wanted financial freedom but I was uncertain this was the way to gain it. The idea was short term. Freedom from Hull was one thing. I hoped geology would peel the world open for me. I'd listened intently when postgraduates returned and spoke about their careers. I noticed they were all tanned and gaunt and possessed a look in their eyes. At first I took it to be fear but as each spoke with conviction I realised it must be their freedom shining through. Whilst waiting, I sat on the boulder and cast pebbles into the water below.

"A penny for them?"

I was startled by the voice. I turned and saw Ricky.

"I've finished the job," he said. "It's such a fine morning; I thought I'd help you. Anyway you looked like someone who needed company. I know, it was all my fault."

I stared at Ricky, "Yes, it's all your fault."

"You said that like you believed it," Ricky sat cross legged, his body rising tall and thin like the ripening grass.

"You're sitting on dinosaur footprints."

Ricky got up and looked. "That's amazing." He ran his hand over their contours and ran his finger round the damp impressions. He looked at me. "You see," he said, "it's simple, if I'm honest. My brother gets in the way. Last night his ex was on the phone in hysterics, blaming herself. She needed calming down. I was the person she turned to."

I warmed to Ricky's humanity, "I thought you'd passed over me for someone else."

Ricky smiled and tapped me in the ribs, "sounds like you've fallen for me."

I smiled and changed the subject, "On the way back I got the jitters, I was being watched by two Germans in a car. I cut across the fields to avoid them. I think they're after me."

"You must be stupid or something," Ricky lay back in the grass.

"I'm not. In the middle of the night I heard someone walk across the yard and try to get in the caravan."

Ricky sat up, "that was me. 3 a.m. I was… I changed my mind." Ricky stood up and brushed his jeans. "Have you reported them to the police?"

"Yes but Birbeck nearly arrested me!"

"Birbeck. Now there's a man to conjure with. Well we'd better get on, Mr. Geologist. There's bones down there!"

"No. This is a day off: a day away from the Ravenscar dome. There's an excellent beach just this side of Sailor's Grave. Secluded."

"Safe?" Ricky asked.

I nodded, "so long as you don't go in the water."

"No fear. Too cold and too full of shit."

I remembered what Barbara had said. Was that really only ten days ago?

The sun was warm on my back and the sand hot beneath my feet. I curled my toes into it feeling the cooler grains under the surface. For a few minutes I sat on a rock and listened to the gentle lap of the waves. The way the sun reflected off the peaks reminded me of a picture I'd seen. I stripped off my t-shirt and jeans and walked down to the water's edge. The chill was refreshing. I waded in up to my knees and felt the waves rise up my thighs and leave a layer of wet flesh. A cascade of water broke over me and I gasped. Ricky had rushed into the water. He was naked. "I didn't say it was that secluded." Ricky took no notice and splashed all the more. I swung my arm round and took both our bodies under. We struggled, and then realising the stalemate pushed each other to the surface gasping for air. We ran onto dry land and wrestled on the shore. Ricky held up his hands in defeat. I looked at his body covered in fine golden sand, he reminded me of pictures of Apollo threaded into Greek myths.

"Let's dry out in the sun, then you can take me for lunch." As he lay there in the sand, his head cocked to one side I felt this overwhelming desire to touch the contours of his body. My finger traced a line down his back and into the cleft of his buttocks.

"Hey, do you mind?" He said. A few seconds later he ignited my senses by drawing his fingers along my back.

I closed my eyes and tried to negate my desires. I opened my eyes again. Ricky was staring at me and smiling. He was about to say something when a family noisily tumbled onto the beach. He pulled my t-shirt over his white backside and grunted.

An hour in the sun and already my flesh was pink and tingling. I brushed the sand off as best I could then pulled on my clothes. Ricky waited in the sun much longer. Finally he stood up as if proclaiming himself to the world. I looked at the family some distance away, *If only…*

Ricky took me to this pokey little café. He'd evidently been there before as the waitress greeted him enthusiastically and she spent the whole meal eying him up. I tried to ignore this. He must have sensed something was wrong because he broke the ice by saying, "This afternoon I want to take you to the most beautiful place I know. I've always joked that my ashes could be scattered there."

"Must be a special place." I replied.

"It is."

We parked at the edge of a disused railway line and walked the rest of the way. We passed a quaint stone-built pub and derelict farm buildings before climbing over a style and following a tree-lined path. All the time the sound of water and sea got louder. Oak trees clung to the cliff their branches contorted by raw easterlies. The path twisted and descended. Now I could glimpse the bay and a peculiar rock formation below. We emerged onto a wooden bridge. The stream beneath was fast flowing and continued towards a great boulder. Here the flow was deflected against the cliff before cascading onto the rocky shore. I followed Ricky as he climbed the boulder and sat with his legs dangling. I pulled myself up next to him. He leant his head against my shoulder. "See what I mean?"

I did. As his head touched my shoulders I bent my lips down to meet his. He moved and looked around. The Coronia sailed into the bay laden with tourists. I could hear their shouts above the commentary. Then as it turned I heard the engine. The individuals became tiles of colour which faded. The boat progressed round the southern headland. I slid down the boulder and ran my fingers through the water. It was cold and somehow restorative. It made me realise why water had been sacred to our ancestors. I leant over the edge of the waterfall and allowed my hand to distort the patterns of the falling water.

"I hope you're not going to spoil the romance of the place by telling me its geology," Ricky stood next to me and looked out over the drop.

"The deltaic beds of the Saltwick Formation and the large boulder you were sat on is a cross bedded sandstone from Sycarham member. But as soon as you said the name I thought, plant bed: a famous layer of shale, rich in plant fossils. Somewhere over there." I pointed.

"I suppose we'd better go and look."

"Day off," I replied, "I'd much rather imagine Celtic rituals taking place. Perhaps they worshipped Cerrunnos…"

"More likely the Mother goddess. There's this friend of mine, a white witch, you know her by the way." He waited to see my reaction before continuing, "Gabby says the place was sacred to the druids. That's why there's so many oaks and mistletoe. The waterfall emptying into the sea must have been a real plus." Ricky pushed me against the rock and pressed his lips against mine. He stood back and looked at me, his eyes filled with passion. "Is this what you want?"

"Absolutely."

Ricky looked up as the sounds of a helicopter built. The craft appeared from over the trees and as it hovered overhead I could see it was a police helicopter. It moved low over the bay obviously searching for someone. When I turned back, Ricky had made his escape.

I walked back through the oaks feeling deflated. He'd done it again, walking out just at the moment. I called his name several times to no avail. In the pub car park there was a yellow sports car.

"You know," Ricky said appearing from behind a derelict cowshed, "I think we've become far too important to the police. My brother, your ex, someone's putting the links together, if they realise we know too much it'll be curtains."

"I've never been much good at detective stories, so you're going to have to spell it out for me."

Ricky smiled, "then let's hope my parents are out. They usually go shopping to the Co-op in Whitby and it will give us time to connect everything."

"Sometime tonight I must ring Carrie and tell her it's all over."
"Why?"

"Because I've fallen in love with someone else. It's the honest thing to do."

"Someone else? Why don't you shout it out? You've fallen in love with me!"

The police helicopter flew over us at higher altitude. Ricky pulled me inside the building. It was dark and despite being summer a fire burnt in the grate. He ordered two pints of bitter shandy and we sat opposite each other, hardly speaking. We both nearly asked the same question at the same time and laughed.

"You first." I said.

"There's no point, I already know the answer." And I saw in his piercing blue eyes that he did.

After a game of pool, we drove back. He concentrated as he negotiated the hairpin bends. "Funny thing, I don't often see Carrie, but last Easter she just turns up on the doorstep asking if her friend, a geologist, could hire the caravan for a month. Now I've fallen for her boyfriend."

I smiled at his confirmation of the fact. "Were you at school with Carrie?"

"Yes, we were at school together but she was always out of my league. I used to tease her on the bus and I remember she once gave me a black eye for my comments. Jevan was never as mean as me, he was always quieter, more cautious. Finally we got dragged in to making porn videos when we hit eighteen. I don't know her very well, but she's always been around."

It was only later as I sat alone in the caravan that the implications of what Ricky said hit home. Carrie had manipulated me into carrying out my field work in North Yorkshire. How we build mountains. Plates move inexorably across the surface of the Earth causing great changes but we are able to forge our own barriers much faster and they're made of sterner stuff than rock.

Chapter 7: Sediment

I think of sediment as dry sand falling through my fingers. Angular quartz and glints of mica reflecting the light. My dreams were filled with the beach and the sounds of the sea. Ricky was stretched out on the sand, his body covered in fine sand and his skin refracting sunlight with a million rainbows.

I woke to my first wet dream in a long time. Afterwards I lay listening to rain on the caravan roof. I picked up the ichthyosaur skull and let my fingers trace round the outline. I mused about the chances of finding such a well preserved specimen just lying on the beach. Once I realised how unlikely this was, I resolved to hide the fossil, to bury it in the orchard. Where ever it came from someone would be wanting it back. Finally my thoughts turned to how my own body might be preserved for millennia.

I found myself asking questions and not knowing the answers. The geology I understood, the motives of those around me I didn't. I was glad Ricky persuaded me not to ring Carrie. Carrie moved to the centre of things. She could have left the note at Whitby Museum. She could have been at the cliff top when Bartholomew fell. I placed all the facts on a piece of paper and tried various connections, none suited the facts as I understood them, possibly I was being naive about one of the names listed. When I slept again I saw the great Liassic Sea under an intense blue sky with the dorsal fin of an ichthyosaur leaving a wake across my dream.

I'd felt sick when Ricky showed me the video. It brought back memories of Drew. The scene revolted me not because Drew was dead, we constantly watch the movies of long dead stars, but because she'd found solace in Mike's arms. I had to ask Ricky to switch it off and when I went outside he came out and comforted me. I remember I broke down in tears. He sobbed as well, so I guessed he was feeling the same emotions about his twin brother.

In terms of geological science the loss of an individual is of no consequence and irrelevant to the fossil record. Without them, the geology of the world would continue unabated. Without a trace of humanity, the processes that shape the Earth would go on. I found this idea humbling and reassuring. There would be a continuation of the Earth, if not life itself, a continuation of life even if not my own. My dad told me we were nothing if we don't have children. That was one of his last pieces of advice to me. Our DNA survives through our offspring and that's all we're here for. I didn't understand the concept then but now I'm certain it's true.

The knock on the door sent my pulse racing. I peeped out between the curtains; two well-dressed men stood there. I hurriedly jumped into my trousers and yesterday's socks and trainers. Answer or run? I thought about the size of the windows. The only viable exit was the front door. I resolved to open the door and jump down, so at least I had a chance to run or shout. As it happened the men separated to look round the caravan. This provided me the opportunity. I opened the door and took a few paces into the yard, "Hello."

"Good morning, I'm Mr. Fibula," the tall thin man in a grey suit put his sunglasses away and offered his hand. "Nice morning," he added.

"Depends how much walking you have to do." I replied.

"I'll come straight to the point. Could you be ready for five? You've a dinner invitation with Mrs. De Vile. It's formal: jacket and tie. Mrs. De Vile has also offered a bed for the night."

"Do I know a Mrs. De Vile?"

"My employer offered you a part in a film."

"Ah! Jocaster," I hadn't forgotten, just misplaced the appointment in relation to now. "I'm here to do a mapping exercise, shirts and ties are a luxury I don't carry. The best I could do is a clean pair of jeans and t-shirt."

"Mindful of that, Mr. Tibia and I will drive you to Whitby to buy the afore mentioned articles."

Mr. Tibia was built like a bouncer and had close cropped red hair. I felt my throat tighten. My voice sounded higher pitched.

"Hi!" Ricky strode across the yard, his face and fingers engrained with dirt.

"Hello, Mr. Moralis," The man waited for him to leave but he came up close to my shoulder. Mr. Fibula added an explanation, "David has been invited to a soiree at Mrs. De Vile's, he's in need of smart clothes, shirt, tie, that sort of thing. I was about to take him into Whitby and…"

"No need. I'll lend him my best. He's just my size and I'll drive him to the event. That way he can enjoy a drink."

"Great!" The man seemed genuinely pleased, "that saves me a journey. We'll see you this evening. Five prompt."

"I wouldn't miss it for the world," I said. The two well-dressed men walked back across the farmyard and regained their silver saloon car.

I looked at Ricky. It was only now that I realised the smell. "Milking?"

"Cleaning out the stalls, yes. How did you know?"

"My other granddad was a farmer. He thought I was a right Nancy because the smell of the milking sheds made me retch. I'm stronger now."

"You mean I smell?"

"Unfortunately," I put my arm around him.

"Don't." he pulled away, "Dad might be looking."

"Did you mean what you said? About taking me?"

"I meant it. I don't want you falling off a cliff in the middle of the night. Several people have lost their way home from the De Vile household after a good meal."

"Does that include Drew and Mick?"

"No one could prove it."

"You mean no one wants to prove it?"

"Amounts to the same thing, either way look after yourself," Ricky smiled.

"Suppose this means you're not in this film? Jocaster told me the scene would be with you," I had hoped that Ricky might also have been invited.

"Did she? I might have changed my mind."

"Well I'm not doing it if you're not!"

"Calm down. It's just a meal, they're not filming a scene. Jocaster never mixes business and pleasure. I bet she genuinely wants to get to know you."

"That's ok then. But don't go frightening me. I've had enough shocks for this year!"

Ricky's dad appeared, "Get back to work you idle shirt-lifter!"

Ricky became meek in his father's presence and sloped back to the sheds. His dad stared at me a moment too long. "And you're not welcome here. Once your month's up, you're out!"

"What have I done?" I asked.

The man turned and trudged back to his chores.

Boggle Hole is reached at the end of a long downhill journey. I managed to hitch a lift in the back of a tractor for some of the way. The path got steeper and I realised a fast flowing stream separated me from the north cliff. The presence of a stream suggested a line of weakness. Something must have enabled the water to erode a channel and the best guess would be the rock disintegrating along a fault. I marked such a line in pencil on the map with a disregard for evidence. Lots of people were just leaving the youth hostel. I recognised several antipodean accents amongst them. We all seemed to be clones wearing grey woolly socks and soft boots, shorts and t-shirts. I was greeted as a long lost friend. An American girl asked me to help her out with her map reading. I obliged.

"I'm walking to Scarborough today." Her voice purred through the New York drawl.

"Some distance but the most fantastic views and walk down to the sea at Hayburn Wyke. It's a beautiful cove."

"Thanks, I will." She said after I'd pointed it out on her map.

This town, is going to be a ghost town…. a radio sang out the lyrics to The Sepecials. I loved songs with words which had meaning and stopped to listen. Just as I rounded the black headland I saw Wojek stretched out.

"Hi!"

"Oh! Hello." He sat up and I saw he had been measuring fossil stems in the wavecut platform.

"That's not very structural geology, looks more palaeoecology."

"You're right. I'm just satisfying myself that I could do the general stuff."

"Well, I could copy your data—that would save me some time."

"Be my guest." So I sat down next to Wojek and copied his figures then added to them. Crinoids are a type of sea animal rooted to the spot. If they are toppled and killed in a storm and their remains covered then the long stems are usually parallel to the direction of the current. This exposure amply proved the theory.

"Thanks for this." I said as Bob Marley and the Wailers struck up with *No Woman No Cry*. I offered my friend a smoke.

"Too early. Besides with the dinner tonight I might overdo my daily allowance."

"Of fucks or fags?" I joked.

Wojek looked at me, he smiled. "I hear you're Ricky's new partner."

"We're friends." I left it at that.

"Don't worry, I'm in no position to judge. I like sex and I like money even more but if my girlfriend found out, she'd kill me. Of course I've often thought what might happen. You know, things change, what would I say if in thirty or forty years time you cold buy porn at the supermarket?"

"You'd probably be pleased to see yourself preserved at twenty and remember the good times. Surely it would all be in the distant past…"

"Women have long memories."

I knew he was right, from mum and Auntie Gertie, I knew he was right.

The best that can be said is that the rest of the day went well. I did all the mapping needed between Boggle Hole and Stoupe Brow. Briefly it went shale, shale with ironstone, and later ironstones with shales. The dark theme of the rocks matched my mood. The evidence I'd accumulated was beginning to suggest there was a displacement if not a fault at Boggle Hole. All that remained was the folklore of the name. I knew that a boggle is a hairy spirit in North Riding myth. A mischievous being who rattles pans, steals eggs and guards the rights of the land against those who'd abuse it. Abuse takes many forms. Drew had been abused by her step-dad. A man in the park had abused me when I was ten. You think you'd be wise after the event but in both our cases it seemed to leave us more vulnerable. For the same reason I expected to be nervous about Jocaster's invitation but instead I found myself excited about meeting new people and pleased that Wojek was going to be there.

I managed to hitch a lift all the way back to Hawsker, so I had plenty of time to get ready. Actually I had too much time and ended up listening to Steve Wright on Radio One: The Human League, The Teardrop Explodes – I'd tried to model my university dress sense on Julian Cope, trousers tucked in boots, a scarf over a new romantic style shirt.

Ricky knocked at the door with about half an hour to spare, "better get a move on," he said brusquely, pushing the clothes down on the table.

"You've had a bad day then?"

"Fucking bad!" He turned to face me. His lip was cut and swollen and one eye puffed up displaying a vivid bruise.

"You didn't get beaten up by those German fossil collectors?" I moved towards him.

Ricky shook his head and stepped away from me. As he backed out of the caravan he whispered, "My dad." He stood on the cobbled yard, on his own territory, "I suppose it's funny. Dad said I didn't match up to expectation. I thought I was doing well to stay here. After all, farming's not the life I chose, that was my brother's lot and much good it did him." Ricky peeled a fiver from a wad of notes clipped in his pocket, "I ordered you a taxi. Getting back's your own affair."

"But…" I moved to the doorway. Ricky had already run to the corner.

The taxi arrived a few minutes later. I looked up at Ricky's window as I passed by. It felt peculiar wearing someone else's clothes. There was the smell of different washing powder about them and the feel only mothers can put into an ironed finish, even when they hate the chore. The journey took us to Whitby. As we got into town we veered left along a private drive. The taxi stopped outside a mansion with an imposing façade. I looked at the large bay windows and the imposing tower roofed in darkened slate and finished with the decorative finesse of Victoriana. Mr Fibula waited at the door. He held it open for me, and then insisted on escorting me to the library and pouring a sherry. I held the glass firmly and wandered along the walls examining the titles of the leather bound books on display.

The bookcases weren't locked so I carefully pulled out a volume that interested me. It was an early edition of John Phillip's *Illustrations of the Geology of Yorkshire*. Even the great get it wrong sometimes. I read the section on the supposed Whitby fault. I'd attended several tutorials on this lesson for all scientists. Phillip's and others had surmised there was a vertical movement or fault between the East and West Cliffs of Whitby. For one hundred and fifty years the idea was perpetuated until someone had the gall to say, hold on where's the evidence? Soon geologists looked again and found, well, nothing. No fault, no fracture in the Earth's crust just a change of sediment. I thought about my own hypothesis at Boggle Hole. It was cast in a less favourable light.

Jocaster entered the room. She smiled at me. "The other guests will join us shortly. We'll be twelve for dinner. Thirteen is unlucky and my brother-in-law, the Canon, wouldn't approve of mimicking The Last Supper."

"It's very kind of you to invite me."

"Kindness had nothing to do with it, it's purely business."

I finished my drink and returned the glass to the tray.

"Another?"

I held up my hand, "I was reading an early geology guide. A beautiful collection you have here."

"It came with the house," Jocaster sipped her drink, "by the way, I took the liberty of preparing a room for you. Do say if it's not convenient." Her suggestion seemed to hang.

"Very Kind. You shouldn't have put yourself out."

"I didn't. That's what I employ Mr. Fibula and Mr. Tibia for." Jocaster draped a deep blue shawl over a chair back, "let me introduce you to the others, though I know you've already met one person." She took me by the elbow and steered me towards the door. As we got out into the entrance hall I realised there were people waiting, every one immaculately dressed. "Everybody, this is David, a research geologist."

People were introduced and then from between the faces Wojek appeared. Without exception they all were unnaturally pretty. No, that was wrong, one guy who I felt was observing me had a deformed face possibly caused by a stroke as his eyelid drooped and his lips hung lopsidedly. Just as everyone was going in for dinner I thought I caught a glimpse of another familiar figure. The short straight hair wasn't quite right but the rest of the proportions were. I almost shouted, "Carrie," But Jocaster took me by the elbow and led me away.

I hadn't eaten French cuisine before. Assiete de crudités was the starter followed by fish stew but it all went by French names. Finally crème brûlée was served in cranberry glass dishes. I'd followed mum's advice and stuck to white wine. The waiter kept topping up my glass but I was pretty certain it amounted to three glasses of Vouvray. Apart from the initial introductions, Jocaster had ignored me and held court at the top of the table. I sat at the furthest end. Opposite me was the man with the distorted face. To my right at the foot of the table an attractive girl called Goldie. On being introduced I resolved not to venture down the missing locks avenue. Goldie was telling me all about a film she was making.

"Terribly nice, a period piece set in Victorian Whitby. I'm the serving wench at the inn who is raped by the sadistic Viscount."

"I play the viscount," it was the first time the man had spoken. His voice was soft but menacing.

"I play Armand, wicked but debonair. It's the only character I do." Wojek raised his glass and saluted.

"Are you doing it for the BBC?"

Everyone laughed. Wojek eventually spoke, "I don't think Auntie would approve. This is the real thing. XXX. Hard core!"

I looked around the table at those assembled. I felt like Jonathan Harker amongst the vampires.

"Will you play the part if you get it?" Wojek asked, "You're to be Goldie's headstrong but naive brother who gets a good shafting by Ricky."

"Getting shafted by Ricky is the only reason for doing the film."

"I'm Richard," the smooth voiced man who sat opposite announced, "I'm also the director." He offered his hand. I accepted.

"And who is the star?" I asked.

"That nobody is allowed to know yet. It's all part of the plot! It ensures our reactions are natural. Needless to say condoms are used for any penetration."

"Hello, Mr. Fibula."

"Good evening, sir," He refilled my glass and went off to do something else. I watched him go into the kitchen. A woman put her arm round him as the door closed.

A crystal glass was tapped. Jocaster pointed with a silver spoon. "Attention please ladies and gentlemen." I listened to the next conversation up the table. This was an even less favourable diatribe on profit in the porn industry and how big companies were slowly, possibly reluctantly investing. I sipped my wine.

"I'm interested to know what Jocaster sees in you. You have no obvious talents," Goldie asked.

"I'm a geologist," I joked, "I don't need talent."

Richard butted in. "I've a ten inch cock. It's very photogenic. You'd be surprised how many of my fans don't realise this," he tapped his face with a finger.

"I had my arsehole specially stretched to accommodate him," Goldie added.

I tried not to look shocked and remembered the exercises I'd been set. The back of my throat went dry and I felt a sudden urge to leave, however curiosity spurred me on. "Carrie always said that punters like to see someone average they can identify with. Well that's me!"

Mr Fibula refilled glasses, though he lent particularly close to Goldie and whispered something. I smelt the fragrance he wore, something expensive with musk at its heart. I knew I'd lost count of the number of glasses and I was beginning to feel light-headed.

"Are you going to say *yes*?" Wojek asked.

"Yes?" I tried to sound cool and calm when in reality I was neither.

Goldie's hand reached for my crotch, she unzipped me and her fingers separated skin from clothing. "Uncut, average, nothing good camera work couldn't sort out." Her hand remained there, caressing. She smiled at me almost willing my reaction. I took her by the wrist and removed her hand. Goldie relaxed in her chair.

"She's a bit of a nympho," Richard leaned forward. "And if she doesn't turn you on, I'm always available. I've always thought being bisexual was literally the best of all possible worlds."

"I've always thought being yourself much more important," I added. I finished my drink. Coffee was brought along. Several people got out cigarillos so I decided to smoke as well. I was stared at as I lit up but I ignored them all. Besides, I needed to do something with my hands, give them a focus. Jocaster walked past me and signalled Goldie to leave her chair. The woman sat next to me, enveloping me in her byzantine fragrance. She stretched out; the emeralds on her left hand caught the light. I lifted her hand, examined the stones then kissed the yellowing skin.

"I hope my little darlings haven't been too much trouble?"

"Very entertaining," I said.

"How's your friend Ricky. I hear his father's beaten him again."

"That was how he told it." I was reluctant to discuss Ricky. "I'm surprised not to see your husband the Canon here," I said innocently.

Jocaster looked at me, "I'm not married," she replied. I think I must have stared a little too long because she gently hid her hand under her silk scarf. She smiled, "but I believe you know my niece, Carrie?"

"Yes, we're friends at university. I meet her most nights at the Queens."

Jocaster smiled, lit a cheroot before getting up and walking off.

An odd looking lad called Nathan began to play the piano. He was elegantly thin and his eyes shone with the passion of the music. I went over and lent on the grand piano.

"Would you like to sing with me?" He asked.

"Sing?"

"You can sight read music can't you?"

I nodded, "Not very well but if it's something I vaguely know..."

"Let's start with a little Elton John." He turned the pages to "Sorry seems to be the Hardest Word." Nathan trialled a couple of keys and began.

> *"What have I got to do to make you love me,*
> *What have I got to do to make you care,*
> *What do I do when lightning strikes me*
> *And I wake to find that you're not there."*

I found myself singing into the almost green irises of his eyes and realising he'd enchanted me. He smiled and for a moment in the chorus I realised everyone in the room was listening. At the end there was applause and I found my singing had broken the ice. Nathan played on alone.

Later several of us got together round a large oak table and played monopoly. Normal life intruded into the surreal atmosphere of the gothic mansion. The game degenerated around midnight and I went into a corner with Wojek to smoke a joint; Goldie took Mr Tibia to her room. The place was quiet. Jocaster had vanished.

"Are you always this late?" I asked.

"We're waiting to film the first scene, at the altar."

The combination of alcohol and cannabis totally knocked me out. I reclined on the sofa. Nathan stood over me. "Come and make some music," he said.

The last thing I remember before collapsing on silk sheets in a dark panelled room was the touch of the piano players fingers as he pulled the sheets over me.

I thought I heard a scream. It was either in my dream or my own scream permeating reality. I sat upright in the bed then closed my eyes and steadied my head.

I heard another scream. I slid off the bed. And felt the door. The handle was cold. The handle turned but the door didn't yield. I had been locked in. I felt befuddled so I filled the sink with cold water and immersed my head under the surface. I thrust my face to the very bottom of the ceramic bowl. My body forced my head into the air once more. I'd read somewhere that drinking plenty of water can assuage the worse effects of a hangover. I managed perhaps two pints before turning on the shower. My head thudded. The en suite was white, almost painfully so. I stood in the stream of warm water. Steam billowed through the room and obscured my image in the mirror. Afterwards I rubbed a section clear. I looked awful even though the shower had revived me and I turned my attention to exploring the mansion.

A locked door. I put my eye to the keyhole. The key obscured any view of outside. There was a gap between the door and wooden floor so I attempted a trick I'd seen in an old movie. *In The Cat and The Canary* this part was done with a thin piece of card. I used some pages from Saint John chapter two from a copy of The Gideon's Bible. I took a match and began playing the key around, I gave it a gentle push. The key fell. I peered under the door. It had landed. The pages had the desired effect. I gained the key and my freedom.

My head pounded as I entered the hall. My vision was disturbed in a way I hadn't experienced since my last migraine. It was at that moment I realised I'd been drugged. Why would anyone drug me and lock the door? Trying to figure it out made my headache worse. I tumbled out onto the corridor and took a deep breath. The only explanation was to keep me out of the way. I allowed my hand to feel the contours of the wall even though my sight distorted the long straight corridor into curves.

I thought I was making for the stairs but instead I saw the smiling face of Carrie. I closed my eyes and rubbed them. A white hand closed the door ahead of me and I heard her silly giggle fade. I tried the door. It was locked. I turned the handle and rattled it. It didn't yield. I knocked. I heard laughter. I turned and emerged on a balcony overlooking the chapel. I concealed myself behind a pillar.

A great battery of lights shone upon the white altar cloth and kneeling before it a couple were getting married.

'This must be part of the film,' I thought. Under the lights sat a woman in a gothic chair. The fingers of her right hand tapped the wood, drawing attention to her ruby clad fingers. I watched for a moment. I watched until nausea welled up inside me. I escaped onto the corridor and by luck found a toilet. I vomited, thought myself finished then retched again until nothing remained. I flushed all away and steadied my shaking legs. More water. I got back to my room. I locked the door, stripped and showered for a second time.

The effects of alcohol, cannabis and some other drug were slowly clearing but I could remember nothing after Nathan escorted me to my room. I opened the window and looked down. The smooth stone blocks would give no purchase and the drop was too great to consider jumping. In the distance the abbey stood silhouetted against the morning sky, its ruins unfamiliar from this angle.

I dressed again and took the opposite way along the corridor. I reached the stairs but the front door was locked and bolted. I followed the tiles to the servants' area. The room was half lit. A couple were playing cards. There was no way out.

I returned to the dining room. It was as though twelve people had never entered the house. The tablecloth was starched, the floor absolutely clean. I ran my finger along the cloth. I ran my finger along the contours of the piano and smiled. At the far end of the dining room where hours earlier Jocaster had held court I saw my opportunity. An open window. I opened it further. I jumped down into the border of marigolds and nasturtiums. I ran. I heard dogs bark and a shout. A car revved into life. A door opened to bar my way.

"Get the fuck in!" Ricky put the car in gear and before I'd closed the door gravel exploded in all directions. We reached the main road.

Ricky drove on for sometime. He took a narrow road that hugged the cliff face. Tyres squealed as we shot round a hairpin bend over a stone bridge. "The old railway line," I asked as I'd got my bearings.

"I thought the fresh morning air would clear your head."

"Wow and something. Someone put me out good style – they wanted me out of the way."

I looked at the multicoloured black eye Ricky sported. He pulled his sunglasses down over his face. "Don't look at me."

"Why not, I love you."

"Don't say that. You've got me into enough trouble already."

"I'm sorry..."

Ricky drove until the road ended at a gravel parking area.

"You know, there are several people who might have wanted you out of the way last night."

"Like?"

"Carrie, she's Jocaster's niece. Jocaster, so you didn't find anything out about the shoot and then there's Birbeck. I followed him. He waited in a lay-by then walked across the lawn just after one in the morning."

"Birbeck? But he's a police officer."

"And a fucking bent one at that."

We started walking down a steep hill. The sound of the sea and a fast-flowing river grew louder. We emerged at the wooden bridge which spanned Stoupe Beck. The air was filled with a fine mist from the rolling waves. I took several deep breaths.

"I saw him murder Drew..."

"Fucking hell you're dead meat."

"Thanks, that makes me feel a whole lot better."

"It surely doesn't make my task any easier."

"What do you mean?"

Something in the way he spoke made the hairs on the back of my neck stand up. I looked at his black eye disguised by glasses. His face still showed the weals from the beating.

"I'm been sent away until after you've left."

"Sent away? Where to?"

"My uncle owns a farm near Ulveston."

"But thats..."

"A bloody long way away and you need a minder."

"I had you ear marked for the job. You could sleep on the problem!"

"Great humour, I nearly laughed!" Ricky moved his hand over my heart. He let it lie there. He took my hand and placed it over his heart. "Promise you'll wait for me."

"I promise, even if I have to wait years."

Ricky snorted, "Weeks hopefully. I'll try and sort something."

"You don't have to say it," I replied, almost at the point of tears.

"I'll leave messages at the Cook Arms but don't be surprised if it's all quiet for a while." Ricky walked away.

"But I thought..."

Ricky stroked my face and smiled, "You're daft, always expecting the impossible when you've already got it."

Ricky flicked a pebble into the sea, "It's no use," he said, "I'll have to leave now."

Ricky didn't look round. He walked at first but finally ran. I resisted the urge to follow. Instead I watched him climb the steps and regain his car. There was long pause. The engine started. Ricky had gone.

Peeling back layers of sediment reveals what is past. Each layer presents some evidence of its deposition and the life it contained. The only thing is you have to be prepared to find something that doesn't immediately make sense. I burrowed through the sand, piling it up in a great mound until I reached the cold damp layer beneath. Nothing is preserved in sediment except death.

Chapter 8: The Angle of Dip

Unlike a geological hammer, a clinometer could by no stretch of the imagination be considered an offensive weapon. I was onto my second hammer as the earlier one was still in police custody. My own clinometer wasn't posh as students from better backgrounds might possess but an old protractor with a plastic edge pinned into the centre. With this piece of equipment I could measure the angle of dip in the rocks. The reason for doing this is to build up data to analyse and generate the probable structure of the area. Structure matters. If you asked my mum about rocks she could tell you only one thing: the oldest rock is at the bottom. Now that's mostly true in North Yorkshire.

The dome of Robin Hood's Bay is the most interesting structural feature in my territory but I have it on good authority, Wojek's, that an igneous rock left over from the opening of the Atlantic, struck its way across Yorkshire like the pulled thread in a jumper. Mr. Caine was pleased to possess a sample of this rock and he'd hand it round the class at every opportunity, much to our delight. The specimen was a standing joke. Then Mr. Caine would eye us suspiciously before closing his eyes. "It is of course a tholeiite with big crystals of feldspar." I've often suspected we could have walked out at one of these times as he contemplated the nature of rocks but on this occasion one eye half opened and fixed me. "And where do you expect the rock originated?" He asked.

"In the Earth?" I said for a laugh and got one. The room quietened and I continued as both eyes were staring and making me feel uncomfortable. "The Scottish Isles when the Atlantic opened."

Mr. Caine smiled but then he countered, "And what is the name for the largest crystals in a rock?"

Drew whispered the name. She coughed to disguise it.

"Phenocryst," I replied relieved to have scored a second victory.

With my eyes closed and the sound of the breaking waves for company I could easily span those three years. I lay back amongst the grass seeded with thrift and reminisced. But it doesn't matter how long ago the event was it is equally beyond our grasp, yesterday, last year or the first day of the Jurassic. It was all the stuff of history; only this special branch of history called geology had captured my imagination.

In my studies to date the history of England and Geology had become inextricably linked. Our advancement as an industrial nation was born out of the greater understanding of the rocks beneath our feet. People broke from Biblical indoctrination and found advancement in the nature of sediments and their angle of dip. Not only did I thirst for knowledge, but geology had become my god. It made a science where there was once creation and relegated The Old Testament to a nice set of fables to frighten children at Sunday School.

There was however a mercenary incentive to this study, I hoped to find employment which paid a lot more than the average salary. All the evidence showed that was the case. One of Mr. Caine's earlier successes had been Alex. He'd got an A and gone to Cambridge. I knew him because his mum and mine were friends. He was ten years older and the sort of person who was absolutely committed to his work. We had a begrudging friendship based on a couple of nights out drinking real ale. Secretly I envied him for loving his work so much and already being there. He was killed when an oil platform exploded. He was burnt to death and his body never recovered. I should have been at his memorial service to say something to his parents but the easy solution was to remain silent, to absent myself. I'm human. I'm not my father. Dad did everything correctly. Perhaps one day I'll be like him. I think in many ways we grow up to be like our fathers no matter how hard we try to avoid it. In my case I don't remember the absolutes. I wasn't old enough when he died and not knowing leaves me vulnerable to becoming more like him.

Five days ago I'd stood here at this same spot and said goodbye to Ricky. Now I was looking up at the vapour trial of a plane and wishing. But it was no use. For the last five days I'd walked everywhere: four miles to the coast and four back. At the end of the day I attempted to hitch a lift. Only once had I been successful which at least meant I had some food by eight and I was in bed before ten.

I'd seen a yellow sports car twice; I'd seen a woman in a pink skirt once. She'd been too far away to make out any detail and after all, it might just be a popular summer colour. I'd not seen anything of the German pair. Nothing out of the ordinary had happened. In this environment, I'd relaxed and the knot in my stomach was beginning to unwind. I walked along the beach to Bay Town and browsed the shop windows on the way up the steep hill. Half way up was a narrow fronted bookshop with a variety of small rooms. I settled to look through a geological guide to the area, to reassure myself there was nothing I'd missed. The owner seemed unconcerned about my presence and sat reading behind his desk. Apart from the echo of seagulls wheeling over the pantile roofs, there wasn't anything to disturb my concentration. After five minutes, I attacked the hill with renewed vigour, counting the steps as I went. I bought an ice cream from the kiosk at the top. At first I let my tongue penetrate the cold creamy layers. Finally, I admired the view of the bay.

"A penny for your thoughts?"

I looked round. The man in a grey Mac was one of the policemen who'd interviewed me after the attack.

"I'm sorry, I don't remember your…"

"DCI Birbeck."

It all came back to me. His breath still smelt of brandy and his skin was peeling over his large nose. I finished eating.

"It's not a social call. I've been thinking about things, putting two and two together and I've realised you've got some connections to this place. You know Carrie Franklin."

"From university, yes. We used to be an item."

Birbeck chuckled.

"Is it a private joke?"

He held up his hand. "She comes back most holidays. You students seem to get a lot of them."

I observed Birbeck carefully, sensing my danger. The man's face puffed up as he spoke and a little ball of spittle formed on his lower lip. I tried not to stare.

"Was it Carrie who told you about the caravan?"

"Yes," I was trying to work out the connection one step ahead of the officer.

"And did Carrie know Drew and Mike?"

"I suppose she might have met Drew at uni but I never heard a Mike mentioned."

"And you knew Drew at university?" He emphasised the last syllables.

"Yes. Is this line of questioning supposed to lead somewhere?"

The DCI smiled, "I hope so. You see I don't think we've had a spate of copycat suicides. I think we've had three murders."

"And you think…" Now I knew he was lying. He needed a scapegoat for the murders of Drew and her boyfriend.

"I don't think, I work on evidence. You are the common denominator as we used to say in maths."

"Well I suggest you go back and work things out," I said with a hint of sarcasm.

"I shall," he turned to leave. "By the way have you met Jocaster?"

"Yes, I went for dinner there last week. It was entertaining and I'm afraid to say I got rather drunk. I hope that's not against the law?"

He shook his head.

As an afterthought I ran after Birbeck, "don't suppose you'd question me further as you give me a lift to Hawsker?"

"It's your lucky day. I'm in a good mood. Hop in."

I cleared the seat of debris: several polystyrene cartons and cups, "It looks as though you've been on a stakeout."

The DCI smiled, "Tell me all about your dinner party with Jocaster."

So I did. Well at least an expurgated version. As we pulled up the hill past the Victoria Hotel, I saw the girl in the pink skirt clearly. I let my head turn. The DCI followed my gaze in the rear-view mirror. When I looked up he pointedly stared forward.

"Pretty," he said, "out of your league I'd have thought. That's Carrie Franklin, but then you know her."

"I just said as much, yes," but I was beginning to doubt whether I really did. "You know, the one thing which confuses me about all of this?"

Birbeck arched an eyebrow.

"Why is it I've never seen the Canon. Jocaster's supposed to be his wife."

Birbeck's face inflated and he spluttered out a great laugh. When he could bring himself to speak he rubbed the tears from his cheeks and said, "Now I know why she wants you here, you're the sacrificial virgin to be rescued by some muscle bound Amazon."

I hadn't taken on board the implications of what he'd said. I couldn't understand what was so funny. I stared at Birbeck. He must have realised.

"You really don't get it do you? Jocaster's not the Canon's wife, it's a joke. They call her that because she's always shooting balls."

I realised how naive I'd been. I felt the blood drain from my fingers as I clenched my fists.

Birbeck continued, "It's her twin sister Josephine who's married to religion. Josephine is Canon Franklin's wife and Carrie is their daughter. To a point I can understand your confusion, they're identical twins. I've known them for years but I can't tell them apart." He negotiated the steep hill and turned onto the A171, "It was worth giving you the lift just for the laugh. Well it's proved to me you're not the brains behind any of this." Birbeck stopped the car.

I got out and gave a mock salute. He'd dropped me a few hundred metres from the village. I knew Carrie could never murder someone but I was a witness to the one man who was. Birbeck. Then there was Barty, how did he get involved? How did he go from the apple of Aunt Gertie's eye to bent cop? Perhaps I'd never find out what had gone on but ignorance is bliss was not a *Bon Mot* I wanted as an epitaph. I realised I'd have to wise up quickly.

After tea, I sat by the window and examined the rough version of the map I'd created. Every angle of dip was marked. Changes in rock type coded by colour, a continuous line for known boundaries and a dotted line for the hypothetical. It was all coming together. Over the autumn term I'd have to convert this into a thesis. Thank heavens for the word processor. Unlike Alex, I'd be able to do my own work, not pay a typist to present the best copy. Despite that, the copy of Alex's thesis I'd read as a sort of expert proof-reader showed the calibre of a top notch student. It gave me something to aim for and something I knew would fill the long winter nights.

Later, when I lay back in bed, something Birbeck said suddenly sent my brain working. Jocaster, Josephine. The problem had been staring at me and as a geologist I should have realised. It was a question of rings. Rubies on the right hand, emeralds on the left. I thought back. Ricky had warned me not to get involved with beautiful women. I'd seen that warning as a green light that he was available, not as a danger signal. What was being hidden from me? I hated the idea of doubting Ricky. He'd been through a lot--the death of his brother, his father's beatings--Carrie on the other hand had already shown a lamentable lack of honesty.

My dreams were haunted by the body falling from the cliff, of my stammered explanations to Aunt Gertie who appeared by my side. She pointed a wizened finger and accused, "it's all your fault. I always knew you were bad." As the dream replayed the woman in the pink skirt stood a moment too long at the edge. Barty's cadaver broke on the rocks, his guts spread over the grey shale, and his eyes went cloudy just as I lifted his head. Only this time when I looked, it was my own face that stared back. I woke in a cold sweat. I thought you were never supposed to be able to see your own eyes in a dream. It was bad luck, very bad luck indeed.

I realised my misfortune when I wiped the condensation off the caravan window and peered out. It was raining heavily. I waited. I pottered about cleaning things but by eleven I knew I had to get kitted up in my Cagoule and make the best of it. I had some work to do on the displacement of the Peak Fault, an earth movement which raised the rocks on one side relative to the other.

I caught the bus to Ravenscar, even though this took my last pound coin. I'd spent so many nights in solitude, even the danger of meeting Jocaster in The Cook Arms was more appealing than my own company. Money was tight. The only way I might alleviate things and get a meal or drink that evening was to sell a couple of ammonites to the fossil shop in Bay Town.

I didn't stop for lunch, the ceaseless rain made eating unpleasant and the biting wind made sitting too cold. It was difficult to believe it was still summer. I worked at the problem I'd set myself. On my map I had to be able to extrapolate the original structure of the dome and work out its height, its age and how it came to be eroded leaving the broad sweep of the bay and the sheer cliffs of North Cheek.

Despite the conditions I felt I was getting somewhere. I pencilled measurements in my notebook. I looked around the deserted bay, grey waves surging under a grey sky, all the surfaces washed in leaden shades. The bad weather brought a different taste to the air.

I walked the cliff path to Bay Town and after some haggling I sold three good ammonite fossils for nine quid. I calculated I'd get a pint, a plate of chips and ten fags for that sum, maybe a second pint if I could dig out some loose change in the caravan. Outside the shop I looked at the wondrous display of amethyst chimneys, polished sections and glinting pyrites. For a moment with water dripping off my nose, I envied the shopkeeper. Indeed I could imagine myself as a middle aged man in such an occupation.

I was so wet, cold and depressed after walking back to the caravan that I could have taken the next bus for Hull. I felt like giving up everything and returning home to mum. If I'd have passed maths, I'd be training for a comfortable life in an office. Everything inside the caravan felt damp, even the clothes hung up in the wardrobe had a clammy feel.

Perhaps my dilemma wasn't unlike William Smith being forced through debt to sell his fossil collection to the state. Of course the bureaucrats held the trump card and forced him to sell for less than sufficient to clear his liabilities. In much the same way the shopkeeper depressed the cash price for my own specimens.

When I counted up the money on the formica table, it didn't quite total the fare home. I smiled to myself and realised this was just as well. I couldn't spend the next nine weeks in Hull. Mum and I wouldn't be able to hit it off for that length of time. What I really needed was a job that paid well, something to provide the readies for the next term or two and maybe ease the number of irate letters the bank manager sent. I found myself fantasising about being in a porn movie. A fleeting image of Goldie beckoning kept me sane as I warmed baked beans in a pan and cut a large slice of bread. After several days of denial I found something appealing about the idea again. Not the act but the money. I remembered what Gabby said about earning enough from adult films to buy The Cook Arms. Was it exaggeration or fact?

I poked my head out of the door. Still the rain came down I kitted up in my cagoule again and despite hitch-hiking no one stopped to offer me a lift. I supposed it wasn't tempting to geologist sitting next to you in a car and steaming up the windows. More likely it was my face hidden under the cagoule hood.

Mrs Moralis, shouted from the farmhouse door. I turned and dodged the puddles as I ran back. She waved a letter. My hopes were raised that Ricky had contacted me but as soon as I saw the envelope, I knew it was from mum. I read the letter under the porch. Mum was ordering me home for Barty Fair's funeral. 11.30am on the 1st August at St Michael's and all Angels, followed by a cremation at Chants Ave. There was at least a ten pound note inside – I couldn't use a lack of money as an excuse. I made a note in my diary.

Even the inside of my waterproofs were damp, making the walk to the Cook Arms a sombre affair. I wasn't bothered about Jocaster anymore. I needed warmth and company, the pub provided both. I'd forgotten it was quiz night, the bar was heaving. Gabby waved me over.

"We haven't seen you for a while," She said and passed me an answer sheet. "Do you know any of these?"

I knew four out of the six and wrote down the answers in silence, "I came in for a bar meal but I can see I've got the wrong night."

"I shouldn't worry," Gabby placed a reassuring hand on my shoulder, "we always give out sarnies and chips. I'll make certain you get a good portion. Best of all it'll be free!"

"Here's the entry money for the quiz. I might as well have a go."

"You could…" I saw Gabby's eyes drift to the door. It was Mr. Fibula, dressed in jeans and a white T-shirt. He folded his sunglasses and pinned them over his shirt. Goldie threaded her arm though his. Her other hand slid gently over the crotch of my jeans and lingered.

She took her hand away and smiled, "I'm forgetting my manners, you're Ricky's virgin meat, though I've heard you made sweet music with the pianist! Still after all that, I might be willing."

I lit a cigarette and blew the smoke to one side.

"You silly boy..." She patted my cheek, "why did you leave us so quickly. You caused quite a stir below stairs."

"I wasn't well."

"I heard you were drugged. Who would do such a thing?"

Mr. Fibula smiled. Had he some inside knowledge?

"Jocaster was angry when she heard. Still you're obviously ok now. Come on Goldie, let's find a quiet corner." Mr. Fibula raised his glass. His face distorted through the curve.

I stood at the bar. I wondered what they knew that I didn't. I remembered the glimpses of Carrie.

"Bad news?" Gabby tapped my arm and brought me round.

I collected the change.

"Carrie."

Gabby went pale, "what?"

"I was thinking of Carrie."

Gabby took a deep breath, "yes, she is a lovely girl."

I looked at Gabby but she had bottled her emotions again. "Yes, she can be," I added lamely.

I squeezed the only free stool into a space at the bar and reflected. Having Mr. Fibula in the same room worried me. He looked like a gangster with his Maori tattoos but seeing him with Goldie put a new perspective on the man. He appeared to touch the woman sensitively with small fine strokes of his large fingers. I decided my vantage point perched at the bar wasn't for me and left for the lounge. Very few people were in this room. A fire burnt in the grate. Jocaster sat alone in the Butler's chair.

"Good evening," I said.

Jocaster looked around. She was dressed more plainly than usual but she wore rubies on her left hand and emeralds on her right. I realised my mistake at once, "Sorry," I said, "you must be Jocaster's sister."

The woman pursed her lips, "Knowing my sister tells me more about you than it does about me." She took a sip of her drink. Perhaps I stood there a little too long because Josephine looked up and said, "Well?"

"I'm sorry, but if I didn't know otherwise I would have said you were the person I changed the flat tyre for."

The sister looked at me. "Observation skills," she said and lit a cigarette. "This by the way is my husband, Canon Franklin."

Her husband's receding hair was jet black. His face tightened as though he suffered from extremely painful piles, "Good evening," he offered his hand and squeezed the thumb joint as we shook.

"I'm here doing a geological map," I said, "I was fortunate enough to be invited to a dinner party at your sister-in-law's." I noticed Josephine move a little nervously.

"We've been away." He picked up his drink, "in fact we only came back today, hence the bar meal. I hate shopping, don't you?"

I nodded.

"So you've seen the ancestral pile? Good," the Canon said rhetorically. "Perhaps you'd care to visit and have the architectural tour? You'll find it a little more informative than the dinner party."

"That's very kind of you. I'm fascinated by history and I love Victorian Gothic," I lied and hoped it wasn't obvious that I was imagining the place being bull-dozed as I spoke.

"Tomorrow at ten?" The Canon shook my hand again.

"Delighted," I walked back through to the bar like a boy dismissed from the headmaster's office.

It was something Barbara said which niggled me. I remembered it when the first blast of cool night air pushed against my face. My cheeks glowed and my stomach was warm and full. What was it? I almost saw her leaning against the lockers, smoking her Park Drive. She said, no one does anything for nothing. It was as good as any of my dad's Bonne Motts. In fact it was better because I was certain it was true and that the expression was as likely to apply to twin sisters as men of the cloth.

I dived under the sheets when I got in. I'd eaten a variety of sandwiches and chips and wrapped a few spares for tomorrow's lunch. Gabby had been as good as her word. She smiled at me before I left and said, I can see you're ready now. She had winked. I knew what she meant, that's why I shivered before the oblivion of sleep.

When I peered through the dirty window of the bus, I caught a glimpse of a yellow sports car. It was gaining on us and as we drew to a halt at the traffic lights, it drew up alongside. I clearly saw Jocaster as I stood up and rang the bell.

I waited on the pavement next to the long brick wall that enclosed the Victorian villa then proceeded down the drive. I stood and looked at the entrance. I hadn't noticed the urns with their great swags of nasturtiums, nor had I noticed the well-manicured lawn and the view across the skyline to the abbey on the headland.

"Hello." The Canon took off his gardening gloves and shook my hand. His thumb squeezed over mine again. "I'm glad you could make it. I'll show you round the garden first as its brighter now." He didn't say anything for a while. I took in the colour of the borders and the fantastic shapes of the Acers which punctuated the lawn.

"There's a lot of hard work gone into this."

"God always provides a way. My sister-in-law brought her film company here and she was generous with hire charges. That enabled me to employ a gardener to help with the chores."

"Yes," I said, "gardening has always struck me as that."

"Wait till you have a place of your own. You'll see things differently." The Canon seemed genuine in his thoughts so I didn't protest. "We have an open day on Sunday in aid of church funds…" His voice trailed off as the sound of two women arguing emanated from the house, "They don't always get on. Opposite ends of the service industry, you might say."

"I've never thought of God and pornography in the same house."

"Remember Mary Magdalene was a prostitute. We are all God's children."

I found the Canon's viewpoint refreshing. I remembered the great fuss our local priest made when they opened a burlesque bar in Hull. He likened the city to Sodom however a massive landslide caused that city's destruction, an act of geology not an act of God.

The rose garden was set out in triangular beds, each of a different colour. The paths met at a statue of a faun. The smiling face of Pan playing the pipes looked down on us. "I expected a saint."

"You forget the role of the clergy in the advancement of even your own science. The Reverend George Young?"

I hadn't forgotten, "I have a whole series of notes on his fossil alligator. I've always though it ironic that he should help set us on the path to replacing God with Science."

"I think you've stood the argument on its head. Knowledge doesn't disprove God; it shows the vastness of his creation. Perhaps," he said, cutting the deadhead from a rose, "we should continue our discussion on theology in the library over a sherry?"

I nodded my approval.

I saw only one of the two sisters sitting at the end of the great dining table. "Good morning," Jocaster rattled the paper up so as to obscure her face. A muffled good morning emanated from somewhere.

"Which one's which?"

"Jocaster spoke. It's a standing joke that people look at their rings to tell them apart. Rubies on the right for Jocaster and emeralds on the right for my wife."

Before I could ask anything else, the Canon escorted me into the library. I remembered thumbing through these leather bound editions a few nights ago but decided to say nothing. Sunlight briefly filtered through the dust. "This might interest you." I was handed an edition of Transactions of the Geological Society of London for 1837. "It's one of my prized possessions." The Canon turned the pages and held the book open at page 215. 'Remarks on a section of the Upper Lias and marlstone of Yorkshire, showing the limited range of the species of ammonites, with their value as geological tests.'

I struggled to remember this geologist and admitted, "I've never heard of Louis Hunton."

"That is the tragedy of his genius. Take the book. Return it when you've read the article, then you'll understand."

"I couldn't. It might get damaged…" I held the book for the Canon to take.

He gently pushed it back towards me, "I would rather it got damaged than remained here gathering dust unread."

I thanked him and promised to return the volume. The clock chimed twelve.

"Is that the time?"

"Indeed, I'll ring the bell for lunch. You must have lunch before returning to your studies." The Canon smiled persuasively. "Besides, in the tower room are my most prized possessions. You'll be fascinated."

It was a simple gesture but I sensed immediately that there was some danger. I climbed the spiral stairs into the turret room with trepidation. Canon Franklin pushed past me and produced keys from his cassock pocket. "In here," his hand gently stroked my back and pushed me forwards.

I felt myself gasp. Every surface of the room was covered in fossils. A complete Teleosaurus chapmani, and ammonites of such size and detail they would fetch vast sums. I doubted the university had such a diverse collection.

"This is my pride and joy. The very fossil which started the advancement of geology. Yes," he nodded eagerly, "the very one Wooler and Chapman discovered…."

I stood dumbstruck. I ran a finger along the contours of its skull. I was going to tell the Canon of my find but I realised there was a gap. The canon was missing one specimen. The card proclaimed: skull of Ichthysaurus sp, Saltwick Bay. The slightly darker felt was about the size of the specimen Ricky had found. I realised something's are better left unsaid. I turned round. Finally I saw an ammonite preserved in fool's gold mounted on the wall. The chipped edges informed me it had been cut from the rock and recently. It put me in mind of the fossil collectors who'd taken such a dislike to me at Ravenscar.

"All these specimens are local," I noted.

"Indeed. I employ two collectors in the summer to furnish me with new material. I'd be happy to buy anything you have of interest when you've written your thesis."

"That's a kind offer. Thanks."

The Canon moved into the doorway. "They are nice boys, German I believe. One of them had a nasty fall recently and has spent a few days convalescing here."

"Here?"

"Yes, I felt guilty at him being injured whilst working for me. Lunch," he added.

It was beginning to connect. I smiled graciously and uttered several compliments before following Canon Franklin out of the room and down the stairs. What I needed to find out was how much he knew about me. Whilst we sipped the beef consommé I started the conversation, "Have you met Ricky Moralis?"

"Yes, a great tragedy for the community and there have been so many of late. I presided at his funeral."

I felt myself go light-headed, "surely you mean Jevan, Ricky's brother?"

"No, Ricky worked hard in my garden. He was a talented man, he'd arrange colours in such an inspiring way. I remember he once did a bed full of different coloured verbenas. I said it wouldn't work. He smiled and asked me to wait. It was a marvellous success. Such a tragedy when he suffocated—carbon monoxide poisoning. He left the engine on and fed a pipe through the window. You can't do that with a modern car but he drove a 1974 Saab. His parents have never got over the loss, you never do, it's not the natural order to bury a child. Of course you are staying there at the Moralis place."

"Yes, in their caravan." I toyed with the mushrooms served with the next course. "Jevan's gaining more experience in farming at his uncles in Ulveston. Now there's a beautiful pace, we stayed there on a field trip a couple of months ago."

"Ah! That's where the young man is. He borrowed an item of mine and I'm keen for its return. I really must get in touch." The Canon added as a conclusion pushing away his empty Royal Worcester dinner plate.

Had I said too much? I was confused about Ricky/Jevan but I didn't know the canon well enough to challenge him. I let the matter drop and continued eating until Mr. Fibula brought in the dessert. "Eve's pudding, sir." The pristine white shirt couldn't conceal the man's build. Mr. Fibula didn't have the physique for polite servitude. As he served my portion Mr Fibula slipped a note onto my lap. I casually passed my plate to him and resumed eating.

"Being out in the fresh air gives a man a good appetite," the vicar said.

I agreed.

"Have you found anything spectacular?" He asked with enthusiasm.

"Several well preserved ammonites. Unfortunately I had to sell one or two to make ends meet," I pushed the note into my pocket.

"It's a shame you haven't found anything to pad out your thesis. A new species, perhaps Teleosaurus jonesi," he teased.

The penny dropped. He knew I had the skull, did Ricky steal it or was it given? I played the game. "I was hoping to find something like that. Something like a plesiosaur skull or even just the teeth would help and I could have passed it on to you afterwards." I saw the Canon smile from behind arched fingers. Did he know I knew what he was up to?

"Well young David, coffee in the conservatory? Then I must let you get on. Where might you go this afternoon?"

"I'll probably walk the disused railway track back to Hawsker and look for any rock outcrops in the cuttings," I looked out at the weather. The clouds were cumulo-nimbus and the attendant blue sky promised a fine afternoon. It was perhaps an hour later when the Canon shook my hand and bade me farewell. "Don't forget Sunday, if you can make it."

"I won't forget," I added as an afterthought realising the original answer might appear rude. As I walked down the drive I paused to sample the fragrance of a yellow rose. I waited until I was well out of sight of the house before straightening out the note and reading it.

Crimine ab uno, disce omnia Virgil, Aeneid book ii

What was Mr. Fibula trying to tell me? The point was lost on me I knew a little Latin from geology but not enough to translate this. I walked into Whitby and found the local bookshop.

I was fortunate. A paperback edition of The Aeneid was in stock and I thumbed through the pages. The quote prefaced book two: *From one crime, learn about them all.*

I left the shop and found a free bench overlooking the Endeavour moored in the harbour. Here I studied the note with greater care. It was written in ink by someone well educated, someone who was able to write in copperplate script. I held the paper to the light and found it was watermarked. I wasn't certain what conclusion to make. Grandpa had written in that type of script. In a box at home I'd placed all the letters and cards he'd sent me. All the stories of the war he'd either written or the notebook I'd kept of snippets of information gleaned. Perhaps that was the only conclusion. The person warning me was older, wiser or nearer the heart of events. I folded the note in my wallet.

On the return journey, I was so tired my head vibrated against the bus window, I realised the quote made sense and the more I thought about it, the more apt it became. As I walked down the farm track to the caravan, I appreciated the truth of this statement. The caravan door swung open and the contents of drawers and cases had been thoroughly searched. I panicked, then forced myself to calmly search my belongings as I tidied. It wasn't money the thief had been after but geology: all the specimens had been examined and left, only the ichthyosaur skull wasn't there. I smiled at my forethought to dig it into a neat hiding place by the apple tree.

I knocked on the farmhouse door. Mrs Moralis peered round a crack in the door.

"Hello, sorry to disturb you but have you seen anyone around, only the caravan's been turned over."

The lady unhinged the safety chain, "No! Is anything missing?"

"A bit of cash," I lied, "and some CDs."

Ricky's mum stood outside in the sunlight, "it's not worth reporting it and it's not worth claiming. The police won't do anything and the insurance will just go up to recover their costs."

She shielded her eyes. Her skin seemed a little jaundiced.

"Are you alright?" I asked.

"Yes," She willed herself to stand upright, "I've been a bit down since Ricky left. It's so quiet without him."

I nodded and looked away.

"He sounded great on the phone a couple of nights ago but today whilst cleaning, I found Ricky's passport. Did he tell you where he was going?"

"To his uncle's in Ulveston, "I said for the second time today. "I don't think he'd need his passport for that journey." I said.

"No," Mrs. Moralis replied.

"I'm sure he's fine. Sorry to disturb you, I just didn't want you thinking I wasn't looking after your caravan."

"No, I know you've been fine." She said and gently closed the door.

I walked away now doubly confused. I cleaned out the caravan and filed everything away again.

When I sat with the maps open on the table, I realised that as much as I'd achieved there was so much more to be done. There were gaps in my knowledge, not just geological ones but chasms in which the lies and deceits of others eroded the bed rock. Yet those others had assumed a greater significance for all their lies. Carrie and her relatives the De Viles, Ricky and his journey, Birbeck's investigations and the Canon's admission that he'd hired two fossil hunters. Perhaps the only certainty was a lie, in which case a truth had been established. There might be one way to find out more, to break into the farmhouse and look through Ricky's possessions. A diary might help, a letter or a photo. What was needed was evidence. Evidence is a dangerous thing, as the Reverend Young discovered with his fossil reptile, it may help disprove the existence of the very god you have faith in.

Chapter 9: 1944

"I can't confirm this," Ernie said as he unfolded his newspaper at the dinner table, "but one of Eldedt's squadron said he'd been shot down in Dutch waters and that he's in a POW camp." Ernie put down the paper and dunked a soldier of bread in the yolk. "Should I tell Gertie or Cyril?"

Marjorie stopped grating apple onto the child's plate and thought about this. "No. Leave well alone. They've been happier since he left." Marjorie wiped her apron and turned her attention to the baby in the high chair.

Ernie put up the newspaper again.

"Ernie, could you help? It's awful without Nanny but she had to go home, her mother's ill."

"Of course. What do I do?"

"Feed Tom little spoonfuls of egg custard."

Ernie rolled up his sleeves and began. Tom responded with the contented purrs of a baby being weaned onto solids. Ernie smiled at the child; it was only when Marjorie placed her arm on Ernie's and squeezed that he realised something was wrong. He looked at Elizabeth, then Tom. Finally he shot an enquiring glance at his wife. He followed her eyes upward. The sound droned through the ceiling then became a clear puck, puck.

"A doodlebug!" He unfastened Tom from the high chair and placed him gently under the table. Marjorie did the same for Elizabeth and stayed there, the three of them were protected by the thick pine.

"Ernie," Marjorie hissed, "what are you doing?"

Ernie vanished into the back yard and looked up at the sky. He shivered. His eyes got used to the dark and the outline of the V1 became clear. The engine stalled. He limped inside and joined his family under the table, "is it close?"

Ernie counted to fifteen. A vibration ripped through the house and glass shattered. The silence outside was replaced by snuffles and cries from the children.

"You'd better go and look."

Ernie took a torch and wrapped himself up in a tweed coat. He toured the outside of the property. Godwyn hadn't been damaged; the shed had protected the house. It stood, peeled open at one side and sitting at odd angles. In the torch light he made out the tail of the doodlebug in the field.

A whistle blew. Ernie put out the light. He heard several footsteps running down the lane, "Ernie, is that you? Are you all alright?"

"Yes. Yes indeed, thanks, it's the shed which got damaged. The bomb is in the field."

"I'll ring the authorities, they'll want a look. Keep everyone inside."

"Check the folk at Galloway's, they're closer."

"Righto."

Ernie pushed open the door and replaced the blackout curtains, "the shed's done for but the house is okay."

Marjorie crossed herself and muttered a prayer, "just our luck after four years of people coming out here to escape the blitz, a bomb goes and lands in Thearne."

Ernie put his arm around her. His warmth was reassuring. "Well, let's get the children to bed and relax with H.H. and his orchestra."

"I'll let you pour me a stiff whiskey."

They both smiled. Outside several vehicles drew up and lights criss-crossed the fields.

In the morning a tarpaulin covered the remains of the bomb, its edges held down with a few bricks from the shed. Ernie rose at first light and put on his gardening clothes. He pushed his way into the shed and began sorting through his photographs and negatives. He boxed up any full plates and put many prints into an old leather suitcase. His darkroom was open to the elements but the equipment was largely intact. It was the old glass plates which had suffered the most. Ernie salvaged all he could but he knew this would be an end to his hobby. There would be little chance of replacing any of the lost chemicals. Still it could have been worse. It could have been a lot worse.

"Ernie. It's seven thirty. You'll need a shave and wash."

Ernie swore to himself and emerged from the shed. He placed the boxes and suitcase in the entrance hall, "a job for the weekend. They needed sorting. It'll have to be done soon or I'll lose some of my work. Well Friday beckons."

Marjorie looked at her husband. He was taking the loss quite well. He hadn't picked up a camera since Birbeck gave an emphatic 'no,' last summer. She'd asked Gertie to intervene or rather Cyril to use his Masonic influence. That had back fired badly.

Ernest's views on the Masons were well known and Cyril flatly refused to help. In fact whatever had been said to Birbeck made matters worse. Ernie had lost ground at work and was now sent out to collect the rent every Friday. He got in late, his temper frayed, in pain with his leg.

Gertie had rung, apologising but Cyril wouldn't even visit. He refused point blank to speak to Ernie. As if there weren't enough bad things in the world without adding this breach.

Ernie walked down the lane for the eight fifteen. He turned and waved once before blowing a kiss for the children. Ernie pulled up his collar. He felt cold, tired and although it wasn't the most important thing, he was put out about the damage to his dark room. He tried to get things in perspective as the bus rattled along Beverley High Road. He saw the barrage balloons being serviced at RAF Sutton. Maybe they had worked and deflected that V1 from its target.

He read the morning paper over someone's shoulder. The Japanese had attacked India. Ernie sighed; he wondered how many more years it might take to get the job done. He walked across what remained of the town centre to the Guildhall, the entrance restricted by sandbags. He touched his titfer as he passed the concierge.

"Morning Mr. Crawford."

"Morning, Davy."

"Good morning, sir," He said to Birbeck.

His boss grunted, took out his cigar and began, "Sculcoates, as usual."

"Very well, Mr. Birbeck."

Ernie managed a false smile.

Birbeck harrumphed and replaced his cigar.

Ernie collected his polished black briefcase and the papers needed for the morning. He smiled as he left the building. It wasn't cold for March, and the flower seller had a few irises and daffodils for sale. The accumulated bomb damage was significant but the streets were tidy and had some semblance of civic pride about them.

Ernie knocked at the first door.

"Is it rent day?" The lady enquired, "Come on in for a cuppa. I'll shout Billy and Charlie."

"Thanks," Ernie sat at the kitchen table. He took out a letter of authority and passed it to the youngest of the boys. They began their well rehearsed routine. The two lads covered one part of the route and Ernie the other.

They met at Aunt Edna's for lunch. "Any problems?" Ernie enquired.

Charlie produced a list of defaulters and bombed houses. There was no change. Ernie copied the amounts and comments into his invoice book. The job was done for another week. "Thanks," he said and passed each of them a florin.

"Thanks cuz," they said almost in unison and hurried from the room.

"You spoil them," Edna said.

"They did a good job and," Ernie smiled, "I found something out about Birbeck, something that'll fix him if I can get the proof. There's a row of prefabs at the back of The Broadway that hasn't been declared on any paperwork I'm aware of. That's a nice earner if he's pocketing the rent from ten houses. Of course I need proof. Next week I'll bring a camera and wait for the old fool. Then go round the houses and ask for rent a second time."

"I can't believe your boss could be so unpatriotic."

"No, neither can I. I'm missing something, there has to be a motive." Ernie finished his lunch then lit a cigarette.

When Ernie got back to the Guildhall there were staff running around searching lockers, drawers, cupboards...

"Birbeck's in a foul mood. Everything's been turned out. A rent book has gone missing." Felicity stood looking very pretty in her poker dot dress and thin waist asserted by what looked like one of her dad's belts cut to size. "Thought I'd better warn you."

"Thanks." Ernie threw his hat onto the stand and sat at his desk. He smiled.

"What are you happy about Crawford?" Birbeck stood and lent over the desk. "I've had a good morning collecting rent, sir." He placed the brief case on the desk and opened it."

"Good. Rent and rent books. There are two signed out in your name!"

"I can assure you I only have one."

"Then explain this." The cigar dropped to the desk and landed on the opened ledger. He brushed the butt to one side.

Ernie looked down. He saw his signature against a rent book on the 14th February and yet another on the 16th.—only on this occasion the copperplate didn't match his own. The signature was clearly a forgery. "That is most certainly not my signature. Someone has very poorly forged it."

Birbeck slammed the book closed and dust rose from the end plates. "Clearly! And that will form the basis of my investigation. I have someone on my staff who's deceiving the Council. There'll be the police investigation to contend with."

"I'm happy to tell them everything I know."

Birbeck studied Ernie for a moment then let the matter pass. "If I find you're involved, I'll have your job and secure you a stiff sentence."

"I don't like your attitude," Ernie replied. "In fact I don't like you at all!" He watched the colour rise.

"Fortunately I'm your superior and my word is law."

"Just remember how those you shat on during your climb to power will react when you fall."

"You are insolent!" Birbeck stormed angrily from the room. Everyone else in the office looked at Ernie then avoided speaking to him.

Ernie sat overlooking Prince's dock as he had his sandwiches. He was still shaken by Birbeck's outburst but now he knew who was fiddling he just had to find out why and Cyril on The Broadway would be a good place to start.

Ernie took the tram down Holderness Road and stopped and walked where the rails had been damaged before collecting another tram and continuing. He arrived by the fish and chip shop at 5.30pm and crossed the road, following the line of intact 1930's semis and seeing the debris of others behind. He knocked on the white front door.

Gertie answered. "Hello. This is a surprise." Margaret peered round her skirt. Ernie wasn't convinced he was welcome but Gertie continued, "Cyril is sitting in the dining room, reading the paper and enjoying his pipe. Would you care to join him?"

"Just for a minute if I may. I'm on an errand at the prefabs – working late before donning my uniform and doing firewatch 8 til 8."

"Cyril, it's Ernie."

"Good evening." Cyril said. He didn't offer Ernie a chair and so Ernie continued to stand, looking at how his friend's male pattern baldness spread from his crown.

"Just on my way to do a job for Birbeck. Thought I'd pop in to see how you're doing."

"I'm fine. I'd better not detain you."

"No, better not," Ernie agreed. He was surprised by his friend's coldness but hoped this didn't show. It was only by the door that Ernie spied an envelope with an Occupied Dutch stamp on it. "Hope you're all safe tonight."

"Safer for knowing you're watching over us."

Ernie couldn't tell if Cyril was being serious or funny. He knew he was watched as he knocked on the first prefab door.

"Excuse me, I'm from the council, just checking everything went well with the rent collection this morning?"

Ernie repeated the question until he got to the door of number seven. When he knocked it took a long time to answer and finally a shy young girl peered round the door. "Is your mummy in? I'm from the council checking..."

"I live here alone."

"Alone, you don't look sixteen."

"I am!" The girl replied in high dudgeon which made Ernie suspect her all the more.

"Well, I'm sorry to disturb you Miss..."

"Miss Josephine. I live here with my twin sister Jocaster."

"Josephine and Jocaster. Beautiful names. I'll bid you a goodnight."

Ernie smiled as he walked back to Holderness Road and waited for the bus. Now he knew Birbeck's motive. A week later he'd dropped a letter to the Treasurer asking why twenty five prefabricated houses didn't appear in the City Council's rent books, even though they'd been paid for by public funds. There were also several photographs of Birbeck collecting rent from the same prefabs and emerging from one containing a young girl called Jospehine.

The Treasurer had summoned Ernie. He stood at the opposite side of the mahogany desk. A bakerlite telephone and large blotter were the only visible items on the polished surface. The man who possessed myopic eyes magnified by glasses shifted uncomfortably, "I don't like your methods, Crawford."

"I was thinking of the council."

"Who is this girl? No, don't reply." The City Treasurer stood and turned the picture of His Majesty to face the wall. "Well can't have the king witnessing such events."

"You'd have to ask Mr. Birbeck, sir. I have no knowledge."

"I won't have scandal in the city council. All this will have to be handled discreetly. We'll need to keep things quiet so the press don't find out."

"Quite so, sir." Inwardly Ernie was enjoying this. The officer took out a gold nibbed fountain pen. In the neatest of scripts he wrote a letter to Birbeck. "See this is delivered. Don't wait for a reply." Ernie tried not to smile. He was only sorry he would not be present to witness his boss's fall.

Chapter 10: Unconformity

   Time passes but it doesn't erase the memory. Time passes but to a geologist this never happens quickly enough. If we could live for a million years and watch the parting continents or sample evolution, how much greater would our knowledge be? A million years ago our ancestors were using stone tools and acquiring the skills required to create all we take for granted. I was fascinated when at a history lecture the speaker concluded that the Iron Age ended with Tudor England. It made me wonder. We think we've come a long way but in reality it's just a short step forward and that movement is in part due to our understanding of geology. Knowing which rocks are under our feet and the structures in which they repose helps our understanding of the processes and informs us of the great wealth they contain. I've missed out Divine intervention, because the more I study geology the more uncertain are the foundations of my faith. Religion is mum's prop. It kept her going through bereavement and now provides comfort. I like to think of my dad looking down from heaven but in reality I know his body is in decay. That provides a substantial truth but little comfort. The chances of Dad making it to fossilisation are almost as unlikely as mine of winning the lottery but infinitely preferable.
   "It's all about time," Grandpa said, "I might be sixty nine . I know I look about ninety to you, but I don't feel any different. My brain is still young but it takes an act of faith to make my body respond in anything like the way it used to!" He smiled and pinched my cheek. "Still out of the two alternatives, growing old is by far preferable!" His laughed turned chesty. He pulled an album out from a drawer, "I found this in my shed. It's terribly damp in there now and I want to preserve the past. Soon it will all be past and you'll be singing rousing hymns over my body."
   "Don't talk like that Grandpa."
   He smiled, "Times have changed. I was once asked to destroy all my pictures of Hull in the war. My boss thought it unpatriotic to take pictures of suffering."
   I opened the cover. The first picture showed a pile of rubble with two semis either side.

"A whole family was wiped out by one bomb. I knew them. I collected rent from them every week for two years. I sat in Maisie's kitchen and drank a cup of strong tea every Friday at eleven."

I swallowed hard. The next picture was a close-up of the debris. I'd looked at the picture a few seconds before seeing the hand. The fingers were too detailed to be a dolls. I remembered to breathe, "You attempted to destroy all the negatives when gran died."

"I did, yes. I stood in the shed and shattered each glass plate until there was nothing left."

"I rescued some of the negatives. I have them in a box under my bed at home."

"Thank you, I knew I was right to bring you up the way I have," he sat down and placed his walking stick at the side of the chair. "It's thirty odd years since I took that. It's a powerful photo and very few people have seen it. My exhibitions in the 40's and 50's were all about fashion: light, shade and pretty young ladies. Here you are seeing the serious side to my work. The obstinate side which refused to stop taking pictures even when threats were made. Lots of threats were made, particularly from Uncle Cyril and his Masonic boss, Birbeck. I locked all the photos away and waited."

"You were right to wait. I just hope I've inherited some of your passion and obstinacy."

"Is that how it seems? It was always put to me that children and grandparents were united against a common enemy."

It was my turn to smile. "Mum said something similar about her standing alone!" I coughed nervously. You must promise me not to be upset because mum wasn't best pleased that I'm not taking A level maths and I don't want another argument. I'll have to retake maths O' Level at Sixth Form, but instead I'm going to do geology. I've decided. I read this book called *Landscape Mysteries* about how the hills and valleys are shaped by geological processes and I was fascinated."

"I'm pleased you've found your calling. I was thirty six before I found mine."

"Will you teach me black and white photography? Developing etc?"

"Gladly, but it's not the future. I reckon it won't be long before computers do the job of silver halides."

"You're probably right but there's something special about a real photo. There's the art in taking one, the chemistry in developing it and the craft of making the image permanent. At least that's my opinion!"

Grandpa nodded and took me out into his shed. He stood me at the threshold. The shed still smelt of paraffin and damp, "Let's begin."

Somehow Grandpa had taken over all those roles which dad could not fulfil but I could see he was getting tired. There was a look in his eyes which spoke of a long journey. Throughout the summer of my sixteenth year he taught me everything I know about photography not just developing pictures but composition, lighting, colour. I lapped it all up. I missed his company in that old shed when Uncle Tom arrived to take the family on holiday to Scarborough. Grandpa leant on the gate framed by the almost circular porch he designed. He waved with his stick and smiled as if he was truly happy. He didn't survive the week. I was devastated. I couldn't bring myself to sing the rousing hymns he'd wished to accompany him into the next world. I did carry out his final wish: to have his ashes scattered over a standard rose -- his favourite -- Peace.

It's all about time. Is it really only three years since grandpa passed away? I still think of those hours spent in his shed. Those times are as untouchable as the Jurassic seas I had to imagine.

I've been mapping this coast for a month. It's twenty eight days since I left the bosom of university life: Barbara with her maternal instincts and Carrie with her libido. The end result? I will take home the rough draft of a thesis, some exceptional fossils including the ichthyosaur skull Ricky found. Well perhaps that's debateable, planted might be a better description. I suppose the video in which Drew gains fulfilment with another man is tangible proof of her existence but I don't believe I could ever watch it. The rest isn't tangible but infinitely more pleasant, but what use is that to anything except literature?

The quiet nights in the caravan have renewed my ideas about writing. I haven't written a story since I was fourteen when I did a one off for a youth club magazine: *Ghosts on the Fen*. But a name I'd seen somewhere kept coming back to me: *Foul Syke Farm*. The story accreted from this titular kernel.

Mrs. Moralis popped in to see me this morning. She was smiling. She passed across a post card from Ulverston. "Ricky's been working at a Buddhist Centre. It seems he might have found something to believe in."

"I'm happy for him."

"By the way," she said looking around, "you can do better with cleaning this place."

So that was her motive. She wanted to see the state of her caravan after a month. I'd already had one go at cleaning. If only I could import Barbara. She'd know what to do, how to make a place feel clean even if it wasn't. Barbara was a past master at that. I suppose there must be a magazine for odour removal, which like the Women's Institute booklets on the treatment of stains, sells well, though I'd long ago realised that stains on sheets are much easier to remove than those on character.

Monday, I cleaned the place again. This time using a Domestos with a heavy fragrance. Mrs. Moralis was pleased and returned the deposit even though I had a couple of days to go. I sat at the edge of the main road in Hawsker looking up at the twin carbuncles of the church and school hall. I had just delivered a box of fossils and specimens for the parcel post and given mum her weekly call. All was going well except for the silences in the conversation. They were born out of love, but signalled mother and son drifting apart.

"Don't forget Barty's funeral." Mum reminded. "It's been delayed once more because of forensic tests. I don't understand but Gertie believes that someone pushed Barty off the cliff. Apparently there's one pink fibre. What do you make of that?"

"I don't know." I lied.

"A woman!" Mum said with venom. "They're not to be trusted.

Mr. And Mrs. Moralis stopped their car at the roadside. "Ey up lad, things can't be all that bad."

I looked at Ricky's father and wondered if he could become such a creature. I remembered the beating he'd given his son, "have you heard from Ricky?"

"A postcard from Ulveston," he pronounced the place like a type of insect, "he mentioned you. Said you'd enjoy the geology."

I felt myself smile.

"I don't approve of travel. It doesn't broaden the mind, just fills it with fancy ideas. Ricky has to come back and see to this farm."

I heard the hurt and insecurity in his father's voice.

"Well, we're off for the weekly shop and hair do's," Mrs. Moralis interjected. "I don't want to be late and Whitby gets so crowded in the summer holidays."

I bade farewell. My opportunity presented itself. I'd have an hour to search through Ricky's belongings. I returned to the farm. The house was locked up and the windows all bolted. Such security was inevitable after the caravan had been burgled. I stood looking up at Ricky's window. It was impossible. I went back to the caravan and made a cup of tea. Staring out at the building I remembered there was a patio door. I ventured out again. The patio was locked, but the door felt lose in its housing, so I took a shovel and prised it under the runner. There was a click and I knew I had gained access. I stood at the threshold of Ricky's room. I could hear my heart beating. I turned the handle and took stock of the room until now I'd only seen from the outside. The walls were painted white and on them black and white photos captured light and shade. Each of the images was signed Jevan Moralis. I stood back and examined them more closely. The images were stop-motion views of waves and rocks in high contrast. I looked around. Sets of drawers occupied the gap between the bed and the wall. The first contained socks and underwear, the second t-shirts. I took one out and breathed the perfume. Boxes of cufflinks and necklaces occupied the base but nothing of note. The wardrobe was built into one wall. Ricky's shirts and trousers hung awaiting his return. Old games were piled neatly on the top shelf and favourite videos lined on one side of the base. There was nothing to help my research, no books, no diaries. I stood and scratched my head. Finally I turned on the computer. *My documents* revealed little. I began to worry about the time. I arranged the files by date order and went to the last entry. It had been written within minutes of Ricky leaving me on the beach.

David, I'm leaving. I haven't told you why. It's not because I love you, it's because I love you in a way I thought I could never do again after my brother died. Twins, that's the key. Ricky and I were up-market rent boys. Escorts the Canon called us. For Ricky it was just money but for me, it became something more. A corruption of the flesh my father would say. That's how Ricky and I met Jocaster and Josephine De Vile. Josephine is dead. It was Ricky who told me that. It's the rings. When he informed the police they laughed. I can still see Birbeck standing there with tears of laughter running down his fat cheeks. Within 24 hours Ricky was murdered. His body never found.

David when you read this, you'll know your danger. You'll know why I've run away. Never go into that tower where he keeps his fossils and don't trust Birbeck. Josephine's body must be somewhere and when it's found things might get very unpleasant. Sell the videos in my wardrobe and catch the train to meet me. Doing nothing is always the safest route. Jevan.

I looked again at the videos. On opening the cases, I realised this was the full collection of Jocaster's films. Ricky had given me a very tempting offer but I knew I couldn't take it. He was confused by his conflicting emotions as he left. He even wrote as if he was his twin.

Time passes but it doesn't erase the memory. I was there the night Drew was pushed off the cliff. I wanted to find out if our love was really in the past. The argument we had persuaded me it was. I felt foolish, angry about travelling over seventy miles and being given such short shrift. Drew had told me in no uncertain terms that she didn't love me. I remember saying some unpleasant things. The words can never be retracted. It doesn't seem to matter that I'm now alone in my recollection of that stormy November evening. When I drove back to Hull, I didn't stop and there were no witnesses. When I read in the paper about Drew's suicide, I wondered if I had pushed her. I couldn't seem to account for every minute. Yet Drew and Mike had died together and I'd seen who pushed them. That much I know I didn't imagine.

It had taken so many months to rise to the surface. Drew had broken off from our quarrelling to acknowledge a man. I recognised him now as Canon Franklin. He received a package from a young man and stowed it in the boot of his car. He smiled briefly before driving away. That young man was Mike.

I had broken into the wrong house, examined the contents of the wrong room. I should be at the Canon's, but how to secure an invitation? This thought occupied me until I heard a car door slam. Mr and Mrs Moralis had returned. I switched off the computer. A police car drove down the drive. Ricky's parents stopped unloading the boot and waited. I piled the videos together and edged downstairs. I made my exit though the patio door and pulled it closed. With a little flick of the shovel it clicked back into place.

It was Birbeck talking to the Moralis's. I couldn't hear anything. I waited, being unable to gain access to the caravan without being seen. Birbeck walked over to the caravan then entered. He spent some time inside before leaving. "If he turns up, let me know," he shouted across the yard.

"We will," Mr. Moralis replied.

When everyone had left the yard, I returned to the caravan. I noticed the smell of Birbeck's cheap aftershave lingered in the room.

As I looked around to see what had been disturbed, I saw the dark leather bound volume. Louis Hunton! That was my ticket back into the Canon's domain. I would use it tomorrow. Why should I fail where others had? Finally, I sat down with a cup of coffee and I found a thousand doubts to argue against success.

I flicked through the video titles. Twin Dilemma, Twin Obsession, Twins in Love comprising the first three volumes of Jocaster's collected works. Jevan and Ricky appeared together on the cover of the final edition. The sexual content appeared to pander to the Canon's tastes.

There was a knock at the door. Mrs. Moralis popped her head round as I hastily buried the videos under a cushion. "It's Ricky. He's on the phone and insists on speaking to you," she wasn't able to hide her contempt.

I followed her at a brisk pace across the courtyard. Ricky's dad passed over the phone. "Hi," I said, finding my emotions confused.

"Listen, did you read the file on the computer and take the videos?"

"Yes but, I'm not coming. I've got to work this one out."

"I knew you'd say that. My parents have the contact number. Ring me every night until you get back to Hull. Don't do anything stupid."

"Why?"

"Because I love you," he whispered.

Mr. Moralis shot me a glance as I was about to reply, "Likewise!"

"Don't worry, I understand, that's why I'm here and you're there!"

"How long are you there?" I asked as an afterthought, only the pips started. "Bye!" I wished all my feelings could travel down the telephone line but Ricky had signed off. I put down the receiver.

Mr. Moralis picked it up, "I need to let DCI Birbeck know you're back. He wants words."

"Let him know I'm in The Cook's Arms," I took several paces down the hall then turned, "Thanks," I said.

"What do you know then?" DCI Birbeck swirled his brandy several times, savoured its aroma and downed it in one. He ran his finger round the dregs and sucked it clean.

"Not a lot," I lied, "except that the Canon has a fantastic fossil collection. I've got some great data to work on in order to find how currents shaped the rocks under our feet."

"And have you found out about Jevan?" The DCI smiled.

"Ricky spoke of him a couple of times but when you said he didn't exist…" I sipped my lager, "naturally I assumed Ricky was lying."

"Naturally." Birbeck turned and signalled with his glass and caught Gabby's eye, "and Jocaster and Jospehine?"

"I confused one with the other. In here!"

"The emeralds and rubies are the giveaway."

I nodded and wondered where this conversation was leading. When Birbeck received his drink, I found out.

"After a bit of detective work I've realised you were up here the night Drew was murdered. We traced the hire car records."

I stared at Birbeck, "I left early. By the way it was always reported as suicide."

"Sorry, a slip of the tongue." Birbeck was obviously no better at lying than I was.

"Wouldn't you agree, from my point of view that would make you a prime suspect?" Birbeck downed the second measure as quickly as the first. "You see, unlike TV, policing is inevitably mundane. Involved plots would lower the detection rate still further."

I smiled knowing full well that detection rates being positive at all were down to speeding motorists.

"Will you be arresting me for murder?" I struggled to get the word out and keep control.

"Not likely, unless you'd like to confess. No, I have a better idea, let's go and see Canon Franklin. He's got a vested interest in this case."

I was about to speak but realised this was a dangerous game and that Ricky had been correct in his suspicions. "May I collect a book I borrowed from the Canon? It'll save me some time tomorrow."

"I'd like to oblige," said Birbeck rising and straightening his jacket, "but I fear you are too important to let slip away."

"Where am I going to slip to, the bottom of a cliff?" I smiled in mock innocence.

Birbeck's colour rose. He struggled to contain his anger. His skin had gone mottled red but he managed a fake smile.

I didn't think it worth protesting. I bid Gabby goodnight and saluted Mr. Fibula and Goldie who were smooching in a dark corner. I figured enough people had seen me leave with Birbeck. I pushed the remains of fast food packaging to one side and got in the front seat of the car. Neither of us spoke on the journey.

"Nights are closing in," I commented as we walked up the gravel drive to the door of the villa.

"Ah! Damian. I've been expecting you. David?" The Canon put down the wicker basket filled with dead blooms. "Come in gentlemen. This looks serious." The Canon escorted us into his study and bade me sit down. He poured sherry for each of us. "Now fill me in on a few details."

Birbeck leaned forward until his stomach rested on his thighs, "David, were you in Hawsker the night Drew died?"

I nodded.

"In fact Canon this young man is Drew's ex."

"I didn't realise any of this was news Birbeck?" The Canon gently sipped his drink then closely observed Birbeck who looked flustered by this last remark.

"He knows what is going on here. He's put two and two together."

"Birbeck, that's what a university education does for a young mind," the Canon refilled Birbeck's glass. "What have you got to say, David?"

"I can only tell you that I was here that November night and that I did confront Drew. We'd been friends then lovers and I wasn't about to let all that slip away without a fight. I got here late in the afternoon, just as it was getting dark. We met in The Cook Arms but could hardly speak civilly to each other. Out in the car park I said some pretty unpleasant things. By the time I saw you and Mike our argument had finished. I regretted what I'd said as I drove home. I was devastated when I heard she'd committed suicide. I needed antidepressants and counselling. Carrie managed to help restore my faith in myself."

The Canon looked serious, "Carrie? My daughter has taken the teachings of Christ to extremes. She wants to put people on the straight and narrow."

I felt light-headed, "Your daughter?" so I had seen Carrie the night of Jocaster's dinner party. Had she drugged me? Birbeck's cough brought me out of my reverie.

"So in a fit of jealousy you pushed Drew off the cliff. Mike just got in the way, so he also had to go."

I finished the drink, "I've seen it that way in so many nightmares." I saw little point in hiding the truth.

"There!" Exclaimed Birbeck, "I'm certain I could get a conviction. A confession and he's inside. Fifteen years maybe for murder. It would certainly take the heat off us."

I stared at Birbeck. I hadn't connected the possibility that these two were working together.

"You are becoming a liability, Birbeck," the Canon spoke softly but with menace. "David, I must ask you to accept my hospitality for the night. Not terribly comfortable but very secure up there in the tower room amongst my collection. By the way what did you do with that ichthyosaur skull I lent Ricky?"

So it was true. Ricky had planted the specimen. "You mean…" I searched my memory. "Why would he want to do such a thing?"

"He wanted to win your confidence. He owed me that." The Canon removed a large key from his desk, "what did happen to it?"

"I buried it under the apple tree then sent it by parcel post to the university."

"Good, Mr. Fibula will be able to collect it on Monday. Now perhaps you'd be so kind as to follow me upstairs. Birbeck, do your job!"

The officer moved quickly and searched through my pockets removing my lighter, fags and mobile phone. He frisked my torso and legs, "clean."

"Good," the Canon's voice echoed up the stone stairwell. The heavy gothic door grated open. "You won't be disturbed here until morning,"

I walked into the museum Canon Franklin was so proud of. A hand pushed damp wadding over my nose and mouth. The sweet smell made me feel nauseous. I struggled momentarily.

It was still dark when I opened my eyes. I tried to stand but the room span and I collapsed. Nausea and a blinding headache compelled me to lie still. I was desperate for water.

It was still dark when I came to again. My legs felt cold. I sat up and rubbed my calf muscles. I took several deep breaths but the odour of the chemical lingered. I stood and gained support from one of the cabinets. I closed my eyes and steadied myself. I tried to prevent my rising panic. Carefully I made my way to the door. A thin silver line of light permeated the room. I felt round the door until my fingers reached the light switch. Momentarily the blinding headache returned. I blinked and wiped the tears away. I looked at the display cases crammed full of rare and expensive fossils. Hung on the wall was the ichthyosaur I'd notice last time. Now I had time to study it carefully. The label in faded ink read: *Singular fossil crocodile discovered Whitby, 1819 by Rev George Young.*

This was a find indeed. It had gone missing over a hundred years ago and now resided in the private collection of Canon Franklin. This was not the fate I desired for myself. I tried the door handle. It was locked. I looked around for something to pick the lock with and found nothing but a paperclip. I unfolded the metal and tried to force the lock. The metal was too weak and buckled. I began tapping at the oak panels surrounding the room. I had obviously watched too many old movies, as if there might be a secret passageway! To my surprise one panel slid open to reveal a handle. I pulled gently. The oak panelling exposed another set of stairs. My heart sank. They climbed upward.

I wedged the door open with a museum catalogue. After taking several steps I began to lose the light from the museum. A stale smell gathered around me. I walked carefully upwards until the first light of dawn was dimly detected. The steps ended abruptly in a room furnished with a single chair.

Mice scuttled across the floor setting the chair to a gentle rocking.

I approached holding a handkerchief over my nose. I pushed out my hand and swung the chair round. I found myself scrambling to the wall. I hit it so hard I winded myself. In front of me the desiccated body rocked. Its eye sockets were empty and its jaw gaped. I gagged. An emerald ring dangled from the right hand and a ruby from the left. I steeled myself and picked off both items. The skeleton rocked silently. Light shone upon her face. Maggots emerged from some cavity. I gagged again and returned swiftly down the steps. At the bottom I removed the book and turned the handle. I heard footsteps and quickly moved to switch off the light. I sat on the cold floor breathing deeply. A key entered the lock. It failed to turn. A second key was tried, a third threw back the mechanism.

"David?" The woman's voice was followed by Jocaster's face. She put her finger to her lip and closed the door, "Listen. I am leaving. My bags are packed. My brother-in-law knows that I know too much."

"For how long have you played the part of your sister?"

"Too long, nearly eighteen months."

"Then there's something you must see." I pulled the handle and revealed the stairs a second time. Jocaster followed me.

"I didn't know this was here."

"My guess is only the murderer knows."

"Murderer, you've seen too many films."

"You'd better take a deep breath, the air's not too pleasant."

Jocaster took my hand. The chair still rocked. The body had slumped forward but Jocaster needed no identification. "So she never vanished, she really was murdered! This is my brother's work. He knew all along, even when he asked me to play her part so no one suspected Josephine was missing."

The two of us stood in silence. The chair creaked. Light shone on the decayed flesh.

"No, I do not believe it was the canon. No one leaves a body decaying in their own home."

Jocaster stared at me. She walked round the dessicated remains of her sister. "She was strangled by a scarf or stocking. Horrible. We never got on but this is just…." Jocaster gagged on the words.

"D'you know what I think? The body was left here to incriminate someone. Someone who's being blackmailed, someone like your brother-in-law."

Again Jocaster looked at me. "Why would anyone blackmail a priest?"

"Because they found out about his twin dilemmas, someone who knew Jevan and Ricky were providing personal services."

"You have a quick brain when you use it." Jocaster placed a handkerchief over her mouth. "I need some fresh air."

At the bottom of the stairs I stopped Jocaster. "All of this would make you a prime suspect. You must have known about the canon's predilections?"

"Of course, I made the films for him and his group. You don't think it was a commercial success do you? Look, I may work in porn but I've never considered killing anyone but Birbeck."

I smiled with relief. "Then we have something in common."

"Will Carrie be safe?" Jocaster took my face in her hands, "I couldn't stand any more deaths. I'll explain all I can when we're out of harm's way." She put her finger to her lips and listened intently. "The living must care for themselves. It's now or never. If we're caught, you know what will happen?"

"I've a pretty shrewd idea." I took a deep breath and followed her down the stairs. We emerged into the Canon's study. Birbeck was fast asleep, his head tipped back and snoring loudly. I don't remember breathing again until I was outside. As I got into the yellow sports car, I heard screaming. Jocaster started the car. The Canon flew out of the door. His fists beat upon the ponderous Birbeck as he slouched onto the steps.

"Do you need anything from the caravan?"

"Clothes. Thesis notes. It's mostly packed."

"What time's your bus to Hull?" Jocaster took a corner badly.

"10.15, why?"

"I'll drop you at the caravan, but promise me you won't go anywhere alone!"

Jocaster didn't have to ask. "Don't worry. I want to stay alive."

"They'll only be minutes behind," Jocaster warned.

I leant over and kissed her on the cheek. Then I passed over the two rings. They were identical to Jocasters.

"From?"

"The body in the top of the tower."

"She had a name: Josephine De Vile."

Jocaster turned off and parked by the abbey. The rising sun ignited the stones with a golden hue. The great east window cast shadows on the lawn. I saw her take a deep breath, she went pale and tears filled her eyes. "Josephine and I are Birbeck's half-sisters. We were the secret family of a bigamist. Birbeck's father bought our mother and kept her a virtual slave in a prefab on The Broadway until some fraud he'd committed was discovered. Suddenly we were free, or so we thought.

We walked down Caedmon's Trod with a cool easterly breeze pushing against us. The smell of bacon rolled along the street and I realised how hungry I was. Jocaster pushed open the door. The warmth and steam from cooking had steamed up the windows, so the street view looked like an impressionistic painting. "Two teas and one bacon sandwich."

Jocaster sat in the window seat. I placed a knife and fork on the table and moved a bottle of ketchup from an adjacent table.

"I couldn't eat." Jocaster said.

"As soon as I smelt bacon, I knew I could."

"You're a man." Jocaster didn't elucidate. The tea arrived in large white mugs and finally food. I opened the white bread and looked at the rashers of meat. I poured on ketchup and closed the bun. I ate with enthusiasm. Jocaster was lost in her own thoughts. A radio was turned on and Depeche Mode began singing. I wiped my lips and fingers.

"Better?"

"Great!"

"Good." Jocaster played with her car keys. "Did Ricky ever tell you about the canon's predilections?"

"Partly. Partly I guessed. The videos were a giveaway."

"It was Drew who found out. She thought she'd be able to blackmail Canon Franklin. He refused to pay and set Birbeck onto her. The rest you know."

"But your twin sister?"

She always kept the canon's indiscretions secret. You don't marry someone without knowing who they are. Josephine fell in love with Birbeck. He visited her often and all went well until Ricky was murdered, then Drew and Mike. None of us were that stupid not to connect. It wasn't sex which did for my sister but fossils. Birbeck thought he was on a nice little earner."

"Josephine knew too much and threatened to turn Birbeck in?"

"We received postcards from South America. After she vanished. But Ricky rang up one night. He was in a real panic. He'd witnessed a murder in the tower above the museum. I told him to come round. He never arrived. I don't know why Drew and Mike were killed, perhaps Ricky told them about the body in the tower. There was only one solution. I'm sorry but it's my foolishness which has continued this dreadful chain of events. I played my twin sister. It has infuriated Birbeck. There has to be a solution to end this madness."

I felt a wave of sympathy rise for this woman. I admired her forthright honesty. Yes I confess I was intrigued by her. Now wasn't the time to ask any other questions.

"It's time to go. I have a flight booked."

"A flight?"

"Don't ask."

We climbed the steps once more until we entered the very graveyard which began this chain of events for me, witnessing Drew's murder. We regained the car.

"I'll drop you in Hawsker." Jocaster touched my cheek. "Thank you Davy Jones but I know what to do now. *Au revoir.*"

I got out. Jocaster's car accelerated, then stopped. The window wound down. "By the way it's Jevan you've fallen in love with."

I was perplexed by this statement.

"If ever you need me follow this to its source," Jocaster threw me a small a piece of rock. I recognised it as basalt.

I smiled. I waved. Jocaster retained a strange sort of integrity I thought. I paused a moment, thinking about the best course of action. Finally I ran back to the caravan.

I stuffed my remaining possessions into a rucksack and hoicked it onto my back. As I emerged from the caravan a car skidded onto the driveway. I ran behind the farmhouse and across the fields. From the vantage point of a copse I saw Birbeck barge into the caravan. He looked around then knocked at the farmhouse door. Mr. Moralis appeared on the drive and pointed in my direction. I crouched down. Birbeck used the police car radio.

I crawled from my hiding place and keeping a hedgerow between me and the farm, I moved as quickly as I could towards the safety of Bay Town. It was possible to catch my bus there at 11.05. I checked my watch. I resolved I'd either catch it or hand myself into the police. If I confessed to murdering Drew, that would surely keep me safe from Birbeck. I reached the coastal path and very deliberately said, "good morning," to everyone I passed. Below me the tide was on the turn. The waves of the bay were running upon the sand and engulfing it once more. A helicopter was hovering someway to the north. I hurried along the path which became busier as I neared the town.

I breathed a sigh of relief as I gained the tarmacked road. Three or four people waited at the bus stop. I stood alongside them. A car tore down the road from Whitby. The unmistakeable outlines of Birbeck and his side kick loomed behind the wind screen.

I dropped my bag and ran. I stumbled into the busy post office and pushed to the front of the queue, "Excuse me. Could you ring the police?"

I saw myself on the security camera.

"Why? Has there been a murder?" The postmaster quipped.

"No but there's about to be."

Everyone laughed. I took a deep breath. I stuck my fingers in my coat pocket. "Hand over the cash!" I demanded, "I mean it, I'm desperate!" I felt a real gun thrust into my back. "Turn around and walk outside." I recognised Mr. Fibula's voice.

"You'll have to shoot me here and now," I said hearing my voice quiver.

"Fine!" I heard the safety unlock. He called my bluff and pushed me toward the door.

In the doorway I saw the outline of DS Laing. He screwed up a sweet wrapper and flicked it into a bin. "Don't worry," he announced to the assembled crowd. "A sad case." He tapped his finger on his temple. "Now for the denouement young David." He pushed me through the door. An officer picked up my rucksack and placed it in the boot. I was bundled into the car. Two men sat in the back with me.

"Your last journey," the bearded blonde said in a Germanic accent. "A final piece of research and a tragic accident."

"Can't we subject him to a little pain first?" The other asked matter-of-factly.

I looked at the scar on his forehead. "Did I do that?"

He responded with a blow which left me in no doubt. We were heading down a track south of Ravenscar. First one bungalow appeared, then a second. The car stopped. Mr. Fibula got out. I was pulled out and the Germans frog-marched me to the edge.

"No," said Mr. Fibula. "There've been too many falls. The tide is coming in. A drowning would be more appropriate."

The German I'd assaulted smiled, "I know exactly what to do!" He pulled a bolt gun from the boot. Mr. Fibula nodded. We skidded down the cliff path unnoticed. I kept looking around for an escape but was gripped too tightly.

The sound of the sea grew. The smell of salt grew. The rocks became colder, darker, wetter. The sea crashed over the jagged outcrops. The tide swirled and eddied in deep pools. "There!" The German pointed. The other German ripped off my shirt. He pinched my nipple and twisted it violently. I winced.

"I'd like to rip your body apart," he smiled, "but it must look like an accident with a bolt gun." The guy smiled, he stood close to me, so I could smell his breath.

"We arrive in the world with nothing and so you'll leave it. You'll be grateful. The cold will strike faster and death will be swifter."

The enormity of this comment expanded to fill every cell of my body. There was no way I was going to die here, today. Like most men, I had a plan to live until I was eighty. I looked for an escape.

"Heinrick, Let's finish this."

I was pushed into the water. The cold hit me with such a shock I struggled for breath.

"Hold out his right hand palm down, Remember it's an accident!" The German ordered. He took out his bolt gun and fired.

A moment of disbelief was followed by prolonged agony. I woke coughing. The pain followed. The water broke over me. I tried to push myself up.

"David, how unfortunate." Birbeck crouched down next to the pool.

I struggled to keep my head above the waves and coughed.

"You know… knew too much. You see I used to live at the Franklin's villa. I know every secret of the place. Rooms to hide bodies in, passageways which let you spy on people committing depravities of all kinds. I did it all because I loved Josephine De Vile."

"We don't kill those we love."

"Don't we?" Birbeck smiled, "and something else. Something of an added bonus in killing you. Your grandfather and my father were implacable foes. It was your grandpa's photographic evidence which trapped dad. He was forced to sell up his properties in Hull and repay the City Council or face prison. Fortunately he had the villa in Whitby put aside as insurance. We lived here in poverty until the church intervened. I believe in a purely financial arrangement with god. Well at least you know why you're going to die, it's more of an explanation than Jevan gave to Barty. Game, set and match to me." Birbeck stood to leave. He looked up and down the beach. "Tell me, would you have killed Drew?"

"I never got chance to find out, you got there first?"

"I thought so." Birbeck gave a mock salute and began climbing the path. He didn't turn round.

Hatred and revenge kept me going.

I woke spluttering and coughing. I couldn't feel my arms or legs. I tried to move but collapsed under the water. The blue sky above the surface shimmered and was gone. I looked and saw my hand bolted to the rock. The pain exploded from it to my arm but I had to move, I had to get purchase on higher ground or drown. I regained the air. I turned round. I screamed and blood pulsed from the wound but I managed to move higher on the rock. I coughed up water and breathed again. I recited geological periods under my breath then all the zone fossils of the Liassic. Sometime around Dactilyoceras commune I lost consciousness.

An unconformity is the passage of time which leaves no record of events in the rocks. Time doesn't pass quickly enough to a geologist. I want to see the movement of the continents, the slow progress of evolution. Time moves on, how slowly time moves on.

Chapter 11: Fault.

"Spodumene, spodumene, we all love spodumeme. Li Al Si two O six…" A group of us had decamped to The Gardener's Arms for some refreshment after the exams. I sang as heartily as the rest knowing that from this point I was on my own. Nigel had completed his finals and was going to take up a Masters in Industrial Geology, Tucker to do research on the use of microfossils in oil exploration. Their futures were sorted regardless of the type of degree they received. I was now a year behind and would have to wait until I reached their enviable position. I practised the exercises the physiotherapist set me as we sang.

"Don't worry," Nigel reassured, "I'll only just be along the corridor. Prof Durham set me some summertime reading, so I'll be here until we go down."

"Thanks," I said. All attention was turned on Tucker who was regaling the audience with some non PC jokes. Afterwards he pushed himself off the table and rejoined his girlfriend. They cuddled then kissed passionately.

"Away the lads!" Nigel mockingly shouted.

Angela affectionately touched the back of my injured hand. I smiled.

"We'll see you're alright." Her hazel eyes caught the sunlight. "I'm meeting Carrie at the weekend, any messages?"

"Carrie?" I hadn't seen her since the trial. That was the moment all my preconceptions were swept aside. Josephine Franklin was painted as a bullying monster who deserved to be silenced forever. Birbeck portrayed Canon Franklin as a depraved homosexual who used rent boys. Carrie managed to sit through the trial in absolute silence but I could see the way she looked at Birbeck. Jocaster gave her evidence but she didn't hang around after the trial to defend her reputation. I had been the last person to talk to her. All the time I sat there loathing Birbeck and vowing revenge. When he looked at me I knew he wondered why I wasn't a ghost.

I said, "Tell her she made the right decision."

"Still, it was hard on her, transferring uni, starting it all again."

"Don't look to me for sympathy. No, I don't mean that, I'm confused by it all."

"Don't talk to him, he hasn't got a good track record with girls!" Tucker joked but the group fell silent. All eyes turned on me.

"Or boys for that matter!" I replied feeling the tension evaporate. I thought of Ricky or Jevan as I now knew he was. Of course I'd been warned against him by Carrie. It had been a salutary lesson, a man unable to give his love versus a man not able to receive it.

"Sorry," Tucker said quietly. "Nigel and I spent a boring month at reciprocal parents and well, I'd be lying if I said we did another four weeks last year. More like two! Still you were in hospital and now you've got to go through it all again." Tucker smiled. I couldn't be certain if this was in support or devilment.

"They said I didn't have to but, believe it or not, I want to. I want to put the events of two years ago behind me. I want to prove I'm not afraid."

Tucker finished his pint. "It's not the geology that should frighten you but those in positions of power and influence. On the same day the Canon got his just desserts a drug dealer got let off with an ASBO and an eighty nine year old woman got twenty eight days for not paying £65 of her rates!"

"Justice ceased the day Margaret Thatcher got to power," I replied feeling a little uncomfortable.

"Yes and who voted for her in 79?" Tucker retorted.

"Believe it or not you learn from your mistakes. And my big mistake was not being able to nail Birbeck." I moved my thumb and forefinger. The scar in the centre of my palm would never leave me. Canon Franklin would go to his grave hating me despite the fact that it was Birbeck who turned him in. The police officer gave the damning evidence against his friend at the trial. Nothing I could say was proven.

It was Jocaster's parting comment which perplexed me. She'd kissed me, "Be brave," she said, "and follow your heart."

"Dave, I've got this idea for a cartoon strip. Captain Geology and the coprolites. Would you write the story?" Nigel studied me intensely.

"Coprolites?" I saw the humour in this, "So we're not talking serious with fossilised shit as a title?"

"Not a chance! We're taking the piss. You know how pretentious geology is with all the Latin and Victorian language."

I knew not only how seriously some people take the study of rocks but how others were prepared to kill to keep their fossil smuggling going.

"I think we might take it from life." I said, "Corrupt cop hires German mercenaries to collect valuable fossils. Captain Geology is called in to investigate."

"Think again," said Nigel, "He's not Columbo, more Superman. He's a superhero in tight undies, not a thinker!"

"No, you need to get air to the nuts for that!" I said joining Nigel's wavelength.

"And don't do a Foul Syke Farm, we're not talking literary short story. We're talking pacey comic strip."

"Okay! I've got it," I resented the allusion to my story, particularly as it had been so successful. My tutor had read it in a Sunday supplement and pronounced its theme to be repugnant. I wasn't concerned. I'd been published and earned some money Confined to hospital for several weeks, I'd had time to formulate stories. They flowed from my pen in rapid succession. Each one I believed better than the last but success was followed by indifference and failure. Finally I bundled all the manuscripts together and placed them at the bottom of the wardrobe next to Jocaster's porn videos. I was determined they would stay there until I had the idea of writing Grandpa's life story, well a fictionalised account anyway.

"Do you think you'll ever make it as a geologist after all you've been though?" Nigel asked. He seemed genuine in his inquiry.

"Yes," I said emphatically. "Nothing is going to get in my way. In fact I might join writing and geology together someday. That would be great fun!"

Nigel seemed to think I was joking. I didn't disillusion him.

"But surely…" he thought better of the question, whatever it was. I lit a cigarette.

"Shame about Barbara retiring," he said, helping himself to a fag. "I always liked her, even if she did very little cleaning."

"She made a great cup of tea on a morning and was quite delicate about cleaning round visitors who stayed till late."

"But you're not supposed to have overnight guests," Nigel sounded mortified at the thought.

"Well, I must catch the bus and get packed. Time and tide wait for no man." And for a fraction of a second I was still pinioned in the pool as the tide encroached. I waved, "See you all at the leavers do tomorrow."

I caught the East Yorkshire bus out to my room in Down's Hall. I sat upstairs looking at the summer foliage from the new perspective of the tree tops. I'd feel safer going back if they'd put Birbeck in prison but keeping him out of prison was the pact the four of us had made. Prison has no consequence, no revenge for the victims, no what we had in mind was straight out of Agatha Christie. It was so honest, so obvious that no one would ever convict us. In the end our subterfuge wasn't necessary, Birbeck and Laing had all the angles sewn up, so when I got back to Hawsker he'd still be filling his police car with sundry packaging. Of course staying at the caravan at Jevan's was out of the question, so I was in negotiation to rent a room in a ramshackle old cottage in Ravenscar. I'd been told what it lacked in modern conveniences it more than made up for in location. Location didn't matter as much as price. We'd got as far as three weeks for two hundred quid cash delivered on arrival. I was unsure, particularly as the bus service to Whitby had been cut back.

In my pigeonhole I found a bill from the Academic Office and a post card:
Dear David, Having a lovely time in Durness, the weather is great. See you soon. Love, Mum. There was also a letter. It contained six words cut out from newspaper headlines. I played around with them on my desk but the only message I could make was: *trace the rock to its source.*

In itself it was meaningless until half way through checking the angle of dip on The Dogger beds, I remembered the rock I'd been given by Jocaster. I held it up to the lamp and looked at it under the hand lens. It was a basalt, a common enough rock but it held the key to where Jocaster was living. There was only one way to find out more, I'd have to ask Nigel to use his contacts and have a thin slice of the rock mounted on a glass slide. Perhaps under a microscope the crystals it was made from would reveal the rock's origin. I heard him return in the room next door. I knocked. "Nigel, I hope you don't mind. Could you do me a favour and get a thin section of this done."

"This isn't from North Yorkshire."

"Right," I said, offering him a fag. "It's from a friend. They said I'd never be able to find out where it came from."

"It's basalt," Nigel passed it back, "a very common rock."

I pushed it again into his hand again. "Jocaster's not the sort to give a clue without providing some solution."

"Ah! That woman is involved. Well why didn't you say so? For the good of your soul I'll get the section done, though for a best guess I'd say this was recent." Nigel took the cigarette. "That's the difference between a first and a second class degree." This I realised was Nigel only half- joking.

"I'm going down to the bar when I've finished packing." I issued this as a statement.

Nigel filed through some pages. "I might manage ten," he said after some delay.

"Fine," I said before returning to my room. I filled the void with sound. Perhaps I should have screamed but I found the music calming, a reassuring link to all the previous occasions I'd heard Ravel's string quartet. I ran through its movements: *allegro moderato, assez vif, tres lent* and finally *vif et agite*. Its passion broken on the dedication to an older man. I loved the record library in the Brynmor –Jones and the occasional glimpse of Philip Larkin. He would tap on the doors of the cubicles to make certain students weren't sleeping. I lay on the bed and read the article on structures remaining in metamorphic rocks by my tutor. I must have fallen asleep. I woke to a knocking on the door.

"I'll be ready in a mo, Nigel!"

There was a long pause. "Are you being funny?" It was a woman's voice. It took me a moment to come round and gauge the time.

"Barbara?"

"Who else?" Her key slid into the lock and the door opened. "I've brought you a cuppa and your post. And…"

"Don't forget your exercises," we said in unison and laughed.

"What am I going to do without you next term?" I touched her hand. The contact lingered a moment too long.

She stammered her reply, "I hoped you might visit us retired folk."

I smiled. "They'll be so short staffed I bet you get a call asking you to come back for a few hours a week."

"That would be nice. Here's my address and phone number."

I felt Barbara's gaze.

"Must get on," She bustled out of the room and turned on the vacuum. A little later she began singing. I arranged her present where it could easily be seen. I had wrapped it in brown paper and cut out an oversize tag.

I sipped my drink letting the steam condense over my nose. Finally I turned to the letter. The typed envelope bore no stamp. I remembered I'd not paid the bill to the academic office and ripped it open. It wasn't a reminder or final notice. I unfolded the neatly hand written letter

Dear David,
I'm visiting Dad today. He's very low. No one believes him innocent when he says he didn't murder mum. I don't suppose you do either but do you believe I

would stand by my father if he had? Like you, he has suffered at the hands of Birbeck. Like you he wants revenge on the man and all he stands for. I don't understand why dad gave such a preposterous defence but he's safer on the inside. He allowed his love of fossils to become an obsession, now he's taking a degree in the subject. In prison he can't be blackmailed anymore and can't be implicated in any other crimes. All the same Birbeck must have been rolling in the aisles.

My dad wanted to see you, so I have taken the liberty of attaching the visiting times and procedures for Hull Prison.

I hope eventually you'll forgive me for my part in all of this. I'm not a bad person. I suppose working in my aunt's porn films has altered my perspective, some might say I was damaged goods but I've always looked on each scene as an opportunity, if not a fantasy. I'll contact you when you've visited him, there's lots to talk about and I have an offer you can't refuse.

Yours, Carrie

I thought about Carrie. I had been naive in not realising the familial relationship earlier in my first stay. It would have settled Carrie's position in the scheme of things. I drank my tea. There was nothing Canon Franklin could tell me that I hadn't already heard at the trial.

I stretched and opened the curtains. The morning sunlight entered the room and I unlocked the door and strode out onto the balcony. A gentle breeze rippled through the leaves. The smell of freshly mown grass lifted my spirits. I realised I hadn't packed some of the larger rock specimens including a large ammonite and various other pieces. I decided to leave them. I doubted anyone would notice and the worst that could happen was some conference visitor taking them home. Not everyone is so passionate about geology. I took my towel and gear over to the shower.

"I'll do your room whilst I've a chance." Barbara announced,

"Thanks." I locked the shower behind me. When I emerged in my dressing gown I found Barbara sitting in tears on my bed. She had been crying.

"It's beautiful," she said and kissed me.

The amethyst crystals glistened in the sunlight. "The ancient Greeks thought they protected you from getting drunk!"

"You are silly!" She dried her tears, "I'm going to visit you and make certain you make it."

"What will your husband say?"

"Something similar to yours, if you decide to go that way." She studied me for a reply.

I smiled.

"I always knew there was something about you, something different. You care too much and that's not good in a man."

'I haven't seen Jevan since last summer," I said with sadness.

"Some things are better after waiting for them. I had to wait two years for Freddie to get back from his Cyprus posting."

"Well perhaps you're right." I was a little embarrassed talking about Jevan.

Barbara touched my cheek then left the room. She reappeared in the doorway, "Thank you. You're the best." She shut the door and left me to dress.

I rang the prison and was given permission to visit twenty four hours later. I knew the outside of the prison well and hoped to keep it that way. The building resembled a Victorian castle with more forbidding walls emerging behind its façade. I followed the long line of visitors through the security checks and was surprised to end in a pleasant informal seating area. I'd obviously seen too many films with lovers meeting at a glass screen. Here the attitude was relaxed formality with several security cameras and officers lurking. Canon Franklin shuffled up to me. He looked gaunt and stooped with age. He held out his hand. "There are over a thousand of us lost souls here." He looked around the room. "I've spent some of my time in the new multi-faith centre. I seem to have found my commitment to God in this adversity."

"That's nice," I said looking around, before remembering I was amongst murderers and rapists. "You asked to see me?"

"Yes, I did indeed. Don't cross Birbeck."

"Is that a threat?"

"No, not at all. It's a warning, if you go back you'll be found dead at the foot of a cliff. I know what you're thinking, you might push him." The Canon savoured the idea. "I'd thought of that myself, but as you know I was too embroiled."

"Look it's you that's in prison for…" I didn't finish the word. The Canon pushed a finger to his lips, I got his meaning.

"I didn't do it. It was such a preposterous defence I thought you'd realise it must be true."

I thought about this. "I didn't buy the fact you never knew about the tower room, it seemed unlikely and I guess the jury felt the same. Like you I found myself out classed by both the defence and prosecution lawyers."

"If you push him you'll get life for double murder. They'll pin Barty's murder on you as well. Police homicide, that's got to be twenty years or so with good behaviour?"

"You're a clever man but I can't be found guilty of killing someone when I was witnessed at the bottom of the cliff where he landed. No one has ever traced the girl in the pink skirt and I know she was the guilty one." I concluded by saying,. "I'll get us a coffee."

"Two sugars in mine."

I looked back only once whilst I waited for the coffee to be vended. The canon had folded in on his thoughts. I wondered what he might gain from lying, he had more to gain from telling the truth. I decided to ask the question which had plagued me. I put down the coffee.

"If you don't mind me asking, why didn't you report Josephine missing?"

The canon held his fingers over his mouth. He blew through them then took a deep breath, "You can imagine things weren't easy between us. Not every man of the cloth gets to know his gardener so intimately."

"Jevan or Ricky?" I asked.

"Ricky. He was by far the nicer of the two. You would have loved him."

I shook my head. "No I fell for Jevan."

"So your intentions re Carrie have changed? I'd hope she would settle down with someone nice."

"Don't worry, I'll see she's alright but now she's in Leeds we don't meet as often." I found the white lie comforting but even as I spoke, I realised that when I thought of Carrie it brought back pleasant memories.

"You see I thought I could rid myself of Birbeck. I implored Jocaster to come back from California to impersonate her sister. When she swapped the rings over and let him kiss her hand he was stunned. I nearly broke him. He took to drink but like all good cops he eventually worked it out and began blackmailing me. Remember Leviticus?"

I shrugged. I didn't, there appeared to be too many rules catering for man B.C, rather than 20th century.

"So for two years Jocaster and myself were stuck in a trap of our own creation. Therein lies our problem, Birbeck murdered Josephine, Carrie's mother. Josephine had an affair with him. You're surprised we managed to keep that quiet. There was a second piece of information we all agreed to keep silent. Birbeck went on to kill the wrong boy. He didn't murder Jevan, he murdered Ricky -- an easy mistake to make with twins but one easily solved."

I took a deep breath, "How would we prove what you say?"

The Canon stroked his stubbly chin, "I don't know. It's very weak but get Birbeck to confess."

I thought about this. "If you're right, it won't be long before I meet him again. I'm going back to my mapping area tomorrow; I only put off going to see you."

"You can't leave ghosts but you can leave your body."

I suddenly thought of Josephine's skeleton sitting waiting in the tower and felt queasy.

"Ah!" The Canon guessed at my vision. "The transition to adult can be a challenge."

"Yes," I agreed.

We sat in silence for many minutes, "Have you seen Jevan since the trial?"

"No, nor Jocaster. It's funny, every time I see a yellow sports car I think about her, how she played with the rubies on the right fingers."

"Did I tell you I'm taking an Open University degree in geology? I know ruby has monoclinic symmetry and its colour is due to chromium."

"I'm impressed. You'll be able to explore the Yorkshire coastline when you're out. Hopefully the mistake will be rectified." I left my pouch of rolling tobacco on the table.

"I'll hope you are right. Indeed I pray you are right." The Canon began rolling a wafer thin cigarette and placed it behind his ear.

"Which may be sooner than you think."

Not knowing what else to say, I replied, "Let's hope so." We parted on the bell with the Canon extracting a promise that I'd send a postcard or he'd assume I'd fallen a long way. I smiled and told him I'd fallen a long time ago. He seemed to think the comment amusing.

I took a deep breath once outside the prison, like hospitals the pervading odour clung. The air outside was also tainted with cocoa from the factory by the River Hull. As I walked toward the bus I was deep in thought, it took a few moments to register that my name was being called. I turned round. It was Carrie, "I wanted to know someone had visited Dad. He gets very low."

"Yes, he's changed," I said coolly.

"So have you," Carrie regarded me. She took my injured right hand and stroked the scar.

"I'm on my way to mum's for tea. She's just got back from sunny Scotland but I'm sure there'll be enough scones for three."

"Does that mean we can still be friends?" Carrie slipped her arm through mine. "Friends? Perhaps. At present there's something much more important. We're on the same side now. Until your dad's free I don't think we'll ever be able to get Birbeck."

Carrie pushed herself close until I could smell the perfume on her. "I have waited far too long to avenge mum's death. The wait ends this summer. I'll be with you all the way. In fact why don't you stay?"

I suspected the motive. I still had the problem of who slipped me the drug the night of Jocaster's dinner party. I suppose three people presented themselves: the canon, Birbeck and Carrie. Now was not the time to ask. I thought about the gothic pile with its black slate roof and infamous tower. On the plus side the gardens were great and so was the library. "Is there a production team nearby?"

Carrie laughed, "Aunt Jocaster's abroad. I don't know where."

"More money?"

"Let's say the bottom's dropped out of the home market." Carrie's hand slapped mine playfully.

"You must know that I fell in love with Jevan."

"My dad told you. Good. That will make the summer easier. Let's not plan anything, just get your map done and Birbeck trapped."

"That sounds like one hefty plan." We walked off toward the bus stop and waited for a blue and white.

Mum was pleased that I'd chosen to take a young lady and she beamed when Carrie told her she'd look after me over the summer. I don't believe I've drunk so much tea over so little conversation but mum was happy and that pleased me.

"Aunt Gertie and I were going to go for a week just to…"

Carrie immediately intervened and invited them, "The more the merrier!" She explained as we sat in the front room looking through the same net curtains I played with as a child.

"Well," I said. "We must be going. Carrie has to get back to Leeds and I've got stuff to get ready."

"Yes Love." Mum kissed me gently. I gave her a hug.

Outside in the ten foot Carrie asked, "Is there anyone else you'd like to invite?"

I could only think of one name, "Jevan."

She stroked my cheek the kissed it. "Only you can secure that."

"See you in Whitby tomorrow."

Carrie waved as I boarded the bus to Cottingham.

The halls of residence were quiet. It was the end of term and before last orders at the bar. As I unlocked the door, I saw the envelope stuck to the wood. Inside was a slide with a thin section of rock mounted on it. A note from Nigel explained: *This seemed to mean a lot so I got it done. If it helps, we're agreed it's a recent basalt. There are a lot of iron minerals in the section which broadly indicates Iceland and the fissure volcanoes associated with the mid-Atlantic ridge.* I smiled and burnt the letter. I placed the slide with all the others prepared for my mapping area.

"Spodumene, spodumene, we all love spodumeme. Li Al Si two O six..."

I woke to singing. I checked the clock through half open eyes. Eight thirty. I heard Barbara's insistent tapping on the door, "David there's these mad geologists outside who claim they're escorting you to Whitby." I pulled on my dressing gown and emerged into daylight on the landing.

"No time to lose!" Tucker announced. At his side was a rucksack and a carrier bag full of bottles of Newcastle Brown. "Carrie's invited us for a few days and well…"

"It's on the way home," Nigel announced to cover up the subterfuge.

"Well thanks. That'll put mum's mind at rest for a few days, until she arrives. Is there anyone else Carrie has invited?"

"Sounds a big place, but then you'd know," Tucker's voice trailed off. "We thought if we set off by nine we'd make Whitby in time for a pub crawl, and if the weather holds, a couple of spliffs in the graveyard where Dracula's buried."

I opened my mouth to speak. I changed my mind. "That's great! Some party and a few rocks!"

"Leave the rocks out! Just some frocks!" Tucker collected his stuff. "See you in the car, I'm going out for a fag."

"Are all geologists mad?" Barbara asked placing a cup of tea in front of me. "You'd better get a move on, don't keep them waiting."

I picked up the cuppa. "Thanks, I won't."

I was ready in record time. I folded myself into the back of Nigel's old mini and stretched out between the rucksacks. "Do you want some cash for petrol?" I asked noticing the petrol gauge was showing empty. "Not at the moment. It's broken. And don't open the window at the back as it's only held in with super glue!"

"Anything else I should know?"

"We push up anything greater than one in five!"

"That's not very encouraging for the North Yorkshire Moors, Nigel."

"No but its good exercise," Tucker cut in. "Or a good excuse for studying a valley from a pub. We'll have to drive round Scarborough foreshore to get a good look at the lasses."

"I can't see why we've set off so early."

"Wait until you've experienced this car. Every journey's an adventure," Tucker replied.

"I don't like adventures," Nigel admitted.

I closed my eyes and let the vibrations of the car lure me back to sleep. I jolted awake when the exhaust scraped over the uneven Wold's road.

"I should have chosen chalk."

"Why ay man! That'd be about as interesting as our pal Nigel!"

I laughed. I noticed Nigel didn't.

Chapter 12: 1945

The sense of excitement had been building for days. After six long years it was finally going to happen. When Ernie picked up the local paper on the way home from work he couldn't suppress his smile as he read, *German War Ends, S.H.A.E.F Official.*

Usually Mondays were dour but this one was different. By lunch time Birbeck's replacement had circulated a memo. The Guildhall would close one hour after the Prime Minister's announcement and remain closed that day and the following. At the bottom of page 2 of the paper was the information Ernie had been seeking. Mr. Churchill's broadcast would be at 3pm.

Everyone in the Treasurer's office at the Guildhall gathered round the radio at 3 o'clock and listened to the Home Service. The peel of bells on the radio was joined by every church in Hull. Ernie wiped away a tear. Surprisingly he found himself hugging colleagues and sharing several glasses of home-made wine.

Later as Ernie walked through the park, he noticed that multi-coloured electric lights had been put up between lamp posts and flags and bunting fluttered in the breeze. Children were dancing round a bonfire and everyone was chattering excitedly. A group of flying officers began splashing in the fountain. Seeing their uniform made Ernie think of Eldedt.

Eldedt had been liberated from a POW camp by the Americans, just before Christmas. He'd written a card thanking Ernie for his hospitality. There had been no further communication. As far as he knew Eldedt had never contacted Gertie or Cyril, nor his daughter, the baby. The baby! Margaret was a tot of four and much more talkative than Elizabeth.

On the bus home passengers started a sing song and when he wasn't singing, Ernie's attention was drawn to all the gaiety on the streets, particularly the bonfires, with *guys* dressed up as Hitler, awaiting the flames.

He got off the bus at Thearne Lane End. He stood for a moment to regain his balance and checked his watch. The lane was utterly transformed. Bunting stretched from house to house and there were Union Jacks everywhere. Marjorie had put up the Christmas lights in the bay window in a defiant 'V.'

She ran out to hug Ernie as he walked down the street. "It's over!"

"It is, it really is," he said. "I think we'll have glass of sherry, darling."

Ernie brought the glass to the gate and looked up into the evening sky. The colours faded from light blue to dark over the river and for several minutes he heard nothing but the birds and smelt hedge parsley instead of diesel fumes. He lit a cigarette. Marjorie and Elizabeth had put on coats.

"We'll join you. Let's walk to the river."

"I've a better idea, you push Tom in the pram and…" Ernie went back to the shed. It lent at a precarious angle but showed signs of being hastily patched up make it into a darkroom again. From its dark interior he produced a rusty three wheeled scooter. Elizabeth cooed with excitement. She soon got the hang of it, leaving the couple to walk behind the pram. The mayflies lazily took to wing, clouds of them rose from the ditches and danced in the evening light. Three hurricanes flew low in a wide 'v,' Marjorie waved vigorously.

"Steady on there, I'll get jealous."

The bicycle squeaked as it was ridden towards them. "Hello there!" Ernie offered his hand.

Old Wozza stopped his bike and doffed his cap. He firmly cemented it over his hair and wiped his hand down his jacket. "Never thought I'd live to see it," he looked into the now empty sky, "but since meeting Moira, I'm a new man. I might get to ninety the way I feel now."

"I hope so," Marjorie put her arm round the old man.

"Here, steady on there gal!" He pushed down on the peddle and unsteadily regained the saddle.

"How old do you think he is?"

"Seventy five, so his son told me one night in The Ship." Ernie steadied his daughter and looked around, "Maybe we should head back?"

"No, for once let's finish what we started."

Ernie agreed.

The banks of the river were churned up by cattle but there was a clear path to the ferry. Ernie waved and Bob pulled the punt back along its chain. "Three for the Bluebell."

"Ernie."

"We'll sit in the garden and take in the view."

Ernie lifted Elizabeth into the ferry and placed the scooter next to her before going back for Marjorie and Tom in the pram. As they were heaved across the river the sounds of singing got louder. Marjorie pursed her lips.

"There's a rare old party in there tonight," Bob said.

"So long as you can get us home in an hour."

"Drunk or sober, I can cross this river so don't you worry."

The crowd were on *There'll be bluebirds over the White Cliffs of Dover* before Ernie got to the bar. When he returned, Elizabeth was playing with a kitten. He passed Marjorie her drink.

"It hit me again," she said, "I just saw them there lying on the white sheet just like they were asleep."

"Don't, it wasn't your fault, you were very ill after Tom." Ernie put his arm around his wife. She shivered. He placed his jacket over her. "The twins are at peace beneath the apple tree. There was nothing else we could do. We'll have to be content with our two beauties."

"We've lost so much to this war, Ernie. Friends, relatives, our babies we can't just erase six years."

"No one's asking us to but we're lucky. We have our home and each other. There are a lot who can't say that."

Marjorie snuggled up to Ernie, "it was a good idea to come here and see the world from the other side of the river."

"And watch the sunset on the first night of peace."

They saluted with their glasses as Elizabeth played and Tom span his rattles.

Chapter 13: 1959

Usually Mondays were dour but this one was different. By lunch time the boss had circulated a memo. It was a simple statement. Ernest Crawford would be the new treasurer of Hull City Council. Elizabeth had to wipe away a tear. Surprisingly she found herself hugging colleagues and then having to beat a retreat to the ladies room to reapply her lipstick.

Later that day as Elizabeth walked through the park, she noticed that multi-coloured electric lights had been put up between lamp posts. A group of children were dancing round a bonfire. She chided herself for not remembering it was bonfire night. A group of flying officers walked past and one wolf whistled. She made it plain she disapproved by ignoring them. Seeing their uniform made her think of William, a lad from the village she hadn't seen since he was reported injured on National Service. The bus was busy and Elizabeth pushed next to a wizened old woman who smelt of eau de Cologne. The transverse seat over the wheel was uncomfortable but beat standing. She sneaked a glance then relaxed. "Hello Mrs Turnbridge."

The lady unfolded her glasses and examined her neighbour. "Why it's Elizabeth Crawford. How are you dear? Been shopping?"

"Back from work. I've taken a couple of hours off to help prepare for tonight's festivities."

"Fireworks. I hates the noisy ones but I'm partial to a Roman Candle."

"You could join us, if you don't mind the walk down the lane."

"That's very neighbourly. I'm sure I could spare an hour now him in doors has gone."

Elizabeth remembered it had only been a few months since Old Wazza died. He'd become a local legend. A talking point all the way from Woodmansey to Dunswell. Everyone knew how the German's tried to strafe him. The frightening incident had renewed his vigour for life and he'd reached the grand old age of ninety.

"I couldn't be doing with marriage at my age, so we lived in sin!" Mrs. Turnbridge joked. "I think my cooking did him the power of good."

"I'll have to remember that when buying pies from the YCA!" Elizabeth helped the old lady off the bus at Thearne Lane End. "We usually start festivities at seven thirty when Tom gets back. Don't worry if you don't like bangs, you can watch from the dining room windows with mum and the poodle."

"Ok dear. I'll see you later." The old lady walked on down the road towards the river. Elizabeth skipped through the gate, finding Marjorie by the door. Her mum was smiling. "Dad couldn't resist phoning. He wanted to tell me and knew you wouldn't be able to contain yourself!"

"He was right." She hugged her mum.

"Let's celebrate with a glass of elderberry wine?" Majorie vanished under the stairs and emerged with a dusty bottle. "There's a firework party for the kids tonight. Her ladyship down at the big house is organising things. A double celebration now William's home."

Elizabeth blushed slightly. "Is he fully recovered?"

"Lady Alice says the plastic surgeon has worked a miracle."

"Was it so bad?" Elizabeth asked with real concern.

"He's booked in for several more operations on his hand but his face is sorted."

"Face?" Elizabeth put the glass down and sat at the telephone seat. "I knew he was injured but..." Her mother's hand reassured her.

Elizabeth picked up her hat. "I'm going to cycle down to the river to clear my head. Oh! By the way I sat next to Rose Turnbridge on the way home, so I asked her to come down for the fireworks."

"Another one. With Cyril, Gertie, Margaret and baby Bartholomew we'll be busy. It'll be a real houseful, like during the war." Marjorie stopped at this recollection. This would be the first time Cyril and Ernie had met since she'd asked for his help. She automatically crossed her fingers. Sensing this Elizabeth hugged her mum. "It'll be fine."

"But will there be enough?"

"Mum, stop fussing, you know there'll be enough for a feast. Besides your heart..."

"Now you're fussing, dear."

Elizabeth clipped lights onto the bike and fastened her old coat. She cycled past the big house and round the double bends. No one seemed to be about until she reached Galloway's. The old farmer leant against the gate. She waved, he doffed his cap.

She propped her bike against the fence, then clambered over the stile and up the river bank. She sat on the bench overlooking the rotting remains of the ferry. She looked towards the lights of Hull. She hadn't been to this spot since William told her about his plans for National Service.

"It seems a long time ago Elizabeth."

Startled she turned and flashed the cycle lamp in the direction of the voice. "William?"

He turned away. "I wanted you to see me before the big party. I wanted to see your reaction."

Elizabeth turned to walk back down the bank. "I don't want to remember you at all!" She cursed herself for sounding angry when that was not what she meant.

"What do you mean?" She felt William's hand pull her round and for the first time she saw the extent of his injuries. Very gently she touched the skin round his cheek and temple. He recoiled then stammered an apology. "I wanted to see you but mum told me you were courting Barnaby Blyth."

"I went to the Regal to see The Best of Everything. We hardly said a word to each other all night."

"When did you get back?"

"Sunday night. East Grinstead is a fair distance from here. I stopped off in London.

I was going to take in a show but I lost my nerve. He held up his bandaged hand and arm. "The metal catches of the cockpit were red hot but I knew I had to undo them or ... well I'd rather not think of it."

Elizabeth rested her arm on his shoulder.

They started to walk back down the lane. "Damn it! I can't hide away forever; I'm one of the good guys!"

Elizabeth clipped the light back on the bike. "Injured in the line of duty. Did they say you'd make a full recovery?"

"Eventually, with support."

"I'm not working tomorrow, so I suggest an outing, if you can stand me driving the old Humber. I'll pick you up at ten and take you for lunch in Beverley, this brand new place has opened, all chrome and formica, you'll love it."

"I'd love doing anything with you." William confessed.

Chapter 14: The Geology of Desire

"Christ, did you see that!" Nigel exclaimed as he swerved up the grassy bank. The radiator hissed and steam erupted through the grill.

I only saw the police car shoot off up the road to Whitby. We all got out of the car. Nigel opened the bonnet with a thick cloth and looked inside.

"Can you fix it?"

"Why ey man. Nigel's got a litre of water stowed somewhere." Tucker rooted around the boot and produced a squash bottle of water. We waited for the radiator to cool, then refilled it. The car started and we regained the A171.

"Look over there, so it wasn't fiction?" Tucker pointed out *Foul Syke Farm*.

I looked at the concrete drive curving toward the hilltop. "Every story has some basis in reality even if only slight."

I was more concerned about the incident, it was curious. Did Birbeck have an accomplice in uniform? Or was it Birbeck's way of reintroducing himself? I smiled because I knew my life couldn't go on until everything had been resolved. I wasn't naive enough to think Birbeck provided all the solutions. It was too neat. In any case there was the murder of Bartholomew Fair I witnessed at Bay Town. I had seen a woman in a pink skirt push the victim. There was a lot of speculation during the Canon's trial but no evidence. It would make sense if it was Carrie removing Birbeck's right hand man, however she never admitted guilt and by the end of the trial I doubted it entirely because of the lack of evidence. For Carrie, revenge only concerned killing Birbeck, no one else would do. If nothing else, staying with Carrie would provide a new opportunity to fill in the blanks. She probably knew more than her father who'd put up such a preposterous defence.

"Where is this place? It's getting on for twelve fifteen and I'm starving," Tucker cracked open a bottle of warm Newcastle Brown, drank, then belched.

"If we hadn't gone round the foreshore twice we'd be there," I explained.

"Well there was such hot totty."

I smiled at Tucker's description.

"Still, you wouldn't appreciate that." Tucker looked in the vanity mirror. His green eyes fixed mine.

I decided not to rise to the bait and smiled, holding his stare.

"You queer!" he said half in jest.

Again I ignored the remark. "You can't miss the house it's on the left as you go into Whitby. A great gothic pile with a tower."

"That's where…" Tucker didn't finish the sentence.

"That's where David found the body," Nigel said. "We can't have any pussyfooting around. We're scientists, things happened, now they're in the past and we move on."

"Nice speech," I said.

"Glad you liked it; I've been rehearsing it for the last hour. Is that the place?"

"Yes!" The grey stone building emerged from its gardens. They looked untended and the pea gravel was choked with weeds. I pulled myself from the back seat and stretched. "It has a great view over the port and abbey," I ventured.

"What do you think, Tucker?" There were whispered consultations.

"Carboniferous limestone from Askrigg? It must have cost a fortune to ship in the 1870's."

"There were trains," I offered.

"See that's the difference between a first and a second. We don't mistake bricks for felsite."

I held my hands up in surrender. It had been a silly mistake on the practical exam but there were so many rock sections to identify and I'd dwelt too long on an Icelandic basalt.

"Hello!" Carrie appeared at the top of the steps wearing a short black skirt and black stockings. I wasn't going to touch her but she grabbed me and planted a kiss firmly on my lips.

"You're wasting your time there," Tucker announced.

Carrie smiled, "Not always. Welcome to my home. I'll show you round and you can sort out your rooms. It won't be as you remembered, David, I had to let all the staff go. We fend for ourselves."

"No problem, some of your servants were very good at pain…"

"As well as being in Birbeck's employ."

"How many of them are left to murder?" Nigel asked as we mounted the stairs.

"I've never murdered anyone," Carrie stated.

"There was Birbeck's right hand man. The one who fell from The North Cheek."

Carrie laughed, "You've a lot to learn about people who wear pink skirts."

"Like?" I ran my hand along the accumulated dust on the windowsill.

"They don't have to be girls." Carrie stared at me and watched for the penny to drop. I took a deep breath and felt my stomach tighten. She patted me on the cheek.

"I thought I'd put you opposite me, where I can keep an eye."

I entered the room. It smelt of polish and had a view down the Esk valley to the Abbey. "Thanks." I threw my bag onto the bed and sat down next to it. The springs creaked. I toured the prints decorating the panelling, then opened the window and looked out on the world. I took in the vista of a marvellous landscape composed of Jurassic rocks, from the Tabular hills of the Moors to the deeply eroded valley of the River Esk, the sediments which made them all appeared as paragraphs in my thesis. At least I hoped there was a place for each of them.

I wondered what I was really doing here. Laying to rest the ghosts of that last summer here or forcing myself to face the truth. One thing I knew was that I couldn't move forward without unravelling the story.

There was a knock at the door. "Hello, is it ok?" I heard a slight hesitation in Carrie's voice, "I wanted to find you alone. I have this for you. It arrived whilst I was in Hull." She passed over a letter. I recognised the writing and my heart raced. I carefully slid open the envelope.

Dear David,

I have found a special friend. Andrea is beautiful. My parents are delighted and I want you to be happy for me as well. I don't know if that's possible. I'm sorry if it isn't and I'm equally sorry if it is. It's a no-win situation. The wedding is planned for November and I know you'll be disappointed not to be invited. I hope you'll understand.

Yours, Jevan

I felt light-headed and sat down in a cane chair. I heard the letter drop and I felt the tears rise and emerge uncontrollably. Carrie must have left during my outburst. When I'd composed myself a little I stood up and locked the door before throwing myself on the bed. Later, much later--as the evening sun was shining through the window-- I picked up the letter and read it again. The words scanned exactly as the first time. I could find no hidden meaning. Finally I noticed the envelope and picked it up. It was franked in York. I looked out of the window. Ricky was somewhere nearby. I had to remember his duplicity. Ricky was dead and now Jevan was dead to me. I hit my fist on the windowsill before going to my rucksack and unwrapping some green. I opened the window and rolled the joint. I drew on it deeply.

"Are you coming out?" It was Carrie again.

I looked at myself in the mirror, my eyes slightly bloodshot and my cheeks with a higher colour. "Where are you going?"

"To St. Mary's graveyard via a few pubs."

"Thanks, but not tonight."

"Are you sure?"

"I'm not sure of anything. No, I'm sure. See you in the morning."

"Okay. I'll lock you in."

"Thanks."

Carrie's footsteps faded as she descended the stairs. The front door closed. There was silence. I smoked again then slept.

"Right, that's it!" I thought as I woke up. It was a beautiful morning with fair weather clouds skidding across a blue sky. I sorted my backpack with hammer, notebook and map, clinometer, and waterproof. I left a note on the kitchen table before letting myself out.

I sat in a box pew in Saint Mary's Church. I knew this had been one of John Betjeman's favourite places. A mediaeval church done out to enlightenment specifications with mystery playing second fiddle to the word of god. I stretched my feet and rucked up a runner of old carpet. Even in summer the nave was unpleasantly cold as if the damp from decaying bodies had permeated the stones.

Outside in the graveyard I admired the view over the cliff edge and out to sea. It was high tide and boats of all sizes were emerging from the harbour in a colourful procession.

"Excuse me?"

I jumped on hearing the man's voice.

"Have you a light?" The old man held out his cigarette.

"Sorry, yes. You startled me, I was deep in thought."

"It won't be long before I'm like them," the old man surveyed the headstones.

"I'm afraid there's no cure for mortality." I lit his cigarette.

"Mind I don't regret anything. I first came a courting here in 1929. After the war we settled."

"Whitby's that sort of place; my Grandparents courted here but then settled in Hull." I'd researched that part of the family history. Grandpa first came here on a Norton with his friend as pillion. He fell in love with Whitby and took loads of photos. His best friend Cyril accompanied him. They stayed at The White Horse and Griffin. Sometimes on a winter's night I'd take out the album and flick through the pages. Grandpa had carefully labelled each photo: time, place, people.

"Don't suppose you remember who you danced to at the spa in 1938?"

"Well, now you ask, I do! It was Percival Mackey's Band," the old man smiled and doffed his cap then walked back towards the abbey.

"*Let's be sentimental, romance is accidental,*" Grandpa used to sing that whilst developing his photos or he'd hum *Charmaine*. As he dipped the paper in developer the image would form. Slowly he'd wash the solution over the sheet until the contrast was just right before submerging the photo in fixer and pinning it up to dry.

Grandpa's life was like the song. Across the dance floor of Whitby Spa, he first spied Marjorie. It was love at first sight and they courted in Whitby most weekends until Grandpa plucked up courage to go to Stockton to visit her father and ask permission. They got engaged. On the return journey Grandpa lost control of his Norton and broke his leg. He spent the night in agony amongst the heather. A milk van found him in the morning. He was already in traction when Marjorie saw him again.

It was a complex break but throughout the spring of '39, Marjorie nursed him. She had him taking the first tentative steps round the ward when war was declared.

I looked out at the headstones. Mostly they were a good quality sandstone but even those who had paid for immortality were rendered anonymous by the weathering of two centuries.

Later, walking along the cliff tops in the July sunlight lifted my spirits. Birds sang and the corn swayed in the breeze but all the time the cool salt air fanned me. I finally reached the caravan park above Saltwick Bay. It was here that Ricky *discovered* the ichthyosaur skull he'd somehow planted. The same fossil languished in the bottom of my wardrobe at Down's Hall. If I wrote about it the university would insist on receiving it as a generous gift and I had half a mind to return it to its previous owner, the Canon. If however it meant the difference between an upper second degree and a first, I would succumb.

I heard the groans before I saw the arched legs and buttocks emerging from the long grass. For a moment I watched then slipped quietly away without disturbing the couple. I felt a momentary pang as to what I was missing. I wondered if Carrie would take me back. I wondered if I wanted Carrie. The revelations from the trial were painful. What sort of aunt allows her niece to develop a career in pornographic films? The Canon's defence team had grilled Jocaster on the point. Had it been child abuse? The question was asked more than once but Carrie had been blunt. She enjoyed sex. She saw nothing wrong with enjoying sex or in providing that enjoyment for others. She asked the barrister if he'd seen any of Jocaster's work. The court dissolved in laughter when he replied only in the line of duty.

"Well perhaps I should provide you with a personal copy?" Carrie had said. There were no more questions on the subject.

The route down to the bay was a muddy path cut into the cliff. In places the descent was easy but towards the base, boulders jutted out at odd angles. I unpacked my bag and began to work.

I spent several hours in the company of a sideritic sandstone. This I knew was a continuation of the Dogger bed which had

protected Wojek and me from the incoming tide. I shivered and looked out to sea.

I was fascinated by the lone sentinel of Black Nab. I remembered thinking when I first saw it, the outcrop of hard Jurassic sediment was a harbinger of death. How many boats had foundered here? How many sailors drowned? Boats full of coal bound for Hull, boats full of piss steaming for the Alum works at Ravenscar. The poor souls who looked on the blackened edifice and knew they were lost.

The waves were calm and near low tide. I drew some of the bivalve fossils and attempted to glean something from their position within the bed. If nothing else the fossils provided evidence of the age of the rock but evidence as I knew to my cost wasn't proof.

"I'm glad you let me know where you were working," Carrie pushed her hand round my waist and bend down to kiss my lips.

"I thought it sensible."

She stood astride me and prevented me from getting up. She moved a little closer. I realised she was wearing no knickers under her skirt. I felt myself smile, "it's a bit crowded for sex."

"Yes," she looked up to the cliff, "and we're being watched."

I turned and saw a man disappear from view but the sunlight reflected from his binoculars as he hid in the grass, "Birbeck?"

"No, his assistant, you'll know him as DS Laing."

"I have particular reason to remember him. He arrested me at The Post Office. It would be easy enough to get behind him and give one almighty push."

Carrie patted my cheek. "You're learning. But this is a deadly game we're playing and we hold no trump cards yet. Besides, we have a pact -- Birbeck."

I looked at Carrie's legs and followed their line upwards, "but we know far too much."

"And Birbeck can't touch you or I. He's blown that. Anything happens to us and he's joining my dad in Hull jail. They say cops have a hard time behind bars…"

Carrie smiled and held out an arm. I allowed her to help me up. "Rocks must be awfully boring?"

"No, they're fascinating." I said with passion and she laughed. "Look at that cross bedding showing the position of a river in the early Jurassic. Dinosaurs might have drunk from that very spot and given enough time we might find their footprints!"

"What is it about boys and dinosaurs?" Carrie picked up my rucksack and offered it too me.

I looked around to check I had all my belongings.

"Women prefer relationships, subjects you can talk about and discuss. That's why I'm doing sociology. As far as I'm concerned beaches are for sandcastles and sex," she winked.

I stammered a few words in reply.

"You see, men get so tongue-tied about sex. They want it; they want it desperately, even when they think they should refuse. One thing you can guarantee is they can't talk about it."

"Hang on there; we just can't talk about it to the person who matters most."

"And that's me?"

"For the moment, if you'd like it to be but…"

"But you'd rather be sucking Ricky's dick or putting Jevan in heaven? I suppose we should call him Jevan now?"

I thought about that. What Carrie said was true despite his announcement of a wedding. "I still can't believe Jevan would do that. Get married."

"There are lots of reasons to get married; very few of them involve love." Carrie picked a pebble up and flicked it against the cliff.

"Is that from your sociology lecture? I'd thought of being a social worker but I'm not inadequate enough yet?"

"You have a poor opinion of social workers," Carrie waited.

"Does it show? Drew always said her care worker was the first person to bugger her."

"Yes and a friend of mine married the mother of the kids in his care, so he could do the touchy feely bits for real. Shit happens and we might as well acknowledge it instead of handing out prison sentences. There are some parts of the world where I'd be hung for that scene I did in Jocaster's video."

"Likewise if I ever get Jevan's cock up my arse. I've read the news, I know Thatcher hates Peter Tatchell and ILEA"

"Jenny Lives with Eric and Martin."

"It's ludicrous, they want us to accept people from different backgrounds but not people of different sexuality. It makes me angry."

"Well do something about it."

"I might very well do just that. There's a publisher called GMP. They're looking for gay themed stories."

"Bravo. That's a start."

"Of course I'd have to live in London. You see I've not considered the consequences," I turned over a few pieces of rock before asking, "What's your real interest in me?"

Carrie stood and blocked my way. "At first just sex, then a way of seeking revenge, now I see you as a friend. There is however one thing you can do for me. It's day fourteen and I want to get pregnant."

I stared at Carrie, not knowing what to say.

"You can close your mouth. I don't want to marry you. It's just a simple biological act I'd like you to perform. I've completed my degree and I want to experience motherhood whilst I'm young. My mum left it until she was thirty five."

"You're lucky. Mum was twenty and grandpa was so angry with dad for having sex out of wedlock he banned him from the house. His heart melted when he saw me."

"You must have been a beautiful baby! This isn't a fad. Gabby and I really want a baby, we want to be a family, so you can forget any notions about it not being looked after like other social worker's kids."

"Aren't there moral implications and fatherly responsibilities?"

"There are but I absolve you of them," Carrie looked at me intently.

"You want me to be the biological father but with no strings?"

"That about sums things up. What you can't provide financially, the proceeds of Jocaster's porn films can and will."

"Why?" I tried to search through the debris of our relationship for an answer.

"I'd have thought that was obvious. You're bisexual, so am I. My girlfriend and I are quite capable of bringing up a baby. The only problem is her oviducts are blocked, mine are all ready to receive and on day fourteen, they're waiting!"

"There's a condition." I hesitated whilst collecting my thoughts. "I want the child to know I'm the father."

"Look, you can visit on Sunday afternoons and Christmas as far as I'm concerned. I don't want you out of the way but I certainly want you in!" Carrie tugged at my arm.

I pontificated, "I'll have to give it some serious thought. I can't just start a baby without thinking of the consequences."

"No neither can I," Carrie agreed. She started teasing me and I fell hook line and sinker.

One minute you're studying currents 225 million years old, the next you're propositioned to be a father. Maybe there was something in the air. Mother swore it was the ozone at the seaside which made people *different*. More likely it was the company I was keeping. Everyone I knew was challenging the barriers of normality, whether it was sex or murder.

Carrie smoothed back my hair and eased herself up on her elbow.

"Gabby, the landlady of The Cook Arms? The thing is I'm not really surprised. She talked about meeting someone special in gender neutral terms."

"I didn't realise until after the trial." Carrie got up and brushed the sand off her thighs.

"I think you should cover up before that party of school girls arrives."

"What!" I said hurriedly pulling on my clothes.

Carrie laughed. When I looked I saw the beach was deserted. I'd fallen for another of Carrie's jokes. If I could be taken in by her how was I going to avoid Birbeck's traps?

"That was immensely satisfying. If Jevan could see you now he'd be jealous, not you." she laughed and danced away down the beach. I did not follow.

Chapter 15: 1975

"You tire me out David. I'm sixty five you know and doing much better than most of my contemporaries, who are pushing up daisies."

I thought about this as we planted out alyssum and lobelia along the borders. Grandpa sat on his trade mark mat. With one leg shorter than the other he had to sit to weed or risk falling as he bent forward. He was a man of meticulous method. He changed into old clothes and shoes to garden as though Gran were still around to chide him for dirtying a best shirt.

The garden was mostly lawn with narrow borders along one side and interrupted on the other by a path to the shed. This wooden creation had stretches of new wood sitting incongruously next to old. It still leant as a result of a doodlebug exploding nearby, or so Grandpa claimed. Adjacent to this, the white and pink heads of japonica swayed in the gentle summer breeze. A box hedge delineated the transition to the vegetable garden, screened from view like a Victorian lady's legs.

He paused leaving me holding a small plant in its cardboard pot. I watched him do this several times. He sat in silence a moment longer before returning to the present.

"She keeps talking to me." I saw the tears fill his eyes as he spoke. His blue eyes submerged.

We'd been living at Godwyn since Gran passed away. Her heart gave in after years of struggling with angina. Gran's health had received its most serious setback after contracting rheumatic fever. At the end of the illness the babies who might have become my twin uncles were stillborn and buried without ceremony under an apple tree.

"It was the war. Things were different then," mum said in response to my questions on the issue.

I'd heard many stories from *the war*. Aunt Gertie alluded to long ago events on a Saturday tea-time. She was a tall lady, with her hair scraped back in a severe bun. She sported pinz-nez on a chain around her neck. I'd once had to untaffle her pearls from the cheap gold chain of her glasses before she could read an extract from the paper about her son. Bartholomew was an excellent sportsman, holder of the college blues in several athletic events. He was going to be a lawyer. Aunt Gertie always said this with a smile. It scored points as mum had studied law before giving all up to be a mother.

I followed shortly before her marriage much to everyone's chagrin. I've often wondered if I was a disappointment, when all you get is David Jones. A strange fourteen year old addicted to castles and fossils – someone who hates football, loves clothes and touched third base with the only lad doing ballet in the fifth year.

Gran was worried that mum wouldn't survive having her first child. I'm not certain what went wrong but I am an only one. I can imagine Gran fussing and worrying over her daughter, she was a terminal worrier but indomitable at getting her own way.

In the end, the consequences of rheumatic fever, took her from us. Mum and I were called to her bedside in the middle of the night. A taxi brought us out into the country. I remember seeing my breath form vapour in the cold night air and looking up at a multitude of stars invisible at home because of the street lights. Grandpa didn't wait for us to step in, he went straight back to the downstairs bedroom and we found him sitting holding Gran's hand. There was light from a side lamp behind him, but the bed and Gran were in shadow. That's when I heard the noise. The rasping breaths which emerged as a panic for air from someone not ready to die. Finally the sheets didn't move.

"Say goodbye, David."

I kissed Gran's warm but clammy forehead, as I moved into a corner she coughed up blackened sputum. I looked away.

"Go and take yourself to bed."

That was the last time I saw her. I suppose you don't normally think of death but for me it occupied some point of every day. How could you forget finding your dad lying on the kitchen floor? I lay awake in the upstairs room and watched the stars until the window streaked with condensation. I woke and it was silent. I knew Gran had passed away.

When I woke again, I dressed myself and went out into the garden. It was sunny but dew lay on the grass, heavy spheres hung from the tips of each blade. The birds sang and the lilac flowered in the hedgerow. I moved to get my bike out from the shed. As I approached I heard this curious sound almost like the tinkling of bells. I put my ear to the door. Inside something was being broken. I peered through a gap in the door. Grandpa was standing there with a small hammer shattering squares of glass.

I gasped, "Grandpa!" I exclaimed though it was barely more than a whisper.

He stopped and looked at the door. His face was smeared, his eyes blood shot. He stood there helpless, knowing I was there and yet unable to respond. He had frozen mid-action.

I opened the door. I looked at the floor. In front of him was a great pile of shattered glass negatives.

"I'm destroying the past," he said calmly.

I gently pulled the hammer from his hand and put down one of the last negatives. I pulled him out into the garden. He seemed so insubstantial he might be a ghost. I put my arms around him. Slowly he tightened his around me and I heard deep sobs erupt.

Mum ran out, her mandarin dressing gown flowing behind her. She led Grandpa away and ordered me to play. That had been my intention but Grandpa had left the shed unlocked. I stole inside and searched amongst the shards. Carefully I picked up the negatives. I saw a hand, a smiling face, all of them detached from the reality of that moment, frozen in time and many destroyed.

I was in luck however, several slides survived and yet more could be salvaged. I gathered them all up. In the main they were pictures of Gran and mum amongst sites I knew well. Beverley Minster, the Black Mill, Aldborough beach, the boat on the River Hull. I set these in a cardboard box. It was hard to make out this negative: A pile of rock? There was a wall, a ruined house and then I saw the hand emerge from the ruins. The city of Hull lit by a strange light. I felt my heart quicken. These were the photos of Hull being bombed. They were the ones Grandpa had refused to destroy and yet so nearly had after thirty odd years of waiting. I placed the slides in another box and by the time mum called me in for breakfast, I had perhaps a hundred negatives. All of them were hidden under the lose floorboard beneath my bed.

I found the idea of the past so much more appealing than the present but then the present is an infinitely more difficult place in which to live.

Chapter 16: Uniformitarianism

It makes me happy that I studied geology because it is through this science I have come to realise there is no god, indeed there never was one. I can live with this absence of faith where mum cannot. I'm more inclined to the view that it is only our atoms which are reincarnated. We are all the stuff of stars endlessly recycled through time.

The definition of uniformitarianism is that the Earth's surface was shaped by the gradual processes of weathering, erosion and occasional cataclysms like earthquakes and without divine intervention. Geology has the answer for everything. Noah's Flood was caused by the Atlantic spilling back into the Mediterranean Basin. The destruction of Sodom was a mud slide caused by an earthquake. There are those who would not like to believe this. There are those who won't hold a ruler up to the horizon for fear they realise it isn't a straight line.

The bay contained many examples of uniformitarianism -- the present is the key to the past. The large boulder diverting the stream was undoubtedly a product of erosion. The rounded pebbles littering the bay mostly had come from the cliffs and had been washed by two tides a day for 13000 years. The trees sending out roots into the rich soil eventually found grip in the rocks below, growing and splitting their surfaces. There's one thing geology cannot do and that's capture the beauty of Hayburn Wyke. The way trees clinging to the cliff were misshapen by the harsh easterlies, the sound of rocks rolling up with each breaking wave, the cry of seagulls echoing round the cliffs and the indefinable smell of somewhere not yet tamed. All of this framed by sandstone cliffs.

When I think of how many people have been murdered in this vendetta, I try to put myself inside Birbeck's mind. He probably acquired the taste for killing when he strangled Josephine De Vile three years ago. As a long standing lover I can see jealousy as the motive when she insisted on going back to her husband. Next he murdered Ricky, who knew too much and Drew because of what she knew and who she was. Mike was a witness. He had to go. I wondered about the lack of a body and cast a glance out to sea. The girl in a pink skirt pushed Bartholomew in revenge. Maybe that rattled Birbeck, the realisation that those around him weren't immune from being dragged into the affray. This set me thinking about whom else was close to Birbeck. It wasn't our demise he wanted but our implication in some crime which would send us down, preferably a crime he'd committed.

Finally there was that link back to the 1940's. Grandpa spoke of his revenge on a man called Birbeck who stopped him from opening a photographic studio. I felt sure the family moved out here when Birbeck was forced to resign in 1945. He'd been syphoning off rent money from a set of pre-fabs at the top end of The Broadway and keeping the mother of twin girls for what Grandpa described as *'immoral purposes.'* Birbeck as a boy was brought up in the villa but another disaster: the money ran out and the place was sold to the C of E. Sometime in the 1970's The Canon took up residence. How each generation of Birbeck must have plotted revenge. The stories which they passed down had shaped the processes of DCI Birbeck's mind. I wondered how easy it would be to prove these points. How easy it would be to nail Birbeck and use the law against him. I opened the palm of my hand to reveal the scar from the bolt gun. If it wasn't possible to find the evidence then revenge would have to do.

So if Birbeck received an adrenaline rush every time he committed a crime, surely by now he was addicted. Each time he'd have to get closer to the edge to maintain the effect and someone close to the edge can easily be pushed off. I smiled. Smuggling fossils, blackmail, murder. What else had Birbeck done under the cover of Her Majesty's Constabulary?

I examined my morality. This was hardly inspiring. I reassured myself that Carrie was unlikely to get pregnant the first time we fucked although I remembered just as my cock stiffened against denim that we'd come simultaneously. What is the morality in providing a woman with a child who is going to be loved? If it made any type of couple happy, surely the sex of the parent's was immaterial? Carrie deserved some happiness and if a child was born both Carrie and Gabby had made it clear I would always be welcome as the father. Of course I was no better than anyone, except Birbeck. For as doors in my life had closed, there would be others to open.

A girl in a pink skirt waved from the view point between the holm oaks. I waved back. I wondered who it was. I walked back towards the path by the waterfall. The girl did not move. I looked between the Holm oaks and could still see her blond hair was not quite right.

My curiosity was piqued, I wondered if there was any connection. I got within twenty feet of her.

"Have you seen Birbeck?" The girl asked. Only it wasn't a girl's voice.

I struggled to understand what was going on but as I saw her smile I realised it was Jevan. I shouted. He vanished into the woods.

Perhaps I should have run after him but I decided against it and returned to my work. It didn't strike me as odd that Jevan should dress as a woman until several minutes later. I laughed at the implications. So that part of Carrie's story was true. She didn't murder Bartholomew Fair. Jevan had pushed Aunt Gertie's precious son over the precipice. As I examined the plant bed at the southern end of Hayburn Wyke, I remembered the first time I came here, how Ricky – as I knew him then - and I were interrupted by a police helicopter. I'd always meant to come back to this place. It had lost none of its appeal in the interim. The river cascaded onto the beach, the great bluff blocks of sandstone provided a vantage point from which to view the bay. The lush vegetation made me think of those coves frequented by Rupert Bear in his Annual. Here I was trying to distinguish the types of fern from the Jurassic apart and fathom some reason for the jumble of leaves. A storm perhaps but the layer was too extensive. I tried a new tack. If this was a vast swamp and periodically the sea flooded in then maybe that would cause a layer rich in plants. The rocks above and below would confirm my theory and quickly did. Some vast delta, like the Nile of now, alternately laying down sediments in an insect infested swamp or the surface was washed clean away by a rise in sea level.

"It's taken a great deal of courage for me to confront you like this." Jevan said. He folded his arms and waited.

Jevan stared down at me. I brushed my dirty fingers down my jeans. "It's great to see you."

"I couldn't decide," he shifted uncomfortably, "it's not an easy thing to admit. I hoped you would hate me for being deviant."

'I don't hate you but I don't like cross dressing. Call me old fashioned but I like my men as men and women as women." I sat on a comfortable rock. "You look too much like Carrie, which is quite alarming really but explains a lot." I unscrewed my thermos and poured a coffee. "Do you want to share it with me?"

Jevan nodded.

I sipped the sweet liquid, "What would your future wife think?"

"You don't even know her name," Jevan accused. "That's how much interest you take."

"The only time I'll take any interest in your wife," I confessed, "is when she divorces you." I passed him the cup.

"That's great, I thought you'd at least say congratulations." Jevan threw the coffee away.

I stared at him. I smiled, "I managed to write congratulations on the card, even though I didn't mean it. It's a formality."

"So you say things you don't mean?"

"Don't we all?"

Jevan got up and began to walk away.

He'd made me angry again, "At least I'm honest enough to admit I love you, even though you're a transvestite."

"You have a way of saying that which makes it sound sick."

I didn't want to appear rude but Jevan had walked out too often. I still wanted to forgive him. "You wrote to me and said you were getting married, so what do you want with me?"

"I don't know!" He said and walked away

When Jevan turned back I could see the tears in his eyes, he looked at me for a few seconds then ran across the boulders before vanishing into the woods. I was going to follow, to beg forgiveness but anger had hardened inside me.

I thought about the nature of tolerance and what we're prepared to accept in our day to day lives. There's a fine line between liking and loathing and we step over it at our peril. To mum and Aunt Gertie, I would already be beyond redemption if they knew who I loved. I prised open the soft grey rock to reveal a perfect fossil of Ginko huttoni, its leaf spread out like a miniature fan and radiating with veins through which sugars once flowed. The plant was at the beginning of the food chain 200 million years ago and it is still alive now, it's just the herbivores have shrunk, a perfect example of uniformitarianism in action. Please do not mention creation. The Canon writes to me of its significance and how we've overlooked god in all this science. Let's shout it now. Shout into the rising tide. Shout into the clear air. There is no god and there never was. It was a nice idea for the infancy of humanity but geology continues without the benefit of philosophy or religion, indeed it would continue apace without people. The bay echoed to my words. A solitary rock fell. The water continued over the fall and the leaves of the oaks rustled. Everything remained as before. Other pieces of plant material briefly appeared on my hand before the fissile nature of the sediment destroyed their outline.

I had been filling in the gaps and completing the puzzle. A lot more events made sense now. Whilst my grandparents were sitting on the veranda sipping sherry and watching mum and uncle Tom play, Birbeck was using his ill gotten gains and moving his family away from Hull to the quiet resort of Whitby. He'd put enough aside to buy a Victorian villa. The retirement he'd long envisaged was short lived. The police arrived. There was a big scandal reported in all the papers.

The story of grandpa's revenge must have become the talking point of the Birbeck household and his son eventually found himself in possession of a means of retribution.

Birbeck's motives throughout had been to seek revenge and perhaps through this, there was a way to lure this man to the edge and trap him. To give him his moment of glory then cruelly take it away. I smiled. I knew it wasn't pleasant but then vengeance was never likely to be. I thought about the type of message which might get him to the cliff by Saint Mary's. The best bait is always the biggest and in the scheme of things that was me. As history has repeatedly proved, if you want to catch a man in power you need a man who can't get there without the former's removal. It seems a little odd to learn something from the politics of Rome but shows there is nothing new in human nature.

I put down the fossil and had a go at composing the note. It wasn't good enough. I continued my analysis of the plant bed before climbing the clay paths to the top. I sat at The Hayburn Wyke with a pint of shandy and waited for the telephone to become free. I rang Carrie. There was no reply.

"Do they sell Newcastle Brown there?" Tucker asked when I managed to get an answer on the telephone. "I spent this morning chasing birds at the South Bay. Gave one a good fuck on the cliffs below The Clifton. Got a round of applause from some lads who'd been watching!"

I stretched out my legs. I drank. I took off my boots and studied some of the notes I'd made. I drank a little more. In the heat and without food I felt drained. I ordered a chip butty.

"Well, you look very relaxed, for a dead man." Birbeck sat down opposite me and swirled his brandy. He appeared drawn.

"I've seen your friend Ricky, only it isn't Ricky, is it?" He sipped the amber liquid as though it were poison. "That's the trouble with twins, can't tell them apart!"

I squeezed ketchup onto the last part of the butty and took a final bite. "I suppose that's how Jocaster played Josephine for two years?"

Birbeck thought about this. "No, I was never fooled by Jocaster. But to confess I knew was to confess to murder and that would never do."

I raised my glass and saluted the DCI.

"Everything came together in you, David Jones, the past and the present. You don't have a future of course. You know too much."

I felt my throat dry even without Birbeck uttering the threat but I tried a reposte. "Funny I thought that statement better described you."

Birbeck finished his drink and slammed down the glass. He recovered his composure, "Tell me, would you have pushed Drew?"

I smiled it seemed an opportune moment to reveal my hand, "Yes, as easily as Ricky pushed Bartholomew Fair."

"Only it wasn't Ricky. He was dead and buried, it was Jevan, that cross dressing shit shoveller!"

"You sound as though you don't like him much."

"Less than you."

"I find that surprising given our history. Tell me how did you find out about the connection to my grandpa?"

"Now that much is simple, Barty Fair. As soon as I mentioned your name he told me the background. I smiled like the proverbial Cheshire cat."

"So we know where each other stands," I said spying Nigel's car coming round the bend. I felt a wave of relief, although I knew I was safe in such a public place.

"A little nearer the edge," Birbeck joked.

I finished my pint and stood to leave, "I'll see you later."

Birbeck grabbed my wrist, "I enjoyed watching that hole being drilled in your hand. I've got something slow and painful in mind for your demise, a luscious death that will beautifully preserve you. I'm trying it out on a rather unsatisfying victim at present, Jevan's prospective wife, the lovely Andrea. Her screams might have woken the gods if they hadn't all stopped listening a long time ago. And when she squirmed it was such a turn on I had to fuck her."

I could see the evil thoughts light up his eyes. I felt a shudder creep through my body. "You won't get away with it."

"My dear David, I already have."

I walked towards the car. Birbeck was playing mind games but perhaps it wasn't all one sided. I thought I'd also scored a minor victory.

"Was that Birbeck?" Tucker asked.

I nodded. "He looks like a cop, though more Columbo than Kojak. He's holding someone captive. My guess is he'll move soon. Tonight, tomorrow even, but he can't afford to let things drift."

"Who could he hold who'd make a difference?" Tucker looked at Nigel.

Nigel looked at Tucker. He revved the engine and did a handbrake turn out of the car park and up the hill to the main road. "Carrie was fine when we left half an hour ago. Honest? We're going to have to be much more careful if we're to be any use!" Nigel confessed.

"Don't worry," I wanted to sound strong."It's not Carrie. He wants Jevan to hate me, so he's picked on Andrea."

"I thought he was as queer as fuck."

"You don't have to be queer to enjoy men." I said. "He might be bi like me."

"Well they're all queer in my book. Being gay is bad for your health." I saw Tucker's white teeth in the vanity mirror.

"Well, I'm bi and proud of it!"

"Bye, bye bi guy!" Tucker waved and both people in the front found the joke funny. I sat back on the seat and saw my scowl in the mirror. I swung my aching feet up onto the seat and waited to get back to Carrie's place.

The heather was in full bloom on the moors encrusting the flat terrain with an amethyst glow. We descended past Foul Syke Farm. There was a solitary hen house with a pitched roof and metal bars isolated in a patch of green. I imagined the child from my story chained inside the contraption. The image of Canon Franklin sitting alone in his prison cell interrupted my train of thought. The moment was lost.

"You've gone quiet?" Tucker said.

"I'm writing a letter to Canon Franklin," I lied. "Well at least roughing it out."

As we pulled into the driveway of the villa, I spied a yellow sports car in the drive. My heart quickened. Surely this meant Jocaster was back. I met her in the doorway, she was smoking a cheroot and looking as though her nerves were frayed.

"I tried," she said.

"I didn't think you'd ever come back after…"

"No, neither did I but Carrie and you are in danger. Danger is best shared." She moved into the sunlight and smiled, "I think we can defeat Birbeck. He is after all only one very ordinary man."

I took heart from this.

"Walk with me in the garden," Jocaster invited.

We strode past the borders of hostas, peony and salvia to places where snap dragons and great swags of nasturtiums rolled across the neglected paths. We walked until we could just make out Whitby Abbey on the headland with its ruined windows peering vacantly on the mass of humanity below.

"I'm packing everything and leaving for pastures new."

"Iceland," I said. "The rock sample you gave me was good Icelandic basalt."

Jocaster smiled and brushed my cheek. "There'll always be a part for you. Well until you lose that svelte shape of yours."

I lit a cigarette, "I'd do it if I could be with Jevan."

"Ah! Jevan, I must talk to him." She deadheaded some of the Iceberg roses. "There are no guarantees in this life and sometimes we must suffer and move on."

I knew she was right. "It's being back here, all the memories of that summer, the hopes, the promises, some have faded like these roses, others grow apace like these suckers. It is a rare branch which produces white blooms in profusion."

Jocaster smiled.

"I know the end is near. Birbeck has Jevan's wife. I don't think he'll harm her. It's a mind game. Jevan has to turn me in."

"Well, I never wanted him to marry Andrea. He doesn't really love her, so no good can come from a relationship with your brother's widow. I know they haven't tied the knot yet but you get my drift." Jocaster placed her finger over my lips and bent slightly as though the effort of thinking was great. "It must be dark. It must be lonely," she looked up. "I know, meet him at the cliff edge by the abbey."

I swallowed hard. "He'll push me off, I know he will!"

"Yes of course he will but use your brain! Not everyone who is pushed, falls. It will be pitch black."

This set me thinking, there was still time to scout the land, to know it intimately. I agreed. "Whatever happens, it will be poetic justice."

Jocaster kissed me. "Don't worry, I'm on your side. I couldn't bear to see another mum at the funeral of her son, no matter how prodigal."

"I'll bear that in mind. Can I borrow your car?" I was surprised when she passed me the keys.

"Fold back the roof, you'll get more looks. There's more men than just Jevan out there. Jealousy works well as a galvaniser."

Jocaster had given me hope and the germ of an idea. I smiled and I thanked her with a kiss before striding across the lawn. I drove through Hawsker and took the coast road to the abbey. I wanted everyone to see me but there was hardly anyone around. I parked up in the abbey car park and began searching the cliff edge. In places the cliff fell sheer but at one point, almost lined up with the top line of gravestones, a thin band of harder iron rich sandstone protruded a few feet. I double checked the position of everything. I also took the precaution of gingerly climbing down to ensure it took my weight. I had a sudden attack of vertigo watching the waves break and the trawlers making their way back into port on the high tide. I stretched up and could just reach the edge of the cliff. I pulled myself up in a very ungainly fashion much to the alarm of an old man walking his dog. I smiled and looked down over the edge. I gave a mock salute and checked the alignments.

I lined myself with the final grave and walked to the edge. I took a deep breath and again slid down. All was ready. If only Drew had been able to use her knowledge of geology. That thought brought tears to my eyes. All that was past and gone, the lost souls who I'd known once. My own lost soul. Drew's death had defined me in so many ways and perhaps she might be proud.

I drove back through the town to The Monkees singing *Last Train to Clarkesville*. I winked at a dark haired youth who gave the car the eye. His insults reminded me not everyone is tolerant and set me thinking of my own reactions.

Jevan was waiting on the steps as I pulled into the drive. He got up, came over and embraced me.

"Hi."

"I'm going to do this because it has to end," I said, "I'm not doing it for you, still less for your wife. It's just that I was always told to stand up to bullies and clever though he might be, Birbeck is a bully and nothing else."

Jevan stepped back. "Don't you love me?"

"When I think of how you abandoned me I realise you don't deserve me. Then there's the matter of a man who puts on a pink skirt to murder people."

"It wasn't like that!"

I saw the faces of Nigel and Tucker looking through the lounge window. I stepped into the garden. Jevan followed.

"I don't deserve this. Why come back here? Why open up old wounds? Sorry," he said touching my hand.

"As I said, it's a lot to ask of anyone." I sat down next to the carved lion. The concrete was cold. "Perhaps you'd be honest with me?"

Jevan sat down next to me. "I wanted you. I wanted you but I couldn't replace Ricky with someone else. It seemed wrong so I went for the next best thing, Ricky's girlfriend. I know the wedding's three months off but we're living together. We'll soon get to know each other properly and fall in love."

I looked across the garden at the view. "Are you sure? An older man once asked me that and I smiled and ignored his advice. A dishonest love is worse than no love at all. You love me, I know you do. Is that fair?"

Jevan shrugged and lit a cigarette.

I took it from him and inhaled before passing it back. "Because every time I look in your eyes I see this light and it says just one thing to me."

Jevan smiled and looked away. "You ought to write romantic novels, they're the only things I know which end *and reader I married him*. Real life is more complex."

"But it doesn't have to be if we're frank. What's the point of getting rid of Birbeck if we can't be honest with each other?" I said, drawing the conversation to a close. "We're agreed."

'Yes! Yes, but when this is all over, I want you," Jevan moved closer.

We embraced and kissed, tongues moving in unison, "I bet your wife doesn't kiss like this?" I joked.

"No, but my brother used to." Jevan watched me as I took in the implication of his words. We sat for several minutes as the sun set and the abbey was lit with gold then red. As the sun vanished behind West Cliff the telephone rang.

"Don't answer it!" I demanded.

Jevan looked at me with indecision and anxiety before bounding up the steps. He looked back just the once and I knew he was trapped. I lit a cigarette and watched darkness descend.

Chapter 17: 1977

Elizabeth stood by the riverbank and looked out at the bungalow her father had planned and built. Beyond the plot, the trees gave the impression they were floating. They hovered like an ethereal island which the faintest breeze might transport to another realm. Elizabeth realised it was a mirage, a trick created by layers of cold air, a Fata Morgana.

In the lounge there was a photograph of just such an event, a double sunrise over the still fields of Thearne. Here on the flat plain of Holderness they were rare events and so she sat by the River Hull and watched until the sun burnt off the mist and the frost thawed.

The flat landscape allowed the golden light of winter to enliven the bare trees and dull brick of the bungalows as she walked back. Somewhere on the banks of the river she had been conceived. The thought made her shiver as though ancestral spirits where watching from within the crystals of ice. Here she was, a woman heading towards middle-age, thinking of the intimate moment which created her. With mum dead, dad was left to fend for himself and despite recently retiring he'd become frail. He still took photos. He never went anywhere without a camera and David was learning all he could from the old master, that much pleased her.

Elizabeth worried about David. She'd found some photos of naked men in a book next to articles about Auden and Isherwood. She decided she needed to keep a close eye on him, only he wasn't an easy person to keep tabs on. When all those hormones turned on, something didn't quite click with her son, he became distant, secretive and angry. She thought it might be about him losing his dad so young but Grandpa was there, her own dad was catapulted into the frame and had relished the opportunity.

Tom was keen on drilling geology into him but after that accident on Lebberston Cliffs, she wasn't so sure.

The letter arrived out of the blue and was followed by telephone calls from a lady who introduced herself as Hendrika. She claimed to be the daughter of Eldedt and she wanted to find out about her father's tour of duty. She didn't wish to upset people over the phone, which was thoughtful, so she asked if she could visit Thearne and do it in person.

Aunt Gertie appeared unconcerned about meeting Eldedt's daughter, she had heard so much about her during their brief liaison. Margaret was another matter. She was fiercely loyal to the memory of her father. Everyone knew Uncle Cyril wasn't her real dad but she persisted in the belief. Not even Aunt Gertie would discuss this stubbornness.

Even now Hendrika would be waiting at the bungalow, armed with pictures and documents. She promised to have plenty of evidence but presumably wanted more. Elizabeth had spent hours with her dad, sorting through papers and old photographs. She hoped it was all worthwhile and might provide an opportunity for nostalgia at least.

There was a left hand drive Opel parked outside the bungalow. The back seat was strewn with papers but the outside was polished.

With a little anxiety Elizabeth entered the house. It had been a long time since she'd seen the front room full of people, Mum's wake in fact. David busied himself with a camera, dad stared out of the window. The three ladies sat. Hendrika's features clearly showed she was related to Margaret. Margaret scowled obviously fully aware of this incriminating evidence.

"We are all a victim of our genes," she thought.

Hendrika's skin was ivorine and fragile. She held out an elegant hand. "We've made the introductions. You must be Elizabeth."

Elizabeth smiled, "I can see the resemblance."

Margaret shuffled uncomfortably on her seat. Aunt Gertie stared over her cane.

"I am Eldedt's daughter, here is my birth certificate, it is in Dutch as you can see and dated 4th April, 1940. That is why I am here."

The doorbell rang, "I'll get it," Elizabeth said.

"Hello."

"Hello, Bartholomew."

Margaret bounded from the front room, "Thank god you're here. I can't stand anymore of this. Come and talk to me in the kitchen."

"I came to give some support. I'm more than happy making tea."

Bartholomew hung his jacket in the hall, rolled up his shirt sleeves and followed his mum.

Elizabeth explained.

Hendrika's slender frame looked too delicate to sit, she appeared to perch on the edge of her seat as though she might make good her escape.

Aunt Gertie passed over the letters neatly tied with a ribbon. Hendrika sat back and relaxed as she read. She smiled then her face became stern before tears rolled down her cheeks.

"That is what I couldn't understand. I do now. He was frightened of death, frightened of not living each moment, so when he met you he fell in love."

A picture tumbled to the floor. "Did dad draw this?"

"No, that was Ernie."

Ernie turned his attention to the room. He picked up the drawing and scrutinised it, "my hand's not steady enough to do that detail now." He took himself to his chair.

"Are you alright dad?" She saw him rub his chest.

"Just a pulled muscle." He lied. "For a moment I was back there in 1941. It's alright, I'm in the present now." He spread out his arms and eased himself into the chair.

I was nervous about revelations but also curious. I couldn't remember my father well. When I thought of him, my enduring image was of him lying on the floor. I don't remember him reading to me or cuddling up in bed. Of course I knew what he looked like from pictures. I could hear his voice saying, "up the apples and pears to bed," or, "you must wake up now." I remember the smell of his breath: a curious mix of tobacco and mints. I couldn't imagine never meeting him of having no picture in my mind. I couldn't blame Hendrika for wanting to fill the gaps perhaps it's a need we all have – to understand our parents.

Hendrika passed across a picture of a dark haired man with a wide collar open at the neck. He was handsome. Margaret was drawn to his eyes sparkling with mischief. Her mother had always maintained her daughter had Eldedt's eyes.

Hendrika pulled a photo from her bag. She passed it to Aunt Gertie. "This was the last picture ever taken."

Aunt Gertie paused. "Look at him, Ernie. Isn't that just how we last saw him?"

Ernie nodded.

"He was shot in the head. I suppose it must have been quick. He's buried near Arnhem." Hendrika passed over a second photo. It was a simple cross. It read: Eldedt de Zurre: 1910 -1945. There was a long silence in which everyone held their own counsel.

The rickety old tea trolley was wheeled in. "Shall I be mum?" Barty asked trying to break the ice. He poured several cups of tea and passed round the sugar. "Ernie, I knew I had something to tell you.

My new boss, you'll never guess his name, it's Josiah Birbeck the son of…."

The saucer dropped. It split in two on the parquet floor. "Don't worry," I said, "We'll soon have it cleared up." I collected the pieces and left for the kitchen.

"Never mention that name again in my house," Ernie pronounced.

Hendrika took out a pen and notebook. She arranged a microphone connected to what looked like a Dictaphone.

Aunt Gertie didn't need a cue, she launched headlong into her reminiscences, her eyes closed to block out everyone else in the room. "Eldedt was the man I fell in love with. Cyril and I stayed out here when there were air raids.

 That must have been May, 1941. It is all so long ago but I still feel it here." Aunt Gertie touched her heart.

Elizabeth noticed Margaret leaning against the door jamb, her cheeks moist with tears as she listened.

"I still feel the same way about him. If I close my eyes I can experience his lips moving close to mine and I feel exactly as I did when he kissed me for the first time. But I made him play for higher stakes," The old lady continued, "He told me plainly, he was already married. That took the wind out of my sails. We argued. He was called to the airfield. He never returned. Shot down over the Zuider Zee after engaging a Messerschmitt." Gertie remained calm.

The room darkened and outside the rain began. Elizabeth turned on a side lamp and watched a moth dance round the light. Aunt Gertie had been attracted to a similar flame. She stood and looked out at the lane as the rain beat down.

"Was it wrong to love two men?" Aunt Gertie asked. The hail sang on the window panes.

"It can never be wrong to love," Hendrika confirmed and took the old lady's hand, gently stroking the veins.

"Might I have a photo?" Hendrika broke the ice once more. Everyone agreed. They posed. I took the pictures.

"Grandpa, you can help me develop these?"

Somehow the conversations separated. The tense emotions had dissipated and the assembly forgot the past and found some common ground in the present. The best china was cleared away by David who joined Barty and Aunty Margaret in the kitchen. Elizabeth joined them.

"Is there anything I can do?"

David helped himself to another ginger biscuit. The sounds of movement took her by surprise. She wondered into the hallway to find people pressed close to the front door.

"You must visit Texel. It's so easy by ferry from Hull. You'd be very welcome," Hendrika crossed the threshold and walked to her car. The hail storm was over. The ordeal was ended. Elizabeth looked out over the fields toward the river. A rainbow arced in the sunlight. It reminded her of other beautiful illusions. She looked at David. "We must talk," she said

David looked down at the ground.

"Later, when everyone has gone."

David knew she'd found out something but couldn't work out what that might be. Mum attempted to smile. His eyes couldn't meet hers. She breathed in sharply and put her hand on his shoulder. "You'll soon be taller than me."

Chapter 18: Olistostrome

At the very edge of the continental shelf layer upon layer of sediment accumulates until an earthquake triggers a catastrophic slide. The result is a melange of rocks twisted and contorted. I saw one on Anglesey. Professor Piasecki stuck his pipe in his mouth and with the clipped English of a Polish refugee he remonstrated with us to think. We thought. Eventually he took out his pipe and used the stem to follow some of the lines within the bedding. Suddenly it clicked we were looking at the famous Gwna melange.

Now teetering on the brink of disaster, I couldn't function. My stomach wound up in knots. I went to the toilet again. In desperation I sat on the steps and smoked a joint.

Birbeck had arranged to meet at nine o'clock by the Abbey. Already clouds were gathering in the west and promising rain. The wind was also getting up and the feel of the evening was chilly and autumnal.

A full moon rose above the abbey ruins. I promised myself I would never return to Whitby if I was successful then realised that was a stupid thought. If I was successful there would be no reason not to return. I'd be able to appreciate the beauty of any season, a winter storm perhaps when I could watch the waves froth and pound against the defences. I could enjoy the history and character of the port without dealing with sedimentary rocks. I'd mapped out my future and it lay with rocks born from fire. Lavas spewed from the Earth, or granites forced into shape miles beneath the surface and allowed to cool over millennia. These would be my new geology. The unknown. Professor Piasecki had entreated me to study metamorphic rocks with him, to wander Scotland and search for ancient rocks within thin sections. This held a certain appeal but promised to leave me poor as a post-grad studying for a doctorate. The ring of Dr David Jones had an appeal; so indeed did 'professor' but more than anything I wanted money and perversely, adventure. Tonight I would certainly get one of those desires fulfilled. I just wanted to live and experience more.

Smoking the joint relaxed me. Dad's aphorisms returned to haunt me, as though *in extremis* he was close: Where there's a will there's a way. Whilst there's life there's hope.

"Don't worry," I said to Carrie as she sat besides me.

"We'll be there for you. Remember we want him dead, it's our opportunity."

"You might, but Jevan wants his wife back."

Carrie smiled and offered me her hand. "If I'm any judge of Birbeck he'll have told her the unadulterated truth. Let's see if she wants him back after that."

I smiled and allowed her to pull me up.

"Come up to my room. I asked you before to give me a baby, now I want you to try again. I'm ready, really ready. I've decided I'm going to move into The Cook Arms with Gabby. Coming out so to speak, I think it's easier for women to do that rather than men, after all we're not illegal, seem to remember you have to wait until twenty one! So what do you say? Shall we give it one last go?" She grinned and led me through the door.

Often a death is balanced by life. It's the natural cycle. I ought to know that being a geologist. I wondered if my death might enhance the chances of a new life. The process of creation was infinitely pleasurable. I rolled off Carrie and lay facing the ceiling. For some inexplicable reason I burst into tears. Carrie comforted me and finally wrapped a sheet around her body and fetched a whiskey. I felt myself calm down.

"Think positively."

I looked outside. It was already getting dark. "Walk with me into town," I asked.

"Sure. I'll meet Jocaster by St. Mary's later."

"I fancy a pint in The White Horse and Griffin."

"Won't you be late?"

I smiled, "Yes. But that won't concern you will it?"

"No.' Carrie also said, "Waiting to kill Birbeck will be a pleasure. They always say revenge should be served cold."

"So long as you aren't avenging my death."

"That won't happen for a long time. Gabby used the Tarot. She said you'd be a force for good in all our lives," Carrie patted her stomach. "How do you feel about being a dad?"

"I thought you'd absolved me of all responsibility?"

"I thought you'd relish the obligations."

I thought through the implications, "I do, but if all goes well I could be working anywhere in the world when I get my degree. I'll have to send some money…"

"Dad always said time was better spent than money. I still believe that."

"You're right. Did I tell you I visited the fortune teller on the sea front? You know, the lady in the wooden shack with all the pictures of celebrities outside. Well she told me one day I'd be a famous writer and that I'd never get married." I sat back and laughed, even Carrie saw the joke.

It was quiet as we walked through the old town. I'd drunk my pint in the same place Grandpa had stayed. Somehow that helped. Like some Bronze Age priest I had invoked the help of my ancestors and briefly I saw the silver thread which connects us all. It was a moment of calm. If I was religious it would have been that road to Damascus moment but I'm not, so I let it pass. I telephoned mum to see how she was. Aunt Gertie and she were playing cards and my Aunt was winning. Life goes on.

I climbed the 199 steps alone. I stopped half way to look at the town, to see the clouds tare across the full moon. At the head of the stairs the silhouette of St. Mary's beckoned but behind the unforgiving ruins of the Abbey rose. Stars shone through the vestigial windows and clouds gathered from the west. It wouldn't be long before the rain beat down again.

At the top I turned left and followed the cliff path and found my place in line with the graves. I leant over the edge. I could see the breaking waves but no ironstone ridge to protect me. I could see the lights of fishing boats tossed by the waves. Eventually I stood. I was startled by Birbeck. He had been watching me.

"Well young David, I've waited a long time for this. I'm not usually so patient."

"That surprises me," I lit a cigarette.

"They'll kill you." Birbeck observed.

"Rather them than you," I replied. In the distance I saw a yellow sports car stop.

"I brought one of these," Birbeck held a taser stun gun. "A rare import, developed by NASA. I thought it might help."

I was unprepared for the pain and paralysis. Birbeck stood over me and smiled, "I like to see people writhe in pain. I particularly enjoyed those torture scenes with Josephine. I don't think she believed I'd kill her, her face was so shocked when I tightened the nylons around her neck." He stood over me gloating, like an avenging angel. Briefly he looked out to sea.

I thought of rolling away but without looking he gave me a sharp kick. I struggled to breathe then the pain seared through me. I rolled over and curled up, gasping for air. His next blow pushed me over the edge. I managed a scream. I landed flat against the ironstone. The wind was knocked out of me again and my head span. I remained still, very still. I listened to the waves below. I listened to the conversation above. I felt air force back into my lungs. I reached out for the grass to secure me. I gave myself a few seconds more. I heard Carrie's voice and Jocaster's.

"Well Birbeck. One down and one to go." Jevan sounded close.
"Jocaster, Carrie, how nice." Birbeck sounded genuinely surprised.
"This is for mum."
I heard the taser fire again. Someone stuck the boot in.
"No!" Jocaster shouted. "Only the bruises from the fall."
The gun whistled past my head.

I pulled myself up just in time to see Birbeck's arms and legs flail through the night sky. I looked down and when I could no longer see I strained to hear the landing. I was disappointed. I did not say a prayer for him. With my last effort I heaved myself up. Jevan, yes it was Jevan who pulled me up and embraced me. I slid to the ground with fatigue. I know I felt the wet earth beneath me.

"You're a bastard," Jevan said. "You've made me love you. Now you'll have to reap the consequences."

But I was too tired to reply, so I waved him away. I reached a bench with the last of my strength. "Leave me a few minutes. I'll walk later." I took out another cigarette, looked at it then crushed the cylinder. A great many things would have to change. That was the first.

I must have dozed off. When I came too the graveyard was deserted.

I stumbled towards the road. I didn't know where I'd found the vigour to fight but the final act had taken all my strength. I slumped on another seat and waited. Jocaster's yellow sports car turned and drew up. I opened the door and got in. She kissed me and brushed my hair out of my eyes.

"I'm so glad you're alive!" She said this as though she'd expected a corpse to be washed up despite all my careful planning.

"I'm just exhausted," I said. "Take me home."

No one was in the mood for celebrating. I found that surprising, so surprising that the next day I resumed my mapping. Now I was certain, the financial gain of oil exploration had won out over exploring metamorphic rocks in Scotland – at least for a year.

If I expected to be the centre of attention I was sadly mistaken. Jocaster had kissed me goodbye in the middle of the night.

"You know where to find me," she said.

"It's a big island," I replied.

"You can do better than that," she patted my cheek. "I'll be back if there's a trial."

There was a telephone call. Carrie spoke for only a few seconds. "That was Andrea, they've arrested Jevan."

I stopped eating, my stomach had wound into such a knot I couldn't force food down when I swallowed.

"It won't be long before we're picked up," she said.

All three tried to keep me company. Tucker pulled a pack of cards from his pocket. They had salacious reverses and for a while we played gin rummy. After Nigel's second win we played another hand with little enthusiasm.

"I can't wait around," I said, "it looks odd. I'm here to finish my mapping project and I'm going to finish what I started. After all, it's safe now, there's no…" I looked around and didn't bother finishing the sentence. Why say the obvious? "Nigel, would you mind dropping me off in Bay Town?"

He grunted, "Okay. I think I'll take myself off to Scarborough. There's bound to be something going on."

Tucker folded the cards and collected them. He paused just a fraction too long at the image of a svelte dark lady."Don't leave me. I'm sure there's good bitter to be had somewhere in the town."

The three of us got into Nigel's old car and waved at Carrie. I watched her as we left the drive. Perhaps I'd been wrong to blame her.

"If we don't know anything we should behave as normal and act surprised." Nigel said.

"If we don't know anything?" Tucker put his feet on the dash. "They'll see through that. No when it comes down to it, honesty's the best policy. You can always confuse people much more easily by telling the truth.

"I think you're right, Tucker. We agree for once."

"Don't mind me," Nigel said.

I realised he was uncomfortable, almost willing the police to stop him now, so he could unburden himself of his part in events and face the future. I couldn't blame him. He was out of his depth. Maybe we all were. The enormity of murder hadn't sunk in.

"I'll catch the bus back," I said through the open door and watched as Nigel and Tucker drove off.

The clouds cast dark blue shadows on the bay and the wind drove seagulls silently to their roof top perches. The pantile roofs shone with damp. I felt as though a weight had lifted and took renewed interest in all around me. In the book shop I stood and read the opening pages of *Fata Morgana* before buying the novel. I hadn't heard of William Kotzwinkle before and looked at the list of his publications. I stuffed the paperback roughly in my pocket. I remember mum berating me about the way I treated books. They were for one read and off to Oxfam. No matter how careful I was never able to keep a book pristine, except Louis Hunton. Louis wasn't mine to molest but the canon's. I would endeavour to return it when he was released.

Eventually I took the steep winding road down to the foreshore. It was busy, reflecting the warm sunny August day. I walked as far as Boggle Hole and confirmed some for my findings from the previous year. It was all rather an anticlimax and I returned to The Dolphin for a drink and sandwich late in the afternoon. I think the old men sitting by the bar found me amusing. I took out my book and read as I drank a pint. The stories of the faded TV star burst into life in my imagination. I read as I drank, I read as I ate. After the meal tiredness almost felled me and I knew if I didn't move I would fall asleep. I climbed the hill to the echo of seagulls and caught the bus back to Whitby.

I realised as I stepped off the bus that I was experiencing the tiredness of relief. There was no need to look over my shoulder, there was no need to set a trap or kick a man when he's down. As I walked up the drive the police were waiting.

I decided not to cooperate, so I was arrested. A pat down search followed and I was read my rights. I was taken over the moors to Scarborough by DC Laing and a woman in uniform.

The custody suite was not as dirty as I'd expected but cold. I was strip searched. My clothes were passed back and I was reeled out for the photos before being fingerprinted. I realised I hadn't thought that bit through. The imprint of my boot would match the bruise on Birbeck's chest, if the body was found too quickly after his fall. It would only take one stray hair and I'd have to tell the truth. I looked down. I was still wearing the same footwear.

The nurse in the custody suite was pleasant but efficient. I was asked to remove my shoe laces and belt. My belongings were checked into a bag and finally I was lead to a cell.

I was given access to a very tired looking legal representative. I told him what I knew. He appeared satisfied and I was taken to an interview room where DS Laing waited. Now he was accompanied by a bearded man in uniform. I was introduced and the taping began.

For once in my life, everything I said was the truth, until I got to the cliff top. I recounted Birbeck's use of the taser gun and the push which knocked me out. Well it wasn't so far from reality. "Surely it was an accident?" I said.

Laing snapped a pencil.

"How did he fall, there were only the two of us. I don't know."

Laing smiled. He knew I'd lied but then I knew he knew. I smiled.

"The improper use of the Taser gun fits with the evidence," Laing confided in his colleague. He terminated the interview and I was returned to the cell. I knew they'd be back. The only murder the police take seriously is one of their own. Birbeck was certainly one of their own. He had been possessed of all the forces finer qualities with yet more of his own devising.

I didn't sleep.

They took me back in to the interview room after breakfast. Their sole line of questioning concerned Jevan.

"Do you think he followed you to the cliff top?" Laing asked.

"I don't know," I said. "It's possible as he might have overheard me talking to Birbeck on the phone."

"You and Jevan are bum chums aren't you?"

"Is that a homophobic remark?" I asked my solicitor. I wanted to be angry but hadn't the energy. "Jevan and I are friends. I've seen him just once recently when he came to tell me about his forthcoming marriage." I sensed something had changed since last night's interview but I couldn't work out what until Laing remarked I should be given coffee and a cigarette.

"Take him to the custody nurse, give him his property back and check him out."

"Are you releasing me?"

"Pending further enquiries," Laing placed the pieces of pencil in the bin. "You can make your own way back to Whitby."

It was a statement. I knew I had enough money for the bus.

The next day was cold, a foretaste of autumn and a reminder that everything needed to be finished on the North Yorkshire coast so that I could commence my third year of studies.

"Well it's like this man," Tucker chose Monday morning to deliver his verdict on everything. "We've done what we set out to. We've saved you. For what, I can't say." He had just taken last night's bottles of Newcastle Brown to recycling and the rain had dampened his shoulders. "I have a job to go to in Venezuela and Nigel has his

PHD to consider. Professor Piasecki has agreed to take him on so long as he doesn't mind a pipe smoker."

"I don't," Nigel intervened, "I'll be looking at the evidence of past rocks in The Lewisian."

"Why ey, he'll be stuck looking down microscopes at thin sections for three years."

I smiled knowing Nigel was ideally suited for such work. I tried to make light of this with a joke. I forgot the punch line. "I'll be fine now. You've done more than I could ever have hoped," I shook both of them by the hand.

"I'll see you next week, Nigel. Send a post card Tucker. "Send a post card! It reminded me that I was away from home and that I too should spend a few days with mum and Aunt Gertie. Of course I could never tell her that what happened fourty years ago had precipitated all the events I'd experienced. Mum would remember the past but never understand the present.

I spend a day watching old movies. I spent a day waiting for Jevan to ring. I went to bed disappointed. When the telephone did ring it was for Carrie. I knew it was Jocaster speaking. She was safe in some country which she couldn't be extradited. Perhaps all adventures end this way. I understood this was what my grandpa meant about the war ending. The friendships which drifted, Gertie and Cyril living an uneasy peace and Eldedt who experienced the liberated Netherlands only to be shot in Germany.

Aunt Gertie never forgave him for dying. When uncle Cyril died of cancer a few years ago she became a bitter, lonely woman. Grandpa said with regret that Cyril's passing was a relief to all concerned. Yet I always remember the affection in which he was held. The passing years stripped Cyril of his faults and preserved a greater man, the good father, the provider and who am I to disillusion Aunt Gertie regarding the past? I only have grandpa's papers to go by. I only have his opinion of things past. When he stood in the shed and told me of all these events I was too young to appreciate them, now sitting alone in a cabin surrounded by a mosquito net, I remember everything. I have to write everything down, so I always carry a notebook.

I got through the final year with what Professor Piasecki described as a disappointing 2, 2. It enabled me to get my job surveying for oil. I spent three months apprenticeship on a seismic survey in Warrington where the weather was the greatest threat I faced. I learned everything about the survey, carrying geophones, drilling the charges, carrying dynamite. Once I drove from Irlam to Dorset with a thousand pounds of dynamite in the boot of my car. I'm sure that infringed health and safety regulations. Finally I was summoned to headquarters and issued with a ticket to San Paulo.

Every week I sent a postcard to Jevan. He'd been inside for eighteen months. Jevan was the fall guy. He admitted to pushing Birbeck. He claimed he'd followed me to the cliff top. He'd been too late to stop Birbeck using the Taser and when he pushed me over, something snapped. He's lost his temper and with unbelievable violence he'd pushed Birbeck over the edge. Character witnesses came and went. My own evidence was crucial. In conclusion the judge was lenient and proposed four years. Now there's a man I'd like to push off a cliff! Alas there are no cliffs in the Amazon basin. There are the most intense shades of green amongst the trees. I've taken pictures but they somehow render the place flat. There are insects, the jungle writhes with them and most have some predilection to bite.

I work hard. I play hard. Every month the lads go to a big resort in Rio. It has all sorts of pleasures available but I prefer to stay and any free time I help out at a sanctuary feeding injured kinkajou. I have many films to develop when I get back but I've wasted most frames on attempting to photograph the Jesus Lizard, walking on water.

I enjoy my swims with the natives, or taking a canoe out into the swamps and fishing with my guide Aguila. I can spear a piranha but usually end up going in after the catch, much to everyone's amusement. Aguila always helps me back into the boat. He strings the fish we've caught until their bodies reflect the rainbow colours.

That evening we had the piranha and surubim grilled with small boiled potatoes. But tastiest of all was the Tambaqui, which gets its flavour from eating the fruit that falls into the water from the trees overhanging the river. Reaching for ripe fruit is how the kinkajou get injured.

After the meal Aguila painted his body and mine with the spots of a jaguar and we chewed sacred leaves. I stopped when blood poured through my nose. Aguila teaches me to dance but I sway like a slim branch. Afterwards I listen to the mournful songs of his tribe. We have brought something which passes for civilisation: money, greed, disease but above all an insatiable apetite for land.

Of course I am waiting. My life is on hold until Jevan gets out of prison and I receive a letter from Jocaster. She writes to me frequently and her letters are witty and inspirational. Sometimes they contain offers to star in a particular scene before I die of some tropical disease. There are no tropical diseases in Iceland but I've heard there is something worse, AIDS. Jocaster tells me she ensures condoms are worn for all penetration. Apparently all those US GIs at the NATO base love her English porn and buy everything. She says there just aren't enough real people. That suits her well; Jocaster hasn't been disturbed doing her Viking Sagas and judging by the VIDEO she sent, Icelandic men certainly live up to her expectations!

It's easy to feel certain nostalgia for England when you sweat constantly. Daytime is humid, sometimes so humid it rains. Night time is simply close and torrid, like unfulfilling one night stands. The relief is that each hour brings a different type of insect. Some don't even appear to be put off by jungle strength repellent. Of course a lot of money goes into my bank account but the poverty surrounding us on the seismic survey makes me wonder. The body of a child floated by yesterday. A child who'd never had the opportunities, never lived to fulfil any dreams, finally something inside me broke and I cried. When I lay down under the mosquito net to settle for what passes as sleep, Birbeck's face haunted me and also the faces of Drew and Mike. Tears and sweat intermingled. I drank another litre of water and a salt tablet before settling to sleep.

I go swimming with the native lads every morning. They think Aguila is my veadinho. He is not. He sees me as his ticket out of the jungle and nothing more. The guys are teaching me some very bad Portuguese expressions which might come in handy in a brothel in Rio. I want to do something for these people who live in the village. They are welcoming yet so poor and they lack the basic medical needs which would save so many. Giving them money would be just like pouring drink into them.

I am in a moral dilemma with. I do not know what to do for the best.

Today I radioed *medicen sans frontiers*. I think something can be sorted. I've given a lot of money to make it happen but I won't be here to find out. The company also radioed in. They want me away from this barge and back in Blighty. Someone told them I was going native and that just doesn't do. My company likes it's workers to exploit the locals not sympathise with them. I'm only glad I have done a little good. Tomorrow morning I'll tell them I'm leaving and see what happens. They might be glad to see the back of me.

As I'm leaving, why not? I dial up the number on the satellite phone. It takes ages to connect.

"Hello!"

"Hello, Jocaster." The line breaks up and every alternate word comes through.

"How are you?"
"David! Great to hear from you. Where are you?"
"Find the Amazon and go a little upstream!"
"They've fired you then?"
"Guess they might. I've been recalled back to HQ."
"Can you visit?"
"I'll try," There was a pause.
"Good. There's someone here who's dying to talk to you,"
Another pause.
"Hi Dave."

I swallowed hard. I felt faint. "Hi Jevan," I suddenly felt as though someone was tightening various parts of my body whilst letting my heart squeeze one last time.

"Do you love me?" He asked.

"Do I love you?" The line went dead. It wasn't how I was going to end the conversation. I was going to redial but my boss appeared in the control room. I smiled and nodded. I looked at my watch and calculated the hours before I would fly out of Brazil and start my life again. Aguila waved from across the tributary so green with algae I felt I might be able to walk on water. As a geologist I know it's only possible to walk on water when it becomes thixotropic with mud—after an earthquake. My thoughts distracted me from my emotional turmoil. I'd been excited and frightened to be given this placement in the Amazon but leaving after six months made me feel numb.

When I told Aguila I was leaving he cried. I calmed him and said I had unfinished business and would return within the year. He thought I was lying but accepted it. I wasn't so certain.

The journey briefly comprised: boat, shack, boat, seaplane, hotel, jumbo jet, hotel, train. Get the picture: a lot of travel and stopovers. Later I arrived in London, well not so much the capital as a grey southern suburb. Barry greeted me and ushered me into a small office.

"It's like this," he said then took a long drink. "We can't afford for our staff to get on with the natives. It spreads panic amongst the companies who employ us to do seismic surveys. Greg found out about your donation to *medicen sans frontiers* well… you can imagine…"

"Shit hit the fan? I don't regret what I did. I don't regret anything except the insects."

"Tell me. That seems to be a condition of finding oil." Barry looked at me. He displayed no emotion or understanding. "Well, let's move on. I'm not going to sack you. I want you to take a holiday.

There's a really posh playground where some of the lads go. It's in the South of France so even the whores are up market! Two weeks should see you up and running!" Barry smiled, he sat on the corner of his desk, revealing his paunch.

"If it's all the same to you, I'd rather have a return ticket to Iceland. I understand basalt and I've always wanted to see a volcano."

"But beer's so expensive there! Are you certain?"

"Absolutely." I wondered if he was going to terminate my contract. "Only I need three weeks. I need one to visit my mum in Hull and catch up with reality."

"You drive a hard bargain but despite your odd ways you're a good geologist. Back here on Monday the 3rd. The two of us are flying out to a new contract in Malaysia."

"What time?"

"The flight's at four, check in at one pm. Don't be late. I'll forward the tickets and visas to your mum's place." He offered his hand. I shook it. Just as he let it go he took my elbow and looked me in the eyes. "If it's any consolation, I wanted to do something for the natives on my first Amazon stint. I didn't have the bottle." He jumped down from the desk and escorted me to the firedoors. Finally he turned on his heels and walked back to his office in silnce.

I walked down the road and descended to East Croydon station. At last I was travelling north.

Chapter 19: Igneous

There were no problems leaving the country except the look on mum's face when I told her I was flying again. Taking an airplane wasn't something either mum or Aunt Gertie had done. It wasn't environmental principle, in Aunt Gertie's case it was something to do with Eldedt and the war. With mum it was something she might have done when young but certainly she wasn't going to start now. As usual she told me not to get into trouble.

I remembered not to wear my studded belt, so I might get through security without a strip search. Afterwards I queued at the phone booth and managed a short conversation with Carrie. She sounded so excited that Nathaniel was crawling. She said she'd posted some photos for me and even without seeing them I felt that inane *proud father* grin spread across my face. I needed to spend more time in Hawsker with them. I needed to take mum. She was so proud but couldn't understand why Carrie and I didn't marry. I didn't enlighten her. That was what the third week was for. I wondered if I'd got the balance right.

My passport was scrutinised by one official then passed to another. I waited. It doesn't do to upset Customs & Excise even though I'm well travelled enough to give an emotionally neutral look to any officer.

The Icelandair flight was prompt, so as we taxied down the runway, I put in ear plugs to alleviate the pressure changes and waited for that feeling in the pit of my stomach which tells me I'm airborne. I'm not a good flyer, the feeling of 30 000 feet between me and terra firma makes me nervous. Once at cruising altitude I relaxed enough to read my book and listen to Ravel's String quartet on my *Walkman*. The opening allegro moderato soothed me. I looked out of the window at the islands scattered below. Eventually the view was obscured by clouds. I closed my eyes.

Lunch was served. It was a pleasant diversion and the executive I sat next to began a conversation. He told me he worked in fish imports in Hull.

"Small world," I said. "That's where I grew up. Now I travel the world in search of oil."

"I work in fish and drink like one. Gisli," he held out his hand.

"David," I held out mine. "I don't have much grip I'm afraid, not since the accident."

He opened my hand and saw the scar. "Is this your first time in Iceland?"

"Yes, visiting friends. We're meeting up at Seljalandfoss."

"Beautiful. Make certain you take the path behind the falls." He finished his coffee. "Even more spectacular will be the eruption of Hecla. It's been expected for several days now. I think that is why the plane is so full." He looked around.

"Sound's great, I wish it could happen whilst I'm there."

Gisli smiled and put his headset back on and watched the adverts. I returned to Ravel's string quartet. I pulled the note folded neatly between passport and cover. *Nine a.m. behind the waterfall at Seljalandfoss, Jevan.*

It wasn't much to go on. I had seen him briefly as he helped to pull me back onto the top of the cliff. He'd asked me if I was alright. We stood in silence and he told me I was in trouble for making him love me. With that he vanished into the night.

That's my memory of the stormy night Birbeck died. Not Birbeck pushing me clumsily over the edge but the way the conspirators melted into the night, leaving me sitting alone as it started to rain. They left me to peer over the edge and confirm Birbeck was dead before walking back to Carrie's house. Jocaster, Jevan and Carrie had all been there. They had each helped push the man over. Somehow everyone was avenged. In many ways it was the perfect solution, if they could live with themselves.

I wondered why Jevan had chosen Iceland. I was even more intrigued why Jocaster should pay for my flight and leave her yellow sports car at Reykjavik Airport. That was all a matter of hours away. The plane banked and the Westland Islands came into view. The central crater looked like the entrance to the underworld. Next to it a smaller volcano threw out plumes of steam and smoke. It all looked unreal from this height. We took a little turbulence and below us clouds closed. I watched a repeat of *Dad's Army* and wondered yet again whether it was me or everyone else.

I looked around the plane. I couldn't see much except for the stewards pushing their trolleys touting for perfumes and trinkets. I closed my eyes and played *vif et agite* the final movement. I smiled remembering how I'd heard this played in Saint Mary's, Beverley's other beautiful church, and how I'd searched for the pilgrim hare. It reminded me of my visit with grandpa. Was it really six years since he'd died? 1909 to 1978. He didn't quite make three score years and ten, which he thought his due. All those stories from the war, the doodlebug which hit the banks of the River Hull and caused all the fields around to flood. At the time I thought them fantastical. Now I know the truth. The present is the key to the past was an aphorism reversed in my life. The plane began its descent. I turned off the music and inserted my ear plugs once more. I swallowed hard several times. The sun was too bright to see anything of note but as the plane banked Reykjavik came into view, its buildings insubstantial against the backdrop of mountains. We turned again and the ground beneath us became arid, plumes of condensation rose from a geothermal plant. I gripped the arm rests and prayed for a safe landing. We were back on terra firma.

My heart raced with excitement. I waited to get off the plane, we walked to the terminal. Everything was so quiet. I was nodded through customs and was able to pick my rucksack up within ten minutes. I found a cash point and took out ten thousand Kronur. I picked up the car key from an officious young lady at Information. She scrutinised my passport more thoroughly than anyone else had done today.

The air was cool and somehow too clean, too fresh. I smiled. The yellow sports car was exactly where Jocaster indicated. I got in and adjusted the seat. The car smelt of Palma violets and lying on the passenger seat was a video tastefully announcing *The Viking Saga*.

I drove towards Reykjavik, playing Depeche Mode on the CD. I found the youth hostel without much difficulty in Reykjavik's eastern suburb, indeed it was more like a hotel where you share rooms. I showered and brushed my teeth, noticing the taste of hydrogen sulphide as I rinsed and spat. I felt human again. I dined on a cheese sandwich before going outside.

I found myself fascinated by the houses and the streets but most of all the grand sweep of cliffs to the north. Presumably years of volcanic eruptions had accumulated in these. I walked for perhaps an hour before returning to the hostel. My room mates rolled in drunk at two. When I awoke again snow covered the ground.

Breakfast was a feast. I ate enough for two and made sandwiches, not knowing what to expect later. Finally I asked for directions to Seljalandfoss.

The road climbed through rugged terrain. I kept stopping to take pictures. All the colours were intense and for the first time I wished I was an artist. White, green and brown compressed under the weight of the iridescent blue sky.

I arrived at the empty car park just on nine o'clock. I kitted up and took the path toward the great roaring force of the waterfall. The spray got everywhere. The chilled water made me feel so alert I might hear the sound of a whisper a mile away. I climbed carefully over the rocks and looked ahead at the path disappearing behind the waterfall. I laboured on, then stopped to see the rainbows dance through the spray. I watched and felt myself smile. Now the rocks became slippery from the damp and ice which clung onto surfaces as though it was protecting the material beneath. The path ate into a great overhang of lava and the water cascaded violently into the pool below. The roar blotted out all other sounds and slowly the waterfall became a curtain of water beyond which the outside world no longer existed. The figure rose up from the rocks. I tried to make out the face. There was no mistaking those bright blue eyes. We embraced and kissed. I felt the rough texture of his tongue against mine. I think I was crying but the waterfall provided so much spray I was certain it wouldn't be noticed.

"Is it time for us?" I shouted.

Jevan nodded. He took me by the hand and I followed. We took the other path back to the car park and sat watching the rainbows arc away from the falls.

"Amazing." I said.

"I come here often. It makes me feel so… insubstantial." Jevan looked out towards the distance so I couldn't see his eyes. "You waited."

"I waited," I said awkwardly.

"Jocaster had to pull strings to get me here. I think she claimed I was a long lost relative." Jevan laughed.

"When it all came out in court, I knew they'd send you down. I suppose their logic of we can't let people go around murdering policemen came into play?"

"I always felt that was unfair," Jevan looked at me again. "Barty murdered my twin. Ricky didn't deserve that."

I agreed. "But four years was only ever going to be two years and two years wasn't so long. I got to finish my degree and take up a post on a seismic survey."

"I hear you have a son. I got angry when I found out. I thought…"

"Probably what I thought when you told me you wanted to get married. She soon deserted you. I didn't." I pulled back his hood to reveal his black hair. It was short, almost military and I stroked the soft down behind his ear. He held my hand and kissed my fingers. I felt the knot in my stomach tighten and my heart race. I closed my eyes.

"Drive me back to yours." I asked a little later when the cold and damp had permeated my body.

I'd desired this man for so long. I stripped off his t-shirt. He'd bulked up and possessed a dragon tattoo on his biceps.

"Prison gym. I earned the privileges."

He undid my shirt buttons. "Thinner, a six pack and some tan, such golden skin! I think I look too pale."

"Pale and interesting." I kissed him.

He pulled me onto the sofa. We lay there looking up at the ceiling, then both giggled.

"I didn't realise I could just lie next to someone and feel so happy." I said. Clouds had gathered and rain was streaking down the windows in a pale imitation of Seljalandfoss. For the first time in my life I felt complete. All the waiting, all the heart ache, all the false starts…

Afterwards, in the hot tub there was a view across the green fields towards great basaltic stacks standing sentinel at the coast. "Go on, surprise me." I joked.

"What?" Jevan slid under the water to try and avoid answering.

"Who owns the place?"

Jevan became serious. "Jocaster. She films here."

We said the last part in unison and laughed. "Will you ever do another blue movie?"

I thought about this. "I always said no, but I'd do a scene with you. I'd like that, we could keep it and watch it when we're retired."

"What if you changed your mind? I mean went off with a girl and had kids?" He seemed anxious.

"What if you did?" I flicked water at him.

He flicked it back. Finally I answered, "I can't stay here forever but I'm yours for as long as you want me."

Jevan relaxed. "And how I want you!" Jevan turned up the bubbles and sank down in the water. I moved next to him until our skin touched. "I think there's something we must do." He said when he surfaced.

I had no idea where we might be going. A pencil line of silver heralded dawn when Jevan took the driver's seat and we headed north. I was content to look out at the scenery. The road rose then fell steeply into a broad and barren valley.

"Did the earth move for you last night, Mr. Geologist?" Jevan asked.

On quiet Icelandic roads I could reply in a way I couldn't in England.

Slowly an ice capped mountain dominated the eastern view. "That's Hekla," Jevan didn't need to point, "Iceland's most active volcano,"

"Beautiful," I replied and studied the barren expanse of the most recent lava flow. "Can we?"

"I thought you might want to." Jevan turned off down a track, plumes of dust rose behind us. It was further than I thought. The road just ended where the force of nature had dammed the way. To look at the flow was fantastic and frightening. The violence of the Earth stood in stark contrast to the peaceful surroundings.

"'It's a basalt. I'm always amazed by how light it is, how all that gas bubbles and froths from the lava flows. I studied geology, two years of an OU degree, whilst I was inside. I learned all about plate tectonics and igneous rocks. I also learned what it's like to be lonely."

I sat down on the sharp rock. I felt winded. "Was it really that bad for you? I didn't think."

Jevan just nodded and turned away. "Your letters and postcards kept me going."

I put my arm round his shoulder, "I took the job because I'd earn lots of cash and be working eighteen hours a day. Somehow filling time was important. I didn't want to sit and think. Sometimes I'd get angry, really screwed up angry and want revenge on the world. I'd feel my heart pound in my chest and be unable to sleep. I always though they should commend you for getting rid of Barty Fair."

"That was never going to happen. Barty and Birbeck, I copped for both of them."

"You did but then they should at least have got the right person."

"What do you mean?" Jevan sounded angry. "I took the rap. All three of us pushed Birbeck, you know that! Afterwards Carrie and I agreed the story. We cut out Jocaster. You couldn't see because you were climbing back up the cliff so we thought the story was secure."

"It was dark. It was a stormy night and that seemed appropriate to the memory of Drew. I'd gone there to meet Birbeck knowing you'd set me up as bait. So I waited by the supposed grave of Dracula's first victim on British soil. I was oddly relieved when Birbeck appeared because I knew why he hated me. I knew why he'd killed Drew. Fifty years ago my granddad forced his dad out of his job. Birbeck senior had been creaming off the Council's rent money and on a nice earner, if that villa in Whitby was anything to go by. He overstretched himself and eventually went bankrupt. The young DCI Birbeck was chucked out of the family home and into a council house. So everything connected. The past is the key to the present. I unwittingly became the centre piece in his revenge."

"I had earlier lined up the edge of the cliffs with the grave stones. There was a ledge of harder sediment some six feet down and I'd practiced tumbling onto it. I wasn't prepared for Birbeck to use a Taser. I remember Birbeck's smile as he pushed me over. He had his moment of victory. I hardly resisted. That was important. For a second I felt air rushing past me. The lights had been turned out. The rock hit me. I stopped falling. I lay there winded, gasping for breath. I was alive. All I had to do was wait. If Birbeck peered over the edge, I didn't see him. I remained silent as I heard the voices: Yours, Carrie's, Jocaster's. I started to climb back up. I almost lost my nerve despite the fact it was only a few feet. I'd forgotten how difficult purchase would be in total darkness and the surfaces damp.

You already had Birbeck at the brink. I didn't dare move in case I broke your concentration. I saw all three of you give him the push he richly deserved. He screamed and fell."

"Remember I asked you to help me?' For some reason you looked confused, then ran over. As I regained the headland, I regained your arms. It was a beautiful moment, yet you backed away and all three of you dissolved into the night. I didn't understand that. I sat and regained my strength. That's when I heard movement a few feet away. I called out but the wind took my words out over the Abbey. Birbeck's face reappeared, then his arms and shoulders. The iron rich sandstone which saved me had preserved him. My anger burst, I raged and ran. I kicked out and caught his chest. He looked startled. I caught hold of grass and buried my fingernails in the soil to stop myself spilling over the edge. He hadn't expected me! I watched his body flail and I found myself smiling as his body fell into the darkness. The silence was broken only by a scream and thud, then nothing.

"After murdering Birbeck, I washed my hands in the gents, folded my dirty waterproofs into my rucksack and joined the concert goers in Saint Mary's. I sat in a box pew by the door and listened to the Lindsay's play Ravel's Quartet. It's amazing the power of music to heal, to quell the storm."

Jevan sat on the car bonnet. "I never did it?"

I joined him. "More importantly we all did it. Don't you see, we're all equally guilty in our revenge. That's kept me going through these long years."

Jevan laughed. He lay back on the bonnet and laughed into the weakly blue sky of a new day. "Obviously the god's want us to be together."

"I think its geology which connects us, not divinity. You see I knew exactly where the band of sideritic sandstone jutted out from the cliff, a six foot ledge of rock which would break my fall. It all worked out."

Jevan looked at me, "I hate saying I love you, but I do." We got in the car and returned to the road, "Wait till Jocaster hears this. It'll kill her."

The lakeside villa was built entirely of wood and rested on top of a small hill. Another yellow sports car occupied the drive, along with several four wheel drives. Jocaster waited at the door, rubies adorning her right hand and emeralds the other. "The prodigal returns!" She kissed me and held me tight like a long lost relative. "Jevan's been going around like a crazed bull for days, alternately overjoyed you're coming then full of doubt. We're having a meal for the cast and crew. We've just finished Viking Saga 2. The first proved very popular north of the Arctic Circle: all bear skins and bear back."

"I hope you didn't kill too many." I joked.

Jocaster laughed, "No bears are a protected species, unlike porn stars. Shall we dine?"

"Very kind. You shouldn't have put yourself out."

"I didn't. That's what I employ Mr. Radius and Ulna for." Jocaster draped a deep blue shawl over a chair back. "Though my last two heavies met with an unfortunate car accident. And a boot full of fossils." She smiled beatifically. "You'll remember Goldie of course and Wojek and Richard. He plays the evil King Olaf. Typecast I'm afraid but what's an old director to do? This is my latest star, Dale Rise, he's from Burniston and has just been given the ok by the doctor. Of course we use condoms unless the couple are partners. HIV. It's a horrid little word. But we must all do our bit. I'm hoping Dale will arouse a few of the natives in our unique interpretation of the Icelandic Sagas. Will you be taking a part?"

I smiled.

Jevan smiled. "Just each other." He said.

"I'll think of how to get that in the plot." Jocaster clapped her hands and people began to seat themselves round the table. "A toast:

To absent friends. Here's to Carrie, Gabby and their son, Nathaniel. It's not everyday I can admit to being a great aunt."

Jevan and I sat either side of Jocaster. "Why here?" I asked.

"The scenery and more importantly the solitude, we filmed at Thingvellir in the perishing cold." Jocaster picked up her soup spoon and delicately scooped the consommé.

I laughed at the thought of filming an adult movie at the site of the world's first parliament. "Did the locals see the irony?"

"Not yet, It's not due out until October," Jocaster poured another mineral water. "Is it all settled. Are you two a couple or is someone going to run away?"

I looked at Jevan.

He smiled. "I have a little secret up my sleeve," He touched his nose.

Everyone was shocked at the way the villa rocked. Only Wojek remained calmly eating his soup. He looked up. "It's an earthquake. They happen all the time but that was quite powerful. The Earth is brewing something for us."

I took his meaning were others looked perplexed. The food was classy but plain and the wines excellent but not in their usual quantity.

"Price," Jocaster admitted, "alcohol's so expensive here. A pint of lager is a fiver in some bars. There'd be riots in Whitby!"

During dessert there was another tremor. My pavlova vibrated on the spoon as though it was wielded by a palsied man. A third and final tremor followed hard by and simultaneously a thunderous crack rent the air. Everyone went to the windows to look. "It's Hekla," Wojek pointed out the fissure which seemed to erupt in an orange glow. Lightning struck around the summit, illuminating the steam and smoke above the volcano. Jevan brushed up against me. "That's where we must go. We must see if the gods will allow our love or devour us."

I looked at him. "You can't be serious?" I stared into his bright blue eyes. He was serious. "We'll have to wrap up well. It's winter up there."

He smiled and pulled me from the room. We embraced passionately.

"Going somewhere?" Jocaster asked.

"To find a volcano," I replied.

"That shouldn't be difficult here. It's stopping them erupting." She went back into the dining room.

"We're both mad."

"We're both in love and we've both murdered. Let's see if the gods have forgiven us."

"You forget, Jevan. I don't believe in anything other than geology and love."

We borrowed coats and hats and trudged into the night air. The frost was sharp and the sky peaceful until I looked north east. Here an unnatural glow emanated from the mountain. "The eruption's partly under the glacier."

"Vatnajokull. Its name." Jevan sounded pleased with his local knowledge. We walked across the road and took a path upwards. It wasn't properly dark, the long twilight and a near full moon allowed us to pick our way up onto a ridge. I stood and gasped at the sight of fire leaping from a long gash in the Earth and lava cascading into the valley. I was acutely aware of the stupidity of our position.

"I'm going down." Jevan tried to drag me down.

"No," I said. "This is close enough." I watched the lava tumble red hot down the mountain. I've never been frightened of the awesome power of rocks before but this was overwhelming. The molten innards of our planet pouring onto the surface and rolling under gravity until the cooling edges congealed and halted its movement.

"How will we know if the gods have forgiven us?"

"There is nothing to forgive and no one to forgive us. We'll just have to love and live like everyone else."

I turned away from the spectacle leaving Jevan half way down the slope. "I'm not letting you go now."

Jevan eluded me and scrambled further down into the valley. I shouted then followed kicking up clouds of dust as I skidded. I caught up with him. The lava flow oozed its sulphurous path toward us. The red hot insides burst open, cooled burst asunder once more. The air became putrid. "You cannot hold this back." I shouted.

Jevan smiled. He pointed at the pyroclastic display exploding from the crater. I began to feel the heat from the lava. I looked around for a safe haven. There was only back up the slope which now looked terrifyingly steep. I looked again at the lava flow and pulled Jevan upward. His feet scrambled away from the molten flow. I carried him a few dozen paces before I collapsed to the floor. "You don't escape from me that easily!" I shouted.

"Come on!" He ran upward with renewed energy and gained the ridge.

Exhausted, I followed. My hand touched the top but my feet slipped away. Hands reached out for me and pulled me up. Jevan folded his arms around me and from this vantage we watched the lava engulf where once we'd stood.

There are three types of love in my life: one is for my son, the second geology and finally my desire for the man who lies close to me. As I sit here watching the awesome power of nature I am overwhelmed that for once I know what I want and I am happy. This state cannot last, nothing does because there are always hidden processes at work, some natural others more akin to love, lust and the geology of desire.

Keep Safe.

If venturing to any sites to view the geology, please be aware of safety. Only descend to bays where you know there's a **safe path**. **Hard hats** and a **knowledge of the tides** are essential to avoid being cut off.

The years of recent wet weather have made many cliff walks treacherous. Geology is constantly changing and some of the geology in this novel is exaggerated to accommodate the plot.

Other publications available from Stairwell Books

First Tuesday in Wilton	Ed. Rose Drew and Alan Gillott
The Exhibitionists	Ed. Rose Drew and Alan Gillott
The Green Man Awakes	Ed. Rose Drew
Carol's Christmas	N.E. David
Fosdyke and Me and Other Poems	John Gilham
frisson	Ed. Alan Gillott
Feria	N.E. David
Along the Iron Veins	Ed. Alan Gillott and Rose Drew
A Day at the Races	N.E. David
Gringo on the Chickenbus	Tim Ellis
Running With Butterflies	John Walford
Foul Play	P J Quinn
Late Flowering	Michael Hildred
Scenes from the Seedy Underbelly of Suburbia	Jackie Simmons
Pressed by Unseen Feet	Ed. Rose Drew and Alan Gillott
York in Poetry Artwork and Photographs	Ed. John Coopey and Sally Guthrie
Poison Pen	P J Quinn
Rosie and John's Magical Adventure	The Children of Ryedale District Primary Schools
Her House	Donna Marie Merritt
Taking the Long Way Home	Steve Nash
Wine Dark, Sea Blue	A.L. Michael
Chocolate Factory	Ed. Juliana Mensah and Rose Drew
Skydive	Andrew Brown
Still Life With Wine and Cheese	Ed. Rose Drew and Alan Gillott
Somewhere Else	Don Walls
Close Disharmony	P J Quinn
When the Crow Cries	Maxine Ridge
Homelands	Shaunna Harper
Border 7	Pauline Kirk

For further information please contact rose@stairwellbooks.com
Novels and Novellas are in bold type
www.stairwellbooks.co.uk
@stairwellbooks